# ESCAPE
## FROM THE
# PSI ACADEMY
### Psi Wars! Book One

# ESCAPE
## FROM THE
# PSI ACADEMY
## Psi Wars! Book One

Vincent L. Scarsella

DIGITAL
FANTASY
FICTION

# DIGITAL FICTION
PUBLISHING CORP

ISBN-13 (paperback): 978-1-988863-03-0
ISBN-13 (e-book): 978-1-988863-02-3

# Part 1
# Sebastian Drake

# Chapter One
# The New Kid

The new kid in the motorized wheelchair was dropped off in front of Colonel J. B. Weber High School by a special van. After his wheelchair was lowered from the side door by an aluminum lift, the van's driver, a kindly looking, plump middle-aged woman, guided it backwards off the grate onto the sidewalk. She gave the kid a peck on top of his slicked down, dark brown hair, then waited a moment as, with a quavering right hand, he activated a control grip putting the wheelchair into gear and swinging it around. With another push of the grip, the wheelchair finally began gliding down the long sidewalk leading to the front entrance of the school. After a moment, the kid glanced back at the woman and she waved after him with a sad smile. Then, after standing there another moment watching him wheel toward the school, the woman turned, went back into the van and drove off.

A few days ago, and a few times before that, I had dreamt this very scene if not something very close to it. Like most dreams, upon waking, I couldn't recall any details beyond the image of a strange kid in a motorized wheelchair being dropped off in front of school by a matronly lady. But seeing the dream unfold before me now sent a shiver down my spine.

It was the second week of school and Colonel J. B. Weber's student body had settled into a kind of easy morning ritual. On the morning of the new kid's arrival, like every other morning the last few days, the students had gathered on the worn, front lawn adjacent the wide, main sidewalk, in stereotypical cliques— jocks, druggies, geeks and nerds—as well as the moody loners like myself, scrutinizing our smartphones, texting, playing a game on some app or listening to music from the iPods connected to our ears, while waiting for the dreaded bell calling us to school for the start of what I considered another long and boring day.

It didn't take long this bright September morning for the class bully, Frankie Nytz, and his gang of maybe six or seven compliant toadies, to spot the new kid. They had congregated in their usual spot, leaning lethargically against the old oak tree that split from the trunk into two long, roughly equal branches a couple feet from the hard, rocky ground. The usual routine of Nytz's gang was to look up from their smartphones from time to time and ogle the pretty or not so pretty girls, who mostly ignored them, or spend a few minutes mocking some familiar classmate who happened for no good reason that morning to become the object of their interest and scorn. But their usual routine was broken that morning by the new kid's unexpected arrival. And their interest was especially heightened by the spectacular fact that he was tethered to a motorized wheelchair.

"Hey, lookie, lookie," Frankie said after looking up from this smartphone and turning around from his usual spot sitting in the old oak tree. "It's Stephen Hawking's son."

Frankie's toadies naturally joined in ogling the new kid. Some of them pointed him out and laughed as the wheelchair rolled along the main sidewalk toward the school. Leaning decidedly to the right side of the chair, he wore a brand new polo shirt and dress pants plucked right out of a cheap department store catalogue.

I have to say, I was impressed by Frankie Nytz's comparison to the son of the famous, crippled physicist, Stephen Hawking, himself tethered to a motorized wheelchair. The analogy was spot on, clever even: he really could have passed for Hawking's kid. That Frankie had come up with the comparison didn't surprise me. I knew that for all his idiotic, Neanderthal bullying and bluster, he was deep down, a pretty smart kid.

But I was one hundred percent certain that his toadies had no idea who Stephen Hawking was. Their chortling had nothing to do with the cleverness of their leader's observation—it was strictly and purely based on the thrill of helping Frankie inflict cruelty. The new kid was simply another in a long line of unfortunate targets, including yours truly, to be mocked and hounded and harassed for no good reason other than for the perverse joy in it.

Frankie started walking toward the new kid with his toadies right behind. He positioned himself solidly in the middle of the main sidewalk with his arms folded across his chest and waited, looking down menacingly as he approached.

"Excuse me," said the kid. "I need to pass."

Even from where I stood, I could hear the lisp. That sealed it. Frankie couldn't have asked for a better assortment of disabilities to inspire cruelty.

With an amused frown, Frankie glanced back at his toadies and a couple other gawkers who had gathered to watch another Frankie Nytz spectacle. The new kid's head stretched even further to one side as Frankie stood his ground.

"Excuse me," he repeated softly. "I need to pass."

Frankie crouched down and cocked his head to match the slant of the new kid's head. Then, pursing his lips, he mimicked the new kid's speech impediment.

"'Cuse'a me," Frankie said. "You need to piss?"

"I said pass," said the kid, seemingly undaunted.

"No," Frankie said. He stood and glared down at the kid. "You distinctly said, piss. You calling me a liar?"

He turned to his toadies and gawkers, held out his arms and asked, "Did he not say, piss?" There was, of course, a general murmur of agreement.

"I just need to pass," said the kid.

Frankie turned to him and said, "Yeah, I know, you need to piss."

One of Frankie's toadies laughed, then blurted out, "'Cuse me, I need to pee-pee."

"You mean wee-wee," another of the morons shouted and there was more general laughter.

"Yeah, Stephen Hawking's son got to pee-pee, wee-wee," added Frankie.

"Knock it off, Frankie," I called out just beyond the crowd of toadies and gawkers.

In the next moment, there was complete silence and I immediately felt sick to my stomach. Something had forced me to blurt that out, to stop what Frankie was doing, some inner moral sensibility. It was one thing for Frankie Nytz to pick on me or any of the other hapless, no name kids at the school. But harassing a kid in a wheelchair, whose head cocked unnaturally sideways with spittle dripping down his chin, well that was a new low even for Frankie Nytz.

As Frankie slowly turned, the crowd of toadies and gawkers had parted to reveal me as the speaker. With a cocksure smirk, he spotted my skinny, four foot nine inch frame standing back there. I took a breath, furrowed my brow, and met his stare. The toadies and gawkers standing alongside and behind Frankie waited expectantly.

"You say something, Greenpooper?"

My name is Greenberg, Henry 'Hank' Benjamin Greenberg, I was named after the great Jewish baseball player who played something like 500 years ago and who nobody ever heard of in modern times. Whenever I told someone I was named after Hank Greenberg and they gave me a funny look, I quickly added that he was in the Baseball Hall of Fame.

But Frankie never called me by my real name. Always, he used some mocking distortion of it, and it was a funny thing, but he never seemed to repeat the distortion twice within the same conversation.

"Well, Greencrapper."

"C'mon, Frankie," I pleaded. "Kid's in a wheelchair for cripe's sake."

"For Christ's sake?" Frankie's eyes widened. "As in Jesus Christ? Who *your* people killed."

"Just lay off the poor kid, Frankie," I said. "He's harmless. Totally."

Frankie sauntered over to me. By challenging his behavior, I had now become the object of his attention and scorn. Out of the corner of my left eye, I saw that the new kid had glided safely away and was already wheeling through the entrance door to the school.

Frankie reached out with both hands, grabbed my shoulders and pushed me onto my rear-end. Naturally, this resulted in a roar of laughter from his toadies and even some gawkers.

"Stay down, Greenturd," he said. "Don't even move."

I knew that the only way to deal with a bully like Frankie Nytz was through resistance. I hopped right up and went head first into Frankie's midsection. I had my arms out and started pummeling wherever my fists would land. Frankie started laughing as did everyone else who had now gathered around to watch another Frankie Nytz special.

After letting me futilely flail at him for about ten seconds, Frankie grabbed me under my armpits, lifted me up onto his left shoulder and, with a wide, malicious grin, helicoptered me around for all to see. I yelled out something derogatory, having no idea what Frankie intended to do. Finally, after three or four more twirls, he knelt down, bent forward and dropped me onto my back with a small thud. In the next instant he had his left knee on my chest and was threatening to make me eat a clump of dirt that he had scooped into his right hand.

And then, the late bell sounded.

"Lucky for you, Greenpoopster," Frankie said as he stood,

tossed down the dirt and slapped his hands together. He stalked toward the entrance of the school followed by his toadies. After a few steps, he glanced back at me and shouted, "Catch up with you later, Greensheetz. You can count on it."

I quickly got to my feet and brushed myself off. As I started trotting toward the school, I checked the cheap watch I had gotten a few weeks back on my thirteenth birthday. Seeing the time, I frowned. By some miracle, the late bell had sounded a full two minutes early, saving me, for the time being anyway, from eating dirt out of Frankie Nytz's right hand.

# Chapter Two
## Sebastian Drake

As usual I sat alone during lunch near the corner of a long table in the back of the lunch hall minding my own business. I'd shrugged off that my confrontation with Frankie Nytz had been fortuitously cut short because the school late bell rang a full two minutes early. I chalked it up to some glitch in Colonel J. B. Weber High's otherwise, up to then, flawless clock system; or perhaps, it was my cheap watch that had been slow and the warning bell had been right on time. Although, that didn't make sense either because the rest of that morning, my watch seemed back in sync with school time.

Whatever the answer, I had other matters to occupy my thoughts. There were tiresome lectures in boring courses that long morning, daydreams about Molly Scott my current, unrequited love interest (I had never yet had a requited love interest), and a persistent uneasiness that Frankie Nytz was likely to finish at the end of the school day what the morning warning bell had prevented. Thankfully, for the time being anyway, Frankie Nytz seemed to have forgotten all about our morning confrontation and he and his toadies were instead busying themselves harassing some other wretched nerd.

As I was carving a morsel of mystery meat during the lunch period, the new kid in the wheelchair rolled up to the empty space between me and a pimply, freshman geek who was also eating alone and minding his own business.

"Is this seat taken?" he asked, in that slurring, lispy way some disabled kids spoke. "Mind if I join you?"

I shrugged as I shoveled a hunk of the mystery meat into my mouth.

"Yeah, sure," I said chewing. "Whatever. It's a free country."

But I did actually mind. I always ate lunch alone, and every other meal for that matter. In fact, I did most things alone. I was what grownups, with worried frowns, call 'a loner.' Hopefully, I wouldn't grow up and kill a bunch of my classmates or other people with an semi-automatic rifle and be called 'a loner' by the media as if that explained the whole thing.

My loner status was confirmed by the fact that I had no real friends. I spent most of my free time at home reading comic books on superheroes like Iron Man, Spider-Man, Superman, Batman, and my present favorite, The Anonymous Man. I also liked watching science fiction on TV, especially old episodes of *The Twilight Zone* or *Star Trek* or *The Prisoner*. In fact, because of these traits, my father often referred to me, even to my face no less, as a 'quirky' or an 'oddball.'

The new kid struggled to pull a chair out and away from the table and then glided in. He shakily lifted his tray, containing a sandwich, salad, a bowl of pudding and a small carton of white milk that had been balancing precariously on his lap. I helped guide his shaky hands to set down the tray with a thud on the table before him.

"Thank you," he said as he parked his wheelchair flush to the table. His head was barely above the tabletop and he looked uncomfortable as he lifted the sandwich off the tray and took a small bite of it. After another bite, he turned to me and said, "I want to thank you for helping this morning. What you did was brave, heroic."

"Don't mention it," I said with a shrug. "Just learn to stay away from that idiot, Frankie Nytz."

"Mr. Nytz, I take it, is the class bully?"

"You might say that." I shoved another lump of mystery meat into my mouth. "Colonel J.B. Weber High's very own ninth grade bully."

Despite all the programs and warnings on TV and in PTA pamphlets they hand out every other day, every school has one: a certifiable, sociopathic bully. Always have, always will; it's human nature.

The new kid nodded and I noticed spittle dribbling down from the corner of his mouth in a long, disgusting thread that settled onto his lap. I quickly looked away, regretting suddenly that I allowed him to sit next to me. He didn't seem bothered or embarrassed by the involuntary dripping of his saliva. He simply took a napkin from his tray and with his shaky hand, wiped his mouth, then dabbed his chin and lap with it. I had to admire how casual he was about it.

After he put the napkin down, he looked to me and said, "Name's Sebastian Drake. What's yours?"

His head was turned in a cocked, funny way as he looked at me, expecting a return introduction. I let him wait awhile.

"Henry Greenberg," I said. "My name's Henry Greenberg."

"Like the ball player," he said.

"Yeah," I said, and gave him a dubious look. "Like the ball player. Hank Greenberg. My dad named me after him, for some stupid reason. Played in the 1930s and '40s, something like that. He's in the Hall of Fame."

Sebastian Drake nodded enthusiastically.

"'Hammerin' Hank'," he said, "'The Hebrew Hammer'. That's what they called him back then. Played from 1930 to 1947, to be exact. Still holds the American League record for most runs batted in for a right-handed batter in a single season, 183. Lou Gehrig, a lefty, holds the record, 184. Hammerin' Hank's career batting average was 331."

My eyes boggled. "Yes, that's right. 331. How the hell do you know all that?"

Sebastian smiled, then shrugged.

"I love baseball," he said, "and I love statistics."

I went back to eating my mystery meat and mashed potatoes smothered with thick, salty gravy and tried not to glance over at Sebastian drooling as he polished off his sandwich.

"Why'd you move here, of all places?" I asked, chewing. "Your dad get transferred or something."

"I live with my aunt and uncle," he said. "But yeah, my uncle got transferred up here."

I found that curious but decided not to probe for the specifics right then as to why he was living with his aunt and uncle instead of his mom and dad. It seemed to me that poor old Sebastian Drake had been dealt a bad hand. He had inherited something or gotten some bad disease that confined him to a wheelchair and had no parents to really take care of him. Aunts and uncles could be just as good, I suppose, as parents, except if you were Harry Potter. But I reminded myself that Potter was a fictional character, and all that stuff about a mean aunt and uncle and spoiled, mean cousin tormenting him seemed just a little bit too contrived and farfetched for my tastes.

"So are they mean to you or nice?" I asked. "Your aunt and uncle?"

I remembered the plump, kindly looking woman who had dropped Sebastian off that morning. She had looked pretty nice.

"Oh, very nice," he said. "They treat me like a son. They can't have children, I think. At least, they never had any. My uncle, he's my father's brother."

I sat there wanting to know what had happened to his real parents and thought he would offer up the story without me asking. But he just sat there, staring forward for a time, methodically chewing his sandwich with little bites and drooling along the way as if it was normal for a kid to be brought up by an aunt and uncle instead of his parents, and to spend his childhood in a wheelchair.

"So what happened to them?" I finally asked, as I scooped up another hunk of mashed potatoes. "To your parents? Why are you living with your aunt and uncle?"

As I shoved the forkful of mashed potatoes into my mouth, Sebastian sighed and took a breath. He turned his head in a crooked way to look at me.

"My mom, she died in a car accident just after I turned five," he said. He winced then a moment later he added, "And my dad, he died in the army a few years later."

"He get killed in combat?" I asked. "Like in Afghanistan or something?"

"I don't—"

Frankie Nytz had sauntered up to the table behind us. "Well, lookie here," he said, "it's Stephen Hawking's son and his girlfriend, Henrietta Greenscum."

"Bug off, Nytz," I said and went back to eating, gathering another forkful of those delicious mashed potatoes.

Without a second thought, Frankie stepped forward and cuffed me across the top of my head. I turned to him with a hateful expression.

"I had enough guff out of you for one day, Greenbugger," he said. "You're working your way to a real, first-rate ass-kicking."

I rolled my eyes as I turned away from him, and lifted my last forkful of mashed potatoes to my mouth. Frankie promptly bumped my arm sending the saucy mess into the right side of my face and the toadies loitering behind him let go of a unified guffaw.

"Okay, Frankie," I said, trying not to sound too insolent as I used a napkin to clean off my face. "You made your point. You had your fun. Now, go torment somebody else."

"Know what you need, Greenspuke?"

"No, what, Frankie?"

"Manners."

"Manners?"

"Yeah, you got no manners," Frankie said. Then he leaned down into Sebastian's left ear. "Does he Hawking?"

"Name's Sebastian," he said and moved his head up and around to look straight into Frankie's scowl. "Sebastian Drake."

"You don't say," Frankie said and turned to his toadies. "New kid says his name's Sebastian Drake." Of course, Frankie mocked the way Sebastian said it, as if he had wet marbles in his mouth. "Cool name."

Then Frankie bent down again to Sebastian's left ear.

"Just tell me one thing, *Sebastian Drake*—you take gym?"

The toadies howled at that one, and I have to admit, it was kind of funny.

"As a matter of fact," Sebastian said, "I am required to take gym. And I bet I can do more pull-ups than you ever could."

"Whoa!" was the general consensus of Frankie Nytz's toadies upon hearing the challenge. Frankie smirked and bobbed his head as he looked back at them, himself seeming amused and impressed by Sebastian's braggadocio.

"And for another thing, Mr. Nytz," Sebastian said, and he was glaring now deep into Frankie's eyes. "At this moment, I think you need to get to the little boys' room before you wee-wee in your pants."

Frankie made a face like, 'What are you talking about,' but then, in the next instant, his expression changed to one of panic.

And in the moment after that, Frankie was running out of the lunchroom with what appeared to be a wet-spot growing on the crotch of his pants.

# Chapter Three
# **A New Friend**

On my way out of school that afternoon, I sensed Sebastian Drake gliding after me down the long, musty corridor that smelled of sawdust and old locker sweat.

"Hey, Henry," he said in his garbled voice as I approached the front door, "wait up."

I pretended not hear him, but then a thought popped into my head that I should stop and turn around. After a groan, I did just that. Sebastian had almost caught up to me and had to skid sideways a couple feet to avoid running me over.

"What's up?" I asked.

We had become an obstacle in the hallway as our classmates hustled around us heading outside to the glorious after school freedom into the cool, fading September afternoon.

"I was wondering if you'd want to come over to my house later," Sebastian said. "Do our homework together."

I immediately gave him a flat no with a list of excuses—I was busy, no, tired, no, we were expecting a visit from long lost relatives, whatever. Then, without even a goodbye, I turned and strode out the front door with the thought nagging at me that I really did want to go over to the crippled kid's house.

As I hopped on the bus that would take me ten blocks to my neighborhood, I felt bad about giving Sebastian the cold shoulder. Despite being crippled and emitting spittle from a droopy mouth, there was something about him; an eccentricity that was strangely appealing. Maybe it was because I considered myself eccentric and not 'weird', as my father called me. That evening, it bothered me that I had perhaps missed an opportunity to get to know an exceptional kid and become his friend. It even made me toss and turn in bed for a time before deciding that the next day at school, I would go out of my way to befriend Sebastian Drake. And having finally settled on that, I relaxed and fell asleep.

The really weird thing was sometime that night, I dreamed about Sebastian. He was in a dark room with the shades drawn and there was a man in the room with him, in the shadows, and then, suddenly, I was there as well. The man was wearing a baggy clown outfit and, from what I could see, his face was painted with a sad clown grin. I sensed at once that the clown was evil, a serial killer or something. I couldn't hear him speak as he leered at us, but I could hear his thoughts.

*Kill him!* said the clown's voice in my head. He was talking about Sebastian. And then I realized I was holding a knife, a steak knife, in my right hand. I'd brought it up eye level.

*KILL HIM!* boomed the bad clown's voice, totally in my head. *KILL HIM!*

"NO!" I shouted and dropped the knife. I woke up sweaty and thirsty and having to pee.

The next morning, Sebastian arrived in the same special van as the previous morning. The same kindly, plump middle-aged woman, his aunt no doubt, opened the side door and lowered the lift. Like the morning before, she kissed him on the head and waved after him as Sebastian slowly wheeled off toward the school entrance.

For some reason, Frankie Nytz was not around that morning, probably skipping school again, and his toadies were even more lethargic than usual as they hung around that same lone oak tree on the front lawn staring at their smart phones and just mindlessly loitering waiting for the warning bell to sound. They ignored Sebastian like everything else that morning, even the girls.

I hurried over to Sebastian as he rolled along the sidewalk to stand before him.

"Hey, Sebastian," I said. He stopped and smiled up at me.

"Hello Henry," he said cheerfully.

"I had a dream about you last night," I told him.

He looked up at me with a silly grin. "You did? Was it about an evil clown telling you to kill me?"

"Yes," I said. "How did you know?"

"That clown was Colonel Zebb," he said.

"Who?"

"The clown who wanted you to kill me," he said.

"What the heck are you talking about?"

"Your dream," he said.

He had started off again toward the school while I stood there for a few seconds dumbstruck by the idea that he knew what I had dreamt last night. Finally, after mulling it over a few seconds, I trotted after and positioned myself around him, stopping him again.

"Are you telling me you know what I dreamed last night?" I asked.

"Why yes," he said. "I had the same dream."

"You what?"

We were only a few feet from the entrance to the school when the late bell sounded.

"We'll discuss it more at lunch," he said as he glided up the disabled ramp.

"Sure," I called after him, "at lunch."

Three hours later I took my usual, solitary seat at the back of the lunch hall and Sebastian made it over with a food tray balancing on his lap. I helped him get situated at the table and sat down next to him. I was munching on today's special, salty chicken nuggets and fries. Sebastian was munching on a salad.

After a brief hello, we quickly got around to my dream from the night before. "So who's Colonel Zebb?" I asked.

"He's a character in a video game," he said with a matter-of-fact shrug. "It's called *Psi Wars!*. Colonel Zebb is the bad guy who tried to kill good psi-warriors."

"I never heard of a game like that," I told Sebastian.

"It's not a game you can get in stores," Sebastian said, and that's all he said while I waited for more. What did that mean? But he just left it dangling there. And he also left dangling the mystery of how I had dreamed what I dreamed last night of an evil, dark faceless figure, Colonel Zebb, or whatever his name was, had been in the dream. And he had sent his voice into my head commanding that I kill Sebastian.

"So how is it possible that I dreamed that last night?" I asked. "With you in it and the villain from some video game. And that you dreamed it, too. How is such a thing possible?"

I didn't remember much about the dream anymore except the terrible, mocking grin of that evil clown and the sinister voice of Colonel Zebb, or whomever he was, commanding me to kill Sebastian. I would never forget that clown grin or that voice.

And then I remembered—I had also had *this* dream before, or something very like it. And, I'd had it more than once.

"I'm not sure," Sebastian said. "All I know is that I have dreams like that sometimes, with Colonel Zebb in them. And always, he looks different. Last night, he was an evil clown. Before that, he was an insane doctor, a polar bear. Once, he was a snake. And, sometimes he appears as a jumbled set of faces."

As Sebastian stared off with a troubled frown, I recalled, vaguely, that this 'Zebb' had had many different incarnations in my dreams as well.

"But what do they mean?" I asked him.

Sebastian shrugged and went about munching into his sandwich. Drool started down his chin.

"I don't know," he said with a shrug when he had finished

chewing and had wiped the spittle. "Maybe nothing. Maybe a lot."

At the end of lunch, I asked if his invitation to come over to his house and do our homework was still good and he said it most certainly was. I agreed to come over that evening around 7:00pm. We had the same English teacher, Miss Shay, and she had started us out reading Dickens' *Oliver Twist*. We had to turn in an essay about the book the following Friday. My topic was to compare the main character, Oliver Twist with Harry Potter. I didn't know what Sebastian had been assigned to write.

"What topic did you get?" I asked him.

"What significance does the novel's title *Oliver Twist* have for the story." he said.

"Cripes," I replied. His topic was worse than mine. "Maybe together we can figure out something to write, find something on the Internet."

Sebastian said sure, but I got the distinct impression that he already knew what to write.

We also had the same biology teacher, boring Mr. Gomez. All he basically did during class was read from a textbook.

"I'm already stumped on the difference between, what are they called?" I said. "Prokaryotes and eukaryotes."

Sebastian laughed and corrected my pronunciation, which was odd considering his general inability to enunciate normal words.

As we took our trays up to the lunch window, Sebastian asked where Frankie Nytz was.

"He skips school a lot," I told him. "Gets him into trouble. Misses too many days. His toadies would say he's out shoplifting or hanging out in some bar." I laughed. "But after he pissed his pants yesterday, and got sent home for it, I think he's just too plain embarrassed." I frowned. "How the heck did that happen anyway—out of the clear blue sky?"

Sebastian shrugged then thought a moment. "No, it wasn't that, though I agree it was odd, his wetting his pants and all," he said. "But his missing school today, and on a regular basis, involves something else."

"Yes," I said. "Something to do with his father." Sebastian looked down, seeming sad or something. I added, "I heard his father drinks too much and beats him."

Finally, Sebastian looked up and said, "Maybe that's why he's the way he is."

I shrugged, then, laughed.

"What's so funny?" Sebastian asked.

"I sometimes dream about him, Frankie Nytz," I said.

"What about?"

"He's not a bully in these dreams, but kind of a nice guy," I said. "In one of them, he greets me on the sidewalk leading up to the front door. And he asks where I been. As if I was ever going anyplace."

"Well, you never know," Sebastian said after a time. "Sometimes, dreams come true."

I shrugged and Sebastian frowned for a time. Then, I smiled, thinking about Frankie running out of the lunchroom with a wet-spot on his crotch.

"How did you know that yesterday?" I asked Sebastian. "That he needed to pee?"

"Lucky guess," he said with a smile.

But I suspected right at that moment that there was more to it than that.

# Chapter Four
## Homework

That evening just before 7:00pm, my mother dropped me off in front of Sebastian's house. It was a decent looking spread; a three bedroom, two bathroom, red-brick house in a middle class neighborhood on a street of other similar neatly landscaped homes. The special van that dropped Sebastian off at school every morning was parked in the driveway.

"Nice house," my mother said. "What's his father do?"

"He's dead," I told her and she looked over at me with a raised eyebrow. "So's his mother. He's an orphan, like Oliver Twist."

My mother gave me a dubious sideways glance, as if I was making it up. Like my father, I knew she thought I was weird. She never told me that to my face, unlike like my father, who often voiced his opinion about that and a lot of other senseless things. 'You are just plain weird, Henry' he'd say looking over the top of his newspaper as I walked by or sat across from him on the couch reading some weird, science book or watching a *Twilight Zone* episode.

I was a small, plain looking kid despite the fact that my parents were generally good looking, average-sized people. My mother was blonde and apparently had a nice body. (Frankie Nytz had told me that more than once, and that he'd certainly like to bed her down. As if he'd have known what to do.) But my face had sharp lines, and my eyes curved down, giving me a perpetual scowl as if I had been born mad at the world. The only good thing I inherited from my mother was her bright, almost white-blonde hair.

I was fairly athletic although because of my size, no one would give me credit for it. My dad was tall and had been all-state or something in football and all-district in baseball, and my mom had been the star of her high school basketball team almost winning a scholarship to some big-time school. As for intelligence, I was pretty average scoring mostly 'B's—nothing that set me apart. Some of my teachers complained to my parents that they thought I could have done better and that I didn't apply myself. And with that, my father always scolded me that slackers never made it in life and neither did weirdoes.

Not that my parents hadn't tried to make me excel at something. They had put me in little league and karate class and signed me up for piano and guitar lessons. But I was unenthusiastic about most things except, as I said, comic books, video games, science fiction movies and some TV shows. Being a loner I also liked to spend long hours in my room, or outside biking aimlessly around pretending to be driving down busy streets in some fictitious city. I even drew complex maps of these imaginary cities. My mother found a few of these crazy drawings and mentioned to my father that she thought I might turn out to be a city planner at which point he laughed and wondered if I'd be drawing cities on Mars or the moons of Jupiter.

It wasn't surprising that at some point, my mother and father pretty much gave up on me and decided I was destined to be just plain weird, through no fault of their own, either by their genes or upbringing. Sometimes perfectly normal parents beget a strange son, and there was absolutely nothing they could do about it.

Or perhaps my fantasy was true, like every other kid, that I had been adopted and my parents really weren't my parents after all or that I had been fathered by a handsome and debonair mailman who was secretly a CIA agent.

"So who does he live with, your friend?" my mother said.

"His aunt and uncle," I told her.

"He's the only kid they have to take care of," I said, "just like you guys."

Even though my mother mentioned once that it was her 'fault' she was unable to have another child, I would laugh to myself thinking that my parents didn't want another kid based upon their experience with me. Or, perhaps my adoption fantasy was true—my mother was not only unable to have another child, she had been unable to have any, even me.

My mother had seemed quite pleased when I told her upon coming home from school that afternoon that I was going over to a friend's house that evening.

"Sebastian's new," I told her when I saw her eyes brighten by the news, as if going over to a new friend's house might mean that I was growing out of my loner weirdness. Maybe I would also grow a few inches and try out for the football team next year. Become a typical high school kid.

"He started school yesterday," I added. "Moved from Virginia."

"That's nice," my mother said. "It's good to have friends, Henry."

"Oh, and by the way," I said, "he's a cripple. Uses a motorized wheelchair. Talks with a lisp. Drools."

She frowned and made a kind of funny face, her hopes for my normalcy suddenly dashed.

I rang the front doorbell to Sebastian's house and within a few moments, the kindly looking lady with bright, smiling eyes, who had dropped Sebastian off at school the last two mornings, answered the door. She was a lot older than my mom, around sixty or so I guessed. More like a grandmother than an aunt.

"You must be Henry Greenberg," she said with a cheery voice. "Named after a great baseball player."

"Yes, Ma'am," I said. My father had always warned me to call grown ladies, Ma'am.

"Well, come on in." She opened the door allowing me to enter a wide, clean living room. "Seb's in his room waiting for you. It's so very nice of you to visit."

"We'll be doing homework together," I said, as if to assure her that this was no social call, but work.

She led me through a spotless house to a back bedroom, the master bedroom in fact, which Sebastian's aunt and uncle had given up so that he could have a spacious room on the ground floor with an attached, handicap-accessible bathroom.

She stopped at the door and looked down at me.

"My name is Dolores," she said with a smile. "But you can call me Dottie." Her smile widened. "Even Aunt Dottie if you like."

I nodded and gave half a shrug, not sure what to say to that.

Aunt Dottie knocked on the door and announced my arrival. Sebastian's lispy voice called out, "okay, door's open."

His room was fantastic. For one thing, it was huge, not like the virtual closet my parents had assigned me. The bed was low to the ground so Sebastian could easily get in and out from his wheelchair. An antique desk set in the corner of the room covered with papers, notebooks and pens. There were all sorts of neat movie and video game posters on the wall, but not one for the video game *Psi Wars!* Model airplanes, rocket ships, boats, cars, alien and superhero action figures lined various shelves along the walls and on top of his dresser. Along a side wall was a large bookcase crammed with science fiction and other neat books on the paranormal plus a thick textbook on designing video games. There was also military stuff including one title in particular that I noticed with the same funny name as the movie that had come out a few years ago starring that actor, George Clooney: *The Men Who Stare At Goats.*

After taking several minutes getting acclimatized to the fabulous bedroom, Sebastian pointed out a chair at a desk for me to sit at. As I sat down, he asked, "So, you figure out what you're going to say in your essay about Oliver Twist and Harry Potter?"

"Except that they're both British a-holes," I said, "not really."

He smiled. "You are a funny guy, Henry."

I remembered that great scene from the movie, *Goodfellas*, so I gave him my best Joe Pesci imitation straight from the script.

"Funny? What's so effin' funny about me?"

Sebastian frowned, not getting my meaning right away. Then, it came to him, and he said, "Funny, you know. The way you tell a story."

And we both laughed.

Then, we got down to doing our homework.

# Chapter Five
## Another School Day

We made some headway that evening on our respective essays, using the Internet with great effect. But we didn't get to study any biology so I still couldn't differentiate between prokaryotes and eukaryotes. Sebastian assured me that the concept was fairly easy to master and we agreed to meet again the following evening, Thursday, 7:00pm sharp, to type out our English lit essays and study for Friday's biology quiz. We also agreed to meet at his house again as mine was not at all wheelchair friendly. If we worked 'expeditiously', he said, maybe we'd finally get to play *Psi Wars!*

"I never heard of that game," I said, bringing up the subject of that again.

"Like I told you," Sebastian said, "you can't get it in stores. It never went public." Sebastian sighed. "All I know is that a copy came in the mail to Uncle Brad and Aunt Dottie after my father died. I'm really not supposed to tell anyone about it. But, it's really no fun unless you can play it with someone. Someone you like."

Looking back, I guess that admission was my first indication that Sebastian and I were on our way to becoming best friends.

On the way home around eight that night, my mother asked, "So what's wrong with him? I mean, why's he in a wheelchair?"

"I don't know," I told her. "We didn't talk about it."

The topic hadn't come up between Sebastian and me. I had just assumed he had been born with some weird, crippling disease.

"Probably muscular dystrophy," she said. "Or is it cerebral palsy? I always get the two mixed up."

I gave a little shrug and looked out the window, not really sure why it was so important for her to know why Sebastian was a cripple. Maybe she was against the idea of me hanging out with a disabled kid. Like, do weird kids hang together, was that what this sudden, new friendship was about, and not a sign that maybe I was growing out of being weird?

She kept quiet the rest of the short ride home. But now that she had brought it up, I was damned curious as well and vowed to ask him about it first chance I got.

Frankie Nytz returned to school the next day with a vengeance. It was a bright blue, sunny morning in what had been a gloriously warm September and the moment he saw Sebastian dropped off in his special van by his matronly Aunt Dottie and rambling up the walkway, he pushed himself off the oak tree and started toward him.

But as Frankie strolled onward, a football being tossed by Tom Kincaid and Allan Boswell got caught by a hurricane gust of wind that seemed to come out of nowhere and sent the ball hurtling toward Frankie. His hands had come up a second too late and the ball struck him square in the nose, causing him to buckle and stumble sideways. Some kids around him, even some of his toadies, couldn't help but laugh. He cursed harshly and bent over. The ball was a few feet away and he strode over to pick it up. He looked at Kincaid and Boswell who raised their arms defensively, begging forgiveness.

"Stupid asses," he shouted and threw the ball back at them.

But a second gust of wind sent the ball back into Frankie's face to skid off his forehead.

"Damn it!" He shouted as more kids laughed.

While all of this was going on, Sebastian had whizzed forward and was now entering the school buildings.

But Frankie's bad luck wasn't finished for the day. He was so ornery that his homeroom teacher had to send him to Principal McPhee's office to explain why he had spent most of the homeroom period flicking at the top of fat Kim Albert's ears from the seat behind him.

After getting a long, dull talking to from the wimpy, weak-backed principal, about the 'need to be respectful of his classmates' and the 'horrors of bullying', Frankie was released to his first period class in which he spent tossing tiny paper spitballs at the back of Miss Shay. She kept turning around to see who was tossing them but for some reason decided to ignore the onslaught and went on discussing the inner meaning of *Oliver Twist,* ending the class by reminding us that our essays were due tomorrow. Frankie made a yak sound that earned a determined scowl from Miss Shay but the bell rang before she could do anything about it.

At lunch, Frankie sauntered over to Sebastian and me.

"Hey, lookie," he said and turned to the three toadies who had accompanied him, "it's Hawking's son and his girlfriend, Missy Greengirl."

"Aren't you tired of that one, Frankie?" I asked.

"Shut up, Greenfag," he said, "before you get another lump of mashed potatoes in your face."

I looked down at my plate, saw a gnarly hamburger and a pile of French fries and reminded him they weren't serving mashed potatoes today. Frankie looked down and picked up a French fry and squished it into my forehead before I had a chance to slap away his hand. His toadies howled.

"You say potato," he said, "I say po-tow-toe."

"Damn it, Frankie," I said and took a napkin to wipe the mess. "You have a bad day, yesterday? Father beat you up again?" I had never said this before because I felt bad, even for a jerk like Frankie Nytz, to be stuck with a cross like that to bear. But today, I was tired of letting Frankie do as he pleased simply on the strength of that excuse.

I knew at once that it had not been a wise thing to say. Frankie's eyes nearly bugged out. He took a boxing stance as if he was about to send a roundhouse right across my jaw.

"What did you say, Greenkike?" he said.

"Mr. Nytz," Sebastian said, coming to my rescue, "you wouldn't want what happened to you the other day to happen again, would you?"

Frankie lowered his right fist and turned to Sebastian.

"Mizzsher Nitz," he said, "what wouldn't I want to happen?"

"Your pants?" Sebastian said, nodding to the crotch of Frankie's jeans.

Frankie stood before Sebastian and his expression went cold. He looked about to explode and perhaps send that roundhouse right into Sebastian's jaw. But that would really be bad form, even for Frankie Nytz, to hit a disabled kid in a wheelchair. Even his most loyal toadies might not stand for that.

Frankie took a deep breath and backed off. "Screw off, cripple," Frankie turned to his henchman. "Let's leave these two lovers to their romantic lunch."

Then he stalked away followed behind by his gloomy toadies and the lunch bell sounded soon after that before I could ask Sebastian why he was a cripple.

# Chapter Six
# Psi Wars!

My mother dropped me at Sebastian's house at 6:30pm that evening. I had told her I needed to get there earlier than yesterday because we had so much work to do. She seemed pleased with my sudden interest in schoolwork and wondered if Sebastian was a smart kid.

"He's a genius," I told her and she said something lame about most disabled kids being pretty smart.

In fact, Sebastian really did seem to be a genius. He knew so much about just about everything and I hoped some of that intelligence would rub off on me so that I would move from a 'B' to an 'A' average. Most of my teachers told my parents that my average grades were due to my 'lackluster' attitude. The simple fact was I didn't apply myself. But not all that was my fault. For the most part, my teachers were not all that inspiring, and the course materials equally lacked interest.

Although there was some truth in needing to get to Sebastian's house earlier to finish off a lot of work before tomorrow, the real reason for doing so was for the chance to finally play the by now greatly touted, by him anyway, video game *Psi Wars!*

Aunt Dottie greeted me with her usual kindly smile and bright eyes and brought me to Sebastian's room. We got down to business and were fairly satisfied with our English essays by

7:15pm. He nodded as he read my comparison between the characters Oliver Twist and Harry Potter.

"Pretty good," he said.

"Thanks," I replied with a shrug. "Actually, there are some pretty neat comparisons between old Oliver and old Harry. For one thing, they are both orphans with their births shrouded in mystery. Both their lives take a, well, interesting turn with Oliver ending up in Fagin's gang, and Harry enrolled at Hogwarts. And, last but not least, they soon face off against a nemesis: Bill Sykes for Twist, and Lord Voldemort for Potter." I sighed. "Bottom line, I still found Oliver Twist a more interesting character than Harry Potter."

"I'm not too sure the millions of Harry Potter fans would agree with your ultimate opinion," Sebastian commented, "that *Oliver Twist* is a better read than the Harry Potter books."

"Well," I said, "whatever. I realized a long time that I am definitely in the minority. About a lot of things."

Satisfied with our essays we next turned to biology and with Sebastian's help, I finally started understanding what prokaryotes and eukaryotes were.

"Those terms basically describe the structures of cells," I finally said in a eureka moment.

"Right!" Sebastian said.

"Basically, eukaryotes are cells that have nuclei," I said, "and prokaryotes don't." I thought a moment. "Or is it the other way around?"

He let me hash it out in my head for myself.

"No," I finally said, "I was right the first time."

"Right!" Sebastian said.

By 7:45pm, confident that we'd ace the biology test the next day, we quit studying and finally got down to playing *Psi Wars!*, although in truth I could have used a few more minutes of study time. But heck, all work and no play, makes Henry a dull boy, as the saying goes.

The game console was attached by three wires to the

Vincent L. Scarsella

nice, new fifty inch flat-screen TV that hung on the side wall of Sebastian's room. Sebastian wheeled over and grabbed two pairs of what looked to be virtual reality simulator goggles off the top of the console. Each pair looked like expensive, modern sunglasses but large enough to wrap around one's field of vision. I decided that they must be wirelessly connected to the game console because there were no wires. Sebastian wheeled over and handed me a set of the goggles.

"We wear these while playing the game," he said. "They transport you inside. Like you're really there. It's pretty cool."

After handing me the goggles, Sebastian used a remote to turn on the TV, then pressed another button on the remote to turn on the game console.

"Where are the controllers?" I asked.

"*Psi Wars!* doesn't use controllers, per se," he told me. "Just the VR goggles." Sebastian nodded to the television screen hanging on his wall. "Watch."

I shrugged, not quite sure what to make of playing a video game without controllers and instead using VR goggles—except that playing it was promising to be one weird experience.

Sebastian pressed the play button and the screen flashed on. There was a short blast of music and it seemed that we were about to watch an educational video rather than play a game. I frowned with increasing disappointment as the screen remained an antique grainy black and white, a scratchy, foggy hue with none of the color and pizzazz of a modern video game.

Still grainy and dark, the opening scene of the game came into focus. There was a bare stage, with a tattered, gray curtain at the back of it. After a moment, some tall and lean guy entered from stage left wearing an aviator jacket, khaki pants, and state trooper sunglasses. A soldier or pilot, I supposed. His features were sharp, drawn and almost mean, like a cop having a bad day. He must be an actor, I thought, about to give some corny backstory about the game and indicate its general objective. Why we had to avoid and kill this or that bad guy and what

36

happens if we don't. How we went about saving the world, that sort of nonsense.

The soldier strode confidently to a spot at center stage and stopped. He looked straight out at us as if we were among an audience of some auditorium.

"Good morning, cadets," he began in a self-sure voice. Like most military folk, or so it seemed, he had a vague southern accent as if he was a good ol' boy from Alabama or Mississippi. "My name is Major Blake Farnsworth, and I hope you are enjoying your stay here at the Psi Cave, home of Project Mind Bloom. My purpose this morning is to introduce you to a rather clever and fun simulation game that we here call *Psi Wars!*"

"*Psi Wars!*" the Major went on, "has become an important training tool that helps us assess and enhance the latent psychic abilities of our cadets. It will be used by our monitoring and mentoring instructors to determine which of you are capable of engaging in actual psychic conflict. In short, it will help us decide if you have what it takes to become a psi-warrior."

Despite the bad video, perhaps intentionally so to make it look authentic, I was intrigued by the game. It felt real in that moment, like I was really out there, a cadet at something called Project Mind Bloom, watching Major Farnsworth from a seat in some auditorium instructing us about a game call *Psi Wars!* This was so cool.

Through its play, a cadet could learn how to become a psi-warrior, a kind of 'wizard', I supposed. But not the kind of wizard using spells and incantations and wands to fight, but one who uses actual psychic powers like telekinesis, telepathy, remote viewing and mind control to defeat evil psi-warriors.

"You see, cadets," Major Farnsworth went on, "the rumors you may have been hearing around here lately are unfortunately true. As I speak, we are engaged in a secret war with a force of evil psi-warriors that are attempting to use their enhanced psychic powers to subjugate all of humanity to their will and whim. This force is led by none other than Colonel Zachariah

Z. Zebb, Project Mind Bloom's former co-commander. Colonel Zebb and the platoon of traitors under his command have allowed the lure of absolute power to negate the oath each one of them took to preserve and protect the American way of life. And in no uncertain terms, they must be stopped or we face, quite simply, the annihilation of our liberty and freedom.

"Three months ago, Colonel Zebb and his treasonous platoon used these psychic abilities, developed here in this very unit, to ambush and massacre Project Mind Bloom's other co-commander, Colonel Peter Drake, and then escaped to parts unknown to commence their quest for world domination."

The mention of Peter Drake, Sebastian's father, sent a shiver down my spine.

"Peter Drake?" I said, turning to Sebastian in the dark room. "As in your father? That Peter Drake?"

Sebastian pressed the pause button on the remote and turned to me with a shrug and a forlorn expression.

"Yes," he said. "My father. Colonel Peter Drake."

"So you think it's somehow true?" I asked. "The stuff about your father being ambushed by Colonel Zebb? Or is it just some silly backstory spiel in a video game?"

"All I know," Sebastian said with a shrug, "is that my father was killed while serving in the Army. Nobody has ever confirmed how he died. A few weeks after he died, a package containing this video game and the special goggles was mailed to my aunt and uncle, addressed to me. It included a note typed out on a sheet of copy paper that said simply this, 'Play the game and learn.'

"At first, Uncle Brad and Aunt Dottie thought of telling the Army about the game. But Uncle Brad finally decided against it. He said he had a hard time believing the Army had told us everything about my father's death, so why should I cooperate with them?

"Whether or not the backstory is true," Sebastian went on,

"whether Colonel Zebb and a band of psi-warriors killed my father, we just don't know for sure."

With that, Sebastian pressed the play button to resume the game and we focused our attention to the rest of what Major Farnsworth had to say.

"During this simulation," Major Farnsworth continued, "you will be forced to confront and, hopefully, learn how to overcome the psychic powers put to evil use. Some of you will succeed in that confrontation. However, I am sorry to say, most of you will not. Those who do succeed will go onto further simulations in the next level of assessments until the day comes when your superiors decide, if they ever do, that you are ready to join the fight against the forces of evil championed by Colonel Zebb and his treasonous followers.

"Until that day, I wish you Godspeed and good luck."

After a few moments, the screen went blank.

"That was interesting," I said.

Sebastian shrugged indifferently as if to say maybe it was and maybe it wasn't. Or maybe he had seen it so many times, it didn't affect him like seeing it for the first time did for me.

"Put on your goggles," he said, "and let's play."

I looked down at the VR goggles. "These really work?" I asked. "We don't watch the TV?"

"No," he said. "I told you, everything happens in the goggles. You'll be immersed in the action."

I shrugged and put them on. Everything went dark. "Okay," I said. "Start."

"It has started," Sebastian said.

"Then it's not working," I said. "It's completely dark. Black."

"That's the first test of the game. You're locked in a lead coffin and have to use the power of your mind to get out."

"What?"

And then I felt it. My field of vision was not dark as if the goggles weren't working. I was now able to see the outline of a heavy, blank mass above me, it looked like a heavy lid, within a foot or so of my face. Suddenly, I felt extremely claustrophobic, walled in. My arms and legs were heavy. I could hardly breathe.

"How?" I asked, growing slightly panicky and about ready to rip the goggles from my eyes. "What powers?"

"Just focus, Henry," he said. "Think. Use the powers of your mind."

"Yeah, sure," I said. "Easy for you to say. You've played this game before." I said. "How in the hell did you know it was lead?"

Sebastian chuckled softly. "I can smell it," he said. "You have to learn what things smell like, Henry. If you want to become a psi-warrior."

I closed my eyes and tried to imagine what lead smelled like and pretty soon I was smelling something metallic. I sniffed and sure enough, there is was. Like a nickel. "Okay," I told Sebastian. "I smell lead. Now what?" A few seconds elapsed. "Sebastian?"

"Think how to open the lid," he said, sounding out of breath. "What's holding it shut?"

I thought a while. Nails? No. How do you nail lead? The idea of screws came to mind. Metal, maybe lead screws. I closed my eyes and tried to visualize the screws holding down the lid of the lead coffin. Then, thinking of being stuck inside a coffin, I felt claustrophobic again. Jesus H. Christ, this was some weird video game.

I remembered what Sebastian told me. *Use the power of your mind.*

What freaking power?

Telekinesis. Something about using brain waves to move things, to physically alter tangible objects. Like that magician, Kreskin, or was it Uri Geller, who I'd seen bending spoons a while back, supposedly with the energy of his mind on the old reruns of talk shows hosted by Johnny Carson that my father sometimes liked to watch.

So I focused my mind on the idea of unscrewing the screws holding down the lid of the lead coffin I appeared to be trapped in. I imagined screws screwing backwards, and after a short time, I could hear one of them moving. It was the one screwed into the top left corner of the lid and it was actually unscrewing in a barely perceptible, counterclockwise revolution.

But then a moment later, I could hear a voice and someone pounding at Sebastian's bedroom door, and then the door opening, and Sebastian garbling, "Take them off."

I found myself pulling off the goggles despite the tug of feeling that I should stay in the game and unscrew that screw. Instead, I was blinking in the suddenly bright light of Sebastian's room gawking at him and his Uncle Stan who was now looming in the doorway.

"You were playing the game," Uncle Stan said to Sebastian. It wasn't said meanly or anything, just a statement tinged with disappointment. "I thought we talked about that."

"I know we did Uncle Stan," Sebastian said. "But I felt my friend, Henry, might be an exception to the rule."

Uncle Stan and Sebastian looked at each other for a long, uncomfortable time. Finally, Uncle Stan sighed.

"Well," he said, "His mother's here. She's been blowing her horn out there for five minutes."

"I guess we didn't hear it," Sebastian said.

I hopped off the chair and placed the goggles on top of the game console. I gathered my knapsack and headed out of the room.

"Night Mr. Drake," I said as I edged past him.

"Night Henry."

When I reached my mother's car, she seemed annoyed. "Where were you?"

"Learning," I told her with a shrug, then looked out the window as we drove off. I didn't add, of course, that I was learning how to become a psi-warrior.

# Chapter Seven
## Sebastian's Disease

The next morning, right after Aunt Dottie had dropped Sebastian off at school, I trotted up to him as he rode up the main entrance sidewalk.

"What happened after I left?" I asked. "Your uncle seemed upset."

Sebastian stopped, turned slightly, and looked up at me with his head, as usual, cocked on a funny sideways angle.

"He wasn't angry," he said. "Just concerned. But after you left, we talked it out and when we were done, he understood why I let you play. Now, he says you can come over any time and play."

"Really," I said, and started walking with Sebastian down the walkway towards the school entrance. "That's cool. When can we play it again?"

"How's tomorrow afternoon?" Sebastian asked.

"Yeah sure," I told him. Tomorrow afternoon was glorious Saturday. Freedom from school. "I've got no plans. I was just starting to unscrew one of the screws fastening down the lid when your uncle came in."

Just then, I looked up and noticed Frankie Nytz leaning against the split oak tree. He was wearing a funny looking cabana hat that looked like some kind of weird fashion statement. I had to take a deep breath to suppress a laugh.

"Well, lookie, lookie, lookie," he said as he pushed himself off the tree.

He lumbered forward on an angle that intercepted us along the walkway and stood there waiting with his arms folded across his chest. For some reason, none of his usual toadies were around.

"If it ain't Hawking's son and his lover-boy, Greenhamandeggs," Frankie said in that annoying, nasally way.

"A-hole," I muttered under my breath.

"What did you say, Greenbacon?" Frankie snorted. "Oh, I forgot, you can't eat bacon."

"Look, Frankie," I said, "what joy could you possibly get harassing a cripple and a nerd?"

"Greenomelet, there's no better fun than harassing a cripple and a Jew," he said with a sigh. "Like my daddy says, Hitler had it right. All Jews and cripples should be exterminated at birth."

I said a very nasty word to Frankie right then, followed by the word 'off,' and after the sound of that sunk into Frankie's brain, he frowned and stepped forward with his fists clenched. I suspected he was about to punch me in the gut or worse, in the nose. But then, a sudden gust of wind came out of nowhere and blew his stupid looking cabana hat off his head. Propelled by this same gust of wind, the hat rolled across the lawn on its brim right into the feet of Marsha Kendall, the prettiest girl in the ninth grade over whom, like every other boy in the ninth grade, Frankie Nytz had a longstanding, unrequited crush. As, of course, did I.

Frankie gawked at her and stopped in his tracks as she held it up for him. "You want your hat, Frankie?" she asked, smiling deviously at him.

He stood before her, unable to think as he swooned under the spell of her warm, devilish gaze. "Y-yeah," he stuttered.

"Looks like you need a bigger brain to keep it on your head," she added as she handed it back to him.

There was a smattering of giggles from those gawkers

around him as Frankie dropped the hat. Sebastian had gestured for us to get going and we started for the school. Frankie knelt down to retrieve his hat and looked dumbstruck into Marsha Kendall's dreamy blue eyes.

Funny thing was, it had been an otherwise windless, warm September morning in the moment before that gust of wind had conveniently come out of the sky just in time to save me once again from Frankie's retribution for standing up to him. Just like that other time, when the football blew into his face.

I looked over at Sebastian as we neared the entrance to the school and, oddly enough, he winked at me.

Sebastian settled into the same spot next to me at lunch as he had the previous three days. I helped him with his tray and saw that this was to become a regular thing for us. We were officially lunch pals. I could also see that we were destined to become much more than that. Friends for sure, maybe even best friends.

I sighed thinking about that, as I looked over at Sebastian chewing a sandwich, spittle and all, and decided I could do a lot worse than him for a friend.

We ate for a while in silence. Finally, I looked at him and said, "Funny about that gust of wind coming out of nowhere and blowing Frankie Nytz's stupid hat off. Just like that football the other day."

Sebastian smiled coyly and nodded.

"Yeah," he said, but offered nothing else. Nothing even to explain the funny wink he had given me the moment after it happened telling me, of course, that he knew something about it.

But I let it go. I wanted to find out why he was crippled and stuck in a wheelchair.

"So, can I ask you," I said, "if you don't mind, why you're in that wheelchair? Like, what's your disease?"

He sighed and thought a moment. "I wasn't born this

way," he said as he chewed into his sandwich and I watched as a trickle of spittle rolled down from the bite along the side of his mouth to the napkin on his lap.

"You weren't born with it?" I said. "You mean, at some past point in your life, you didn't need a wheelchair? You could walk?"

"Yes," he said. "Up until I was five, when my mother died. There was a car accident." Sebastian halted and looked down at his lap. Telling this story was clearly hard for him and I almost told him to stop, that it didn't matter.

But then he went on, "Anyway, we got into an accident. She was killed, and the accident left me a cripple stuck in a wheelchair. But the doctors don't know why. They say they can't find anything physically wrong with me. Some of them think the whole thing's in my head, you know, psychosomatic, caused by the trauma of the wreck and my mother's death."

He sighed and licked up the small thread that wound down from his lips. I found it hard to believe that the mind could cause him to be this way. His physical deformity had to be a real. Just look at him.

"Some other doctors think it's a form of cerebral palsy brought on by the accident," Sebastian went on. "Believe me, I've had a thousand tests but nobody can quite figure out why I am the way I am. I'm a medical mystery."

"That's, that's weird," was all I could think of saying.

And that was it. Sebastian Drake was a cripple, that was certain, but nobody knew why.

After that, we settled into eating our respective lunches, silently ruminating on the day's events. At one point, I laughed out loud thinking of that stupid cabana hat blowing off Frankie Nytz's head by a sudden, inexplicable, gust of wind and him chasing after it into the beloved Marsha Kendall's feet.

Towards the end of lunch, we agreed to meet around 1:00pm tomorrow at his house, to resume playing the game.

"I was starting to unscrew the screw, you know," I told him.

"Yes, so you said," Sebastian said and smiled. "Well, who knows? Maybe pretty soon you'll be making gusts of wind come from out of nowhere and blowing hats off peoples' heads."

# Chapter Eight
## A Beautiful Friendship

That night, I had another dream about the evil faceless psi-warrior, presumably Colonel Zebb, and again, he was out to get Sebastian. This time, he tried a kinder, gentler approach, telling me that Sebastian was not all that he was cracked up to be, that he may not be among the good guys. When I told him to take a flying leap, that he couldn't talk about my best friend that way, he shook his head and laughed at me.

"Best friend?" he said. "He's your worst enemy."

And then, in the next instant, he turned into a scowling, gargoyle-faced smoke monster, a grayish, brackish thing like something out of a steel plant smokestack. It floated above me for a moment then there was an army of similar ugly smoke wraiths beside it. I ran and they started chasing me. From a distance, I heard Sebastian's voice echoing in the wind.

"C'mon, Henry!" he shouted. "C'mon!"

I woke up and the dream quickly faded from my mind except for the part that when Sebastian called out my name and he wasn't lisping.

When I got to Sebastian's house around 1:00pm the next afternoon, I told him about it.

"It was that Colonel again," I told him. With a laugh, I

added, "And you know what? He told me that maybe you were a bad guy."

Frowning, Sebastian looked away. Finally, he looked back at me, still frowning, tense.

"Zebb's full of it," he said and then, with a sigh, he added, "Did you come over to play *Psi Wars!* or talk about some silly dream?"

I gave him a curious look, thinking his put off reaction somewhat odd. He didn't seem like the Sebastian I had come to know. He suddenly seemed different, unfriendly.

"To play *Psi Wars!*," I said. "Geez. Calm down."

"So let's play," he said.

So Sebastian and I soon became immersed in the game; it was like entering a movie and playing around with the main characters. It was most certainly the best video game I had ever played.

During the game, I used my mental powers, or whatever, to somehow unscrew all the screws and pop open the lid, then escape from the lead coffin into a dark cavern—a dank, murky dungeon of some kind. It took me something like an hour to get that far and I couldn't decide if it was really my mind energy that had done it, that had made eight screws turn backwards and pop out, or whether it was simply a clever illusion the game creators had imposed upon my imagination.

By the time I had escaped the coffin, I was pretty much mentally and physically spent. I took off the VR goggles and told Sebastian I'd had enough. My head was splitting.

I asked him what he thought. Was it a trick or had my brain energy actually filtered into the digital matrix of the game to turn the screws counterclockwise. Sebastian said he wasn't sure. He seemed to have calmed down by then, become his old, unassuming self. All he knew was that you didn't need a controller to play *Psi Wars!* and that it certainly seemed to improve one's psychic powers.

"How do you know that?" I asked.

"Because sometimes," he said, "I do things."

"Like what things?"

"Just things," he said. "I shouldn't have mentioned it. It's probably just my imagination."

"Like what things, Sebastian?"

He shook his head and turned his wheelchair around so that his back was to me.

"Like those gusts of wind?" I asked. "Those gusts of wind that blew a football into Frankie Nytz's face and his hat off into the feet of Marsha Kendall?"

When Sebastian didn't turn around, I added, "Or made the school warning bell ring early? Or made Frankie piss his pants?"

Finally he turned around. "Yeah," he said. "Like those things. I sometimes think things, and they happen."

Now that would be cool, quite a magnificent ability, in fact, like one of the superheroes in the comic books I read. Except Sebastian certainly didn't look like a superhero sitting there in his wheelchair, with his body all disjointed and saliva dripping down from his lower lip.

Over the next few weeks, Sebastian and I continued to eat lunch together on a daily basis and I continued regularly going over to Sebastian's house to do homework, play *Psi Wars!* and other video games and to generally talk about things. Soon enough, I considered him to be my best friend in all the world and, I think, he considered me his as well.

Naturally, Frankie Nytz and his toadies start calling us homos. Frankie also started mixing our names together in silly combinations, calling Sebastian, Greendrake, and me, Drakesgreenqueen, stupid stuff like that. He also wanted to know whose surname we were going to take when we got married and whether I had a wheelchair fetish.

With each stupid comment, I told Frankie and his stupid toadies to flip off. One afternoon, after doing just that, Frankie chased me down in the hallway between classes and cuffed me across the back of the head. One of the stern-faced hall monitors saw and gave Frankie a detention chit for which he paid me back the following morning with a stifling headlock, followed by a half nelson that almost made me pass out. He only let go when a solitary seagull glided over us, circled, and then proceeded to drop a load of slimy, white bird poop on his head. Upon releasing me, he stumbled around wiping the top of his head and emitting a string of curses that an outside monitor heard, earning him yet more detention.

From the corner of my eye, I saw Sebastian rolling along the sidewalk and I suspected that the fortuitous seagull was yet another example of his innate psi powers honed by playing *Psi Wars!*

I spent almost all my free time at Sebastian's house from the middle of September through the end of October. My mother began to say things, drop subtle hints, suggesting that maybe my exclusive friendship with a disabled, wheelchair-bound kid may not be in my best interest. She'd ask where I was going, and I'd say, "Seb's", and she'd comment dryly, "Again". Sometimes, she'd add, "He's the boy in the wheelchair, right? The crippled kid," and I'd say, "Yes, Mom, for the hundredth time. The crippled kid." Once I added, "And I think the politically correct term for him is 'physically disadvantaged'."

One Saturday morning a few days from Halloween, just after I told her I was biking over to Sebastian's house, on my way out the door, I overheard her complaining about my 'obsession' with that 'crippled boy' to my father as he was scrutinizing the sports pages. I stood in the doorway a moment waiting for my father's response. Finally, he said, "I told you. The boy's weird. Just like your brother, Eddie. And weird boys hang together."

From what little I understood, because it was rarely a topic of conversation between my mother and father, Uncle Eddie was an eccentric 'drugged-out dude' as my father called him, who the last time my mother heard, was living in some commune in a desolate stretch of northern California.

Though *Psi Wars!* was the main video game Sebastian and I played during our time together, we did play some other games as well. And, not surprisingly, Sebastian was an ace at all of them. I could never beat him and I was no slouch at video games. I called him, to his face of course, the Pinball Wizard, like the deaf, dumb and blind kid hero from that old Who rock opera. For a competitive kid like me, constantly losing to Sebastian became a source of simmering frustration. This resulted in me acting somewhat like a Frankie Nytz wannabe and I found myself calling him all sorts of terrible and hurtful names upon losing another game to him. I immediately regretted doing so every time and always apologized profusely, but he took my verbal abuse in stride, saying simply that he understood my frustration which sometimes made me even angrier.

He also tried to explain why he was so good at video games, passing it off, partially at least, to having spent hours playing since the onset of his crippling disease. Unlike other kids, he couldn't go out and play. During all these hours of solitary game playing, Sebastian told me that he had perfected a way of being one with the game, becoming part of it, like a Zen master. It was a similar tactic he used in playing *Psi Wars!*

But I thought there was more to it than that. He had an innate ability, psychic or otherwise, a sixth sense, that enabled him to anticipate the next hazard or sequence of events that the gaming software programmers had built into the digital matrix of the game. Sebastian simply knew where the game was going, what was going to happen next.

So time and time again, he was able to beat my score, no matter how well I played. And time and time again, I'd slam my fist on top of his bed, or punch the wall, stamp my feet, slap my own face, or call him a rotten name. A curl of a smile would form on his lips as I finally calmed down and apologized for being such a jerk, such a poor loser. He'd forgive me with a nod and we'd move on to the next game; my next loss.

But mostly, we played *Psi Wars!*. It was the best game ever, challenging and quirky and we couldn't get enough of it. After supposedly using the power of my mind to compel screws to unscrew, pushing off the lid of the coffin and jumping out into a thick, dank darkness, I stood waiting for the game's next obstacle. During the wait, I reached over and touched the side of the coffin I was standing next to. It had a hard, rough metallic feel. And then it occurred to me it was odd that I was able to feel anything at all. I was playing a video game that was being wirelessly transmitted into my VR goggles via the digital innards of a console. I should be able to see things that looked real, but to feel them as well was simply beyond any technology of which I was aware. And it was a moment after having that thought, the recognition of technological impossibility, the realization that I was in Sebastian's room playing a video game that had nothing to do with reality, when I lost my sense of sight and hearing and smell and touch and the game went blank.

"Just concentrate," Sebastian said, sensing my inner sense of doubt. "Play the game. Suspend your disbelief. Pretend that the real world does not exist."

I sighed and focused and pretty soon I was again immersed in the digital imagery of *Psi Wars!* in total darkness in some kind of chamber, alone. I squinted, expecting my vision to adjust to the complete lack of light. And then, far off, toward the end of whatever cavern I was in, I saw black shapes. What came to mind was the word 'wraiths' and they made a low humming sound, like a million bees trapped in a pillow case. The wraiths were coming toward me, for me. In the next moment, they were upon me.

There was the classic comical whizz and whirl sound that video games make when a game is lost. Game over.

"What just happened?" I asked Sebastian.

My VR goggles were off and on my lap, and I was sitting

on the floor leaning against his bed. He was hovering above me in his wheelchair.

"You pooped the bed," he said. "Screwed the pooch."

I looked up at him. "Screw you, gimp," I said and he smiled at me. "Why are you here, then, if you're so great, Zen master?" I asked, "And not still in the game?"

"I signed off when you went down," he said.

I sighed and blinked down hard. After a moment, I looked up. "What the hell were they? Do you know?"

Sebastian nodded. "Mind wraiths. Holographic demons formed by one's brain energy. To fight them, you have to learn how to make your own, white and black wraiths."

"Well, it would have been helpful to know that before I got zapped."

"For some," he said, "it's intuitive."

"That an insult, cripple?"

"Not at all," he said. "Most kids wouldn't have figured out how to unscrew the screws."

"So how does one make a wraith, white, black or otherwise?"

"Well, to make a dark wraith, you think the darkest, ugliest thing you ever thought of," he said. "A black deed. Then a black wraith will appear."

"Sounds wonderful."

"To make a white wraith," Sebastian went on, "you think the best thing you ever thought. Ice cream. Sunny days in July. Disney World. The blast of lightning, boom of thunder and the smell of ozone and rain. What you do, you create an angel. You think of Mickey Mouse, Tinker Bell, Sweet Pea. Marsha Kendall, or Marcia Brady. That's what a white wraith is."

I let Sebastian's description, in all its cleverness, sink in, and laughed.

"Sounds wild," I said. "Neat."

"Yes, it is wild, neat," he said. "Quite wild, quite neat. And it works."

He nodded to the goggles in my lap.

"Try it," he said. "There is nothing better in the world of *Psi Wars!* than to make a white wraith eliminate a dark wraith."

I sighed and lifted up the goggles.

"Okay," I said. "Let's do it."

The game commenced again with me standing next to the coffin. The dark wraiths came to life at the far horizon and just stood there wearily observing me. I thought of ice cream, puffy clouds against a blue sky, wind chimes on a breezy summer night, Marsha Kendall; and, in the next moment, standing alongside me were a team of figures, floating there like clouds. White wraiths. My very own white wraiths. I looked up and there they were, a row of them to the right and left of me. They turned towards me, but they were faceless. Still, I did not fear them. They had come into existence to fight on my behalf, for my survival, for my existence. My guardian angels.

We stood our ground facing the dark wraiths. And then, after some minutes, one of them emitted a fearful howl; it was like a horn sounding a distress call. A moment later, the others howled like that as well. Then, they started growling, shrieking, and screaming with raised arms; and, the sound rose up in a horrible cacophony of dread, straight out of a nightmare.

The white wraiths stood their ground in the teeth of this aggression. From them, I heard a gentile kind of low melody, a charm of sorts, or a prayer hummed by angels, like the wistful chorus of wind chimes.

Finally, moments later, the regiment of dark wraiths started running towards us from across the plain of darkness, a mad rush seemingly without plan or modus operandi. The white wraiths stepped methodically and fearlessly forward to join them in battle.

"What should I do?" I asked the wraith floating next to me. He or she (I wasn't sure what sex it was) turned to me and nodded benignly, but said nothing. I realized at that moment that they were figments of my own mind, incapable of speech or thought and that their sole purpose was to protect me from the attacking dark wraiths. Once unleashed, they would either succeed or fail. If they failed, game over.

On this occasion, they did not fail.

At some point after the battle, as the white wraiths began to fade in the nothingness from whence they came, and as the darkness of the place began to brighten, as if the sun was coming up causing a gray, false dawn, I fell asleep.

The next thing I knew, Sebastian was jabbing at my right shoulder.

"Henry," he whispered. "Wake up."

I opened my eyes and saw him peering down at me from his wheelchair, a line of spittle just starting to drop from his lower lip. I sat up and rubbed my right temple.

"I'm so tired," I told him.

"You will get stronger," he said. "The more you play."

I looked up at him. "So I won?"

"Well, if the light was coming up, you advanced to the next level." He sighed. "But I think you've had enough *Psi Wars!* for one day."

"You got that right," I said. I rubbed my head for a time, let go of a wide yawn and stretched my back. "And you?"

Sebastian smiled. "I am already in level five," he said. "I can already smell Colonel Zebb's ugly breath. It's like brimstone."

"Someday," I asked, "can we play together, as a team?"

"Someday," he said, "I'm sure we will."

I laughed to myself.

"What's so funny?" he asked.

"You know what," I said, "we are just like Captain Renault and Rick, from that movie, *Casablanca*. What we have started is a beautiful friendship. Ever see it?"

"Yes," Sebastian said and smiled and seemed to blush, as did I. "I've seen it."

Enough already of this sentimentality, I thought to myself.

"Yes," he said.

"Yes, what?"

"It is unbecoming of a psi-warrior," he said.

His words sent a shudder down my spine and made my heart miss a beat. That was exactly what I was thinking.

# Chapter Nine
# **The National Defense Mental**

Aptitude Assessment Test

Early one morning a week after Halloween, we got a slushy, messy six inches of snow and cold air that made a lot of it stick to the grass and roads, and I was hoping for our first snow day. But no such luck. I had to trudge out into the cold, damp morning, with leaden, ugly gray clouds low in the sky making the dark morning even darker, wearing my three-year-old musty smelling, out of date, winter coat for the first time of what promised to be another long, dreary winter. Then, I had to wait an extra fifteen minutes for the bus at the corner of my street and by the time I clambered in, I was wet and ornery. We edged along with the slow traffic that morning and finally made it to school around twenty minutes late.

I shuffled into homeroom and took a seat. Mr. Vickers, my homeroom teacher, scowled at me as Vice Principal Zykorski was droning the last of the morning announcements. I yawned and was trying to finally warm up when I heard him state:

"This is to remind all ninth grade students that today, from the start of first period until first lunch, you will be administered the National Defense Mental Aptitude Assessment test in your homerooms and will not, I repeat, will not change classes until lunchtime."

There was a minor shuffling of discontent among some of

my classmates as if having to take a three hour standardized test was worse than experiencing lectures from our boring teachers.

Zykorski ended with his usual, stupid admonition, "Have a pleasant, safe and successful day", as if pleasantness, safety and success were part of what Colonel J. B. Weber High School had to offer.

A minute or so later, the bell rang and several of my more inattentive and inane classmates got up to change classes. Mr. Vickers had to call them back while asking in his most sarcastic tone, 'Hadn't they been listening to Principal Zykorski's announcements?'

There were a pile of blue test booklets on Vickers' desk and with a bored expression, he started handing them out. There was an American eagle emblazoned on the cover of each booklet and each one had fifteen pages of questions with an answer grid stuck in the middle that we were told to carefully pull out along the perforations.

After handing out the booklets, Mr. Vickers passed out No.2 pencils and then gave us what little directions we needed to know. Basically, there were four parts to the test and we had forty-five minutes to take each part, for a total of three hours. In short; we'd be done by the freshman lunch period; it was imperative that we completely fill in the circle indicating what the *best* answer was; if we needed to go to the bathroom, raise a hand.

"What's this test for?" asked Brad Jenkins, athlete extraordinaire, as he looked up from the booklet. He was destined, some said, to be the future star quarterback and savior of the Colonel J. B. Weber varsity football team after his stellar freshman year for the JV. Like the rest of us, he was flipping through the pages of the test booklet, annoyed at having to read so many questions, and think so hard on that cold, snowy morning.

"I mean, does it have anything to do with getting into

college?" Brad asked. Vickers sat on the edge of his desk at the front of the class. He crossed his legs and shrugged.

"I have no idea," he said. "My job is to hand it out and watch you take it. And your job is to take it."

And that was it, the sole explanation why we had to take the NDMAA test. We soon figured out that this was like no standardized test we had ever taken.

"You have forty-five minutes for Part One," Vickers said as he checked his watch. "And that time starts...now."

Part One listed fifty seemingly pointless multiple choice questions. They were grouped in fives, and posted after the description of ridiculous situations giving us five equally ridiculous possible reactions under choices (a), (b), (c), (d) and (e). In answer to each of these questions, choice (e) was either 'all of the above' or 'none of the above.' My best guess was that this part was trying to determine one's personality type.

The directions were quite simple—carefully read the scenario and provide what you think was the best response. For example, the first scenario had us imagining that we were in a bank that was being held up by a gang of bank robbers. The first question wanted to know what we would do if we were told by the robbers to lay on the floor and keep our heads down:

*(a) Obey the directions of the robbers until the robbery is completed.*

*(b) Disobey the directions of the robbers and charge at the one closest to you in an attempt to grab his weapon and foil the robbery.*

*(c) Obey the directions of the robbers, but use your cell phone to dial 911.*

*(d) Obey the directions of the robbers while thinking of a way to safely foil the robbery and then implement it.*

*(e) None of the above.*

I chose (b), probably wrong, but what the hell—it was fake question in a fake test.

At the end of the forty-five minutes, Vickers barked out an order for us to stop.

"Alright," he said, "turn the page to Part Two."

Part Two was also fairly simple in terms of what we were required to do. It seemed like yet another personality assessment test with a series of 'Yes/No' questions asking things designed to determine whether we were an introvert, extrovert, neurotic and etcetera. Each of the questions seemed nonsensical or just plain silly, for example:

*"It's difficult to get you excited" (Yes); "You are almost never late for school" (Yes); "You enjoy having a wide circle of friends." (No); "You often think about humanity and its destiny" (After thinking, "What?" to myself, I answered, Yes); "You find it difficult to speak loudly," (I laughed at this one as well, and finally selected, No); "You value justice higher than mercy" (Yes); "You find it difficult to talk about your feelings" (Yes).*

And, about another fifty more, just like these.

Spliced in among these questions were several questions even more strange and nonsensical than the others, also requiring yes/no answers:

*"When your telephone rings, you sometimes know who is calling?" (Yes); "You can control your dreams?" (No); "You see the shapes of faces and animals in clouds?" (Yes); "You dream in color." (Yes); "What you dream about sometimes comes true." (Yes).*

As for that last answer, the true response should have been, 'I think so but I am not entirely sure'. I mean, I'd sometimes dream something and sometime later, anywhere from a day to a year or longer, something would happen or someone would say something and I'd stop in my tracks with a vague recollection that I'd dreamt exactly what the person had just done or said. It wasn't all that clear, and maybe it was just an overactive imagination, or remembering things wrongly or out of sequence, but despite my misgiving that perhaps I was exaggerating, I still answered, (Yes).

By 10:30am most of us were groggy and tired and sick of all these stupid, seemingly pointless questions. But we still had an hour and a half or so to go. We were finally given a five minute break, and during mine, I had the distinct displeasure of running into Frankie Nytz in the boys' restroom.

"Come to pleasure me, Greenjerkoff?" he asked from his spot in front of the urinal. He had partially turned to face me. I noticed a purplish welt above his left eye as if someone, most likely his drunken father, had smacked him across the forehead.

"You got nothing to pleasure, Frankie," I said, sorry immediately for being smart with him. Frankie took half a step back as if to swat back at me but he was still in the middle of his business and I quickly entered a stall, closed it and secured the lock.

"Ah," he said, "off to pleasure yourself, eh, Greensturbator."

I decided to keep my mouth shut as I lifted the toilet seat in the stall and started taking a leak. After finishing my business, I cautiously open the stall door and looked right and left. Frankie had already left and, after a sigh, I hurried back to class.

After a quick scan I noticed the third and fourth parts of the test were the most interesting, and led me to suspect that psychic ability was the aptitude the NDMAA test was trying to assess—though why whoever was giving the test wanted to know that was certainly beyond my security clearance.

The questions on the first couple pages of Part Three depicted the backs of cards, which I later learned are known as 'Zenner Cards', named after some Dr. Zenner, a paranormal researcher who invented them to help assess one's psychic ability. The face of the Zenner Cards, which we couldn't see, depicted a circle, plus sign, square, star, or two or three wavy lines. It was our task to guess what symbol was on the front of the card after gazing at the back of it for a few moments. We were directed not to rush, but to get through all the questions and not spend longer than twenty seconds with each card.

After the Zenner Card questions, on the next ten or so pages, we were asked to use our minds to move various objects depicted in a series of photographs. Each object existed at some distant location in real time and was connected to our individual tests by a serial number.

My first picture was of a tiny desk pendulum with a lone silver ball suspended from two strings set on a piece of white paper on a table in an otherwise blank room. The task, obviously, was to sway the pendulum ball and I closed my eyes and tried to do just that, to make the silver ball swing on the strings supporting it in the air. The next photograph was a little matchbox truck also on white piece of paper on a small table in that same blank room. I closed my eyes and imagined it moving forward on its own. Then there was a picture of a feather and I closed my eyes and tried to make it move. On and on it went for a few more pages, small objects like that, including an analog clock with a second hand that we were asked to stop. Naturally, that made me think of the late bell's early warning chime on Sebastian's first day at Colonel J. B. Weber High that saved me from Frankie Nytz's wrath.

The last page of this section depicted what appeared to be a sleeping gerbil in a cage. 'Wake it up!' blared the direction across the top of the photograph in bold, red ink. So I closed my eyes and thought of the gerbil awake, running around the small cage. I thought later, the directions could easily have been to stop its heart and kill it, something that psi-warriors might be asked to do to people.

Some of the kids around me groaned or laughed as they went through this part of the test and looked at each other wondering what this could possibly be testing. We were all pretty much zonked by the time it was over and relieved when, at long last, Vickers told us to stop, and we should turn to the fourth and, thankfully, last section of the test.

I quickly saw that this section was equally bizarre. However, it did provide me with a serious pump of needed adrenalin when I turned the page and saw the psi-soldier. He was standing in front of a blue screen, wearing an aviator's jacket, khaki pants and state trooper sunglasses. It was exactly what Colonel

Farnsworth had been wearing in that hokey introductory film to Sebastian's video game.

"Alright," Vickers said, "please take a moment to read over to yourselves the directions to this section." These directions stated the following:

*"Meet Major Tom. Over the next series of questions, you must identify the object or person about which he is thinking. As in the questions above, close your eyes as directed by the test monitor and clear you mind and relax. Begin only when you are directed to do so by the test monitor."*

"Alright," Vickers said, startling me. "As directed, close your eyes and clear your minds."

I didn't think Vickers waited, as it seemed only moments later when he told us to begin.

And so we began. Each question had a little photograph of 'Major Tom' and below it a series of four selections identified by letters (a) through (d). The selections under the first of the Major Tom questions were various disparate objects. For example, in one, there was an apple, a baseball bat, a car, and a cat. I closed my eyes and tried to imagine which object Major Tom had been thinking about. Finally, after guesswork more than real vision, I selected (d), for cat. There were something like forty similar questions after that. Finally, I turned to a mostly blank page. Along the top instructions had us imagine that Major Tom was thinking of a place, a geographical location of some kind, with a building. We were asked, again, to close our eyes and see what place he was thinking about, and then draw the location.

Just as I closed my eyes and attempted to visualize the location, Vickers blurted out, "Five minutes."

I looked up at the large clock up high on the wall behind him and saw that it was five minutes to Noon. We had been going at this test three long hours. I closed my eyes and tried to imagine what place and what building Major Tom wanted me to see to no avail.

"Finish up people. One minute." Vickers said.

Then something came to view. It was a building—squat and secure and all white. It was the White House, where the President of the United States of America and his family lived. But I never got to draw it, because Vickers had shouted, "Time's up! Pencils down. Immediately. Bring up your test booklets and deposit them on the desk."

Then the lunch bell rang and I followed a line of my weary classmates and dropped my booklet onto the desk next to Vickers. I was still quite upset that I didn't have time to draw the White House that I thought I had seen in Major Tom's head and asked Vickers if I could have a moment to draw what I saw.

"No way, Greenberg, test's over," he said and gestured me out of the classroom.

"How'd you do?" I asked Sebastian as he pulled up his wheelchair the lunch table. He shrugged as he lifted his tray onto the top of it. "On the test."

"Alright, I guess," he said.

"Did you notice the guy, the psi-warrior?" I asked him. "Major Tom. He was dressed just like Colonel Farnsworth from *Psi Wars!*. Damned unusual, you ask me."

Sebastian sighed and turned to me. "Yes. I think it was unusual. Most unusual."

"What building did you see?" I asked. "On the last page. What did you draw?"

"What did you see?" he asked, squinting at me. "You tell me first."

"Crap," I said after a sigh, "I didn't draw it. I saw it after a couple minutes. At first, all I could visualize was Marsha Kendall in a bikini." I looked over at Sebastian and he smiled. "But then I saw it, it came into focus clear as day. The White House. The frigging White House." Again, I sighed. "But then Vickers was yapping that our time was up so I never got the chance to draw it. I handed in a blank sheet." After a moment, I asked him, "So what did you see?"

"The White House," Sebastian said with a nod. "Just like you. And that's what I drew."

# Chapter Ten
# **The Yellow Snow**

By the time Thanksgiving rolled around and passed us by, and I started thinking about Christmas and presents and much-needed time off from school, and perhaps, a snowstorm coming off Lake Erie to finally give us one or more snow days, I had mostly forgotten about the test. Every once in a while, however, I'd ask Sebastian when he thought we'd get our grades. He'd shrug and say he had no idea as if he really didn't care.

Between Thanksgiving and Christmas vacation, I developed a crush on Molly Scott in addition to my crush on Marsha Kendall (the one who had in fact started going out with some stud in the senior class in early October). Molly wasn't quite in the same league as Marsha Kendall, but she was not far behind with her square, bright face, long bouncy wheat-blonde hair, firm body and developing breasts that were especially wonderful in a tight sweater.

But like all the other girls in the ninth grade, Molly Scott didn't notice me, or at least I didn't think she did. For one thing, like all the rest of them, she was considerably taller than me and because of that, I developed this idea that she would never take me serious as long as she was literally looking down at me. All the other boys in the ninth grade were sprouting up, growing inches by the week, except for me, seemingly locked forever in my dwarfish four foot ten inch frame.

Finally, at a doctor's visit in early December, he seemed overjoyed to report that I had grown another inch, to four foot eleven, and gained six pounds since my last visit in August, putting me over the century pound mark for the first time in my life.

"He's so worried about his size," my mother told the doctor, but she could have added, 'we' as well, considering at least once a week she and my father discussed my size and from whom I had inherited it, considering they were fairly large people in families of large people.

"He'll get there," old Doc Prescott assured her, though without exuding much confidence. "Some boys just take longer than others to sprout."

To make matters worse, Frankie Nytz, his toadies and some of my other moronic classmates were relentless in calling me names: squirt, shorty, dwarf, hobbit, midget, and my personal favorite, munchkin. To make things worse, Frankie would attach such epithets to the 'green' part of my name changing 'How's it hanging, munchkin' to 'How's it hanging, Green-munchkin'. And sometimes Frankie sang that old Randy Newman song *Short People* just loud enough for everyone around us to have a good chuckle at my expense.

It was not surprising then that I had become sincerely self-conscious about my stature and mostly because of that shortcoming—to use a bad pun—I lacked any confidence regarding my ability to get girls. Naturally, I shunned the bi-monthly dances sponsored by Colonel J. B. Weber High held in the school gymnasium, or going out to socialize with my fellow classmates at places like the Wiggins Fun Emporium where young pre-teen kids aimlessly congregated on Friday or Saturday nights and hung out in the game room or restaurant and sometimes got into serious trouble.

One Saturday afternoon sometime in late November, as

we were lazing around taking a break from trying to overcome the next obstacle on our quest to chase down Colonel Zebb in the nutty psychic world of *Psi Wars!*, I finally admitted to Sebastian that I really liked Molly Scott. Really, *really* liked her, I admitted sheepishly. It was all I thought about some days, I further admitted. Sebastian gave me a long look of appraisal over this breaking news.

"But what's the use," I said. "She doesn't even know I exist."

"Don't be too sure about that," Sebastian said.

I glanced over at him. "Why? What possibly could you know about it—a gimp stuck in a wheelchair?"

That was a low blow, and I immediately felt bad for saying it; but, I also already regretted having revealed my inner secret desire for Molly's affections to anyone, even my best and loyal friend. But Sebastian was nonplussed. Without further explanation, he suggested that I go up and talk to her. I might be surprised.

So right before lunch the following Tuesday (I had chickened out on Monday, to Sebastian's chagrin), only a couple days to the annual ninth grade, semi-formal Holiday Ball and only ten days before Christmas Eve, I did just that. I had been staring at Molly all through English class and thinking about what Sebastian had suggested, and right after the buzzer sounded dismissing the class, I edged through my classmates and said, "Hi, Molly, how are you?" as we stepped out into the hallway. To my utter astonishment, Molly was receptive to this bold and unexpected advance. I had to look up at her, but she truly seemed interested, and even after my own self-deprecatory remark about my 'short-ness', at one point even told me while grinning, "But you have such dreamy, blue eyes, Henry."

Despite such obvious interest on Molly's part, I was unable to pull the trigger. I just stood there looking up at her, trembling a little, my brain and throat frozen. I should have blurted out right then a request that she go with me to the Holiday Ball.

"Well, see ya," Molly said after a time looking down at me when it appeared that I had become mute.

During lunch, Sebastian asked with some annoyance, "Why didn't you ask her to the Ball?"

I shrugged and glumly looked at the mystery meat swimming in unappealing dark brown gravy on my plate. After a time, I looked across at him as he started chewing into his sandwich.

"How'd you know?"

"How'd I know what?" His voice was garbled from both his condition and the wad of sandwich in his mouth.

"That I didn't ask her to the ball," I said. "Or that she maybe likes me, for that matter. You read her mind or something?" I asked, then added, "You crippled freak?"

"She does like you," he said and smiled, a drizzle of spittle ran down the side of his chin. He wiped it as I shrugged. "And reading minds has nothing to do with it. It's the way she looks at you that gives it away. And the way she strains her neck to look back at you almost every day in English class. You just never notice it. She can't keep her eyes off you. That's usually a good sign someone likes you."

After a time, he smiled. "And, I read her mind."

I shoved his arm right then and suppressed a smile.

"Well, can you read her mind enough to tell me if she'd put out on our first date."

"There has to be a first date first," he said.

"Yeah, yeah," I said. "I'm gonna ask her. Right after school. To the damned Ball."

Just at that moment, like a drum symbol shattering a good thought, Frankie Nytz came clambering up to our table with two of his toadies right behind him. He had come to school that day in an especially foul mood and I noticed, as he stood defiantly at our table that he had a purple welt under his right eye socket.

"So what are my two favorite nerdly girly buddies,

Greenqueer and Sa-bad-jun up to this afternoon during this bright happy holiday season?" he asked. "Oral examinations?"

During that entire semester, Frankie had been relentless in his harassment of Sebastian and me, as well as several of our fellow ninth grade misfits. But for some reason, he found the friendship between Sebastian and me especially repugnant and worthy of imperial condemnation.

Sebastian told me often enough that Frankie was the way he was—a bullying, royal jerk—only because of a bad home life, the drunken father excuse, and that deep down, he really wasn't such a bad kid. He can't help himself, Sebastian explained. It was the only way for him to relieve his suffering and to garner self-esteem. But I responded that there was no proper excuse to justify heaping abuse on other kids, especially a *special* kid like him. Sebastian shrugged noncommittally, and in that moment, I knew that he was truly sympathetic for Frankie's plight; and, that Sebastian Drake was truly a 'good egg'.

We ignored Frankie's comment, but, of course, Frankie persisted, seeming to need something more out of us that day than mere thrill of annoyance.

"Oh, I forgot, Greenqueen doesn't celebrate Christmas— the birth of the Lord. Instead, he celebrates by lighting those Jew candles." He looked back to his toadies and made an intentional mess of the name for the Jewish holiday by snorting out a vague semblance of Hanukah.

Our persistent indifference to his harassing presence seemed only to insight Frankie's anger. He stood directly behind Sebastian and, after hovering there a moment, reached around him and plucked a chocolate éclair from Sebastian's tray and took a large bite out of it.

"This is so good, Mr. Hawking," he said. "Thanks for the early Christmas present."

I jumped up and grabbed the éclair out of Frankie's hand.

"Stop it, Frankie," I told him. "He's a damned cripple. Can't you see that?" I looked at the éclair and then at him.

"And I guess I'll have to go up and get Sebastian another éclair because who knows where you mouth has been."

Frankie slapped out at me but I ducked and his open hand went wide. I quickly made my way to the server line and looked back at Frankie and his two toadies still hovering over poor, hapless Sebastian. Still, by now, I suspected that Sebastian could take care of himself. I turned to the lady dishing out lunches.

"He dropped this," I said, showing her the munched into éclair and nodding back to Sebastian. "Can I have another?"

The server looked at Sebastian and nodded. The whole school knew about Sebastian's mettle and eccentricity. When I followed her gaze, I saw the curious sight of Frankie Nytz patting Sebastian on the back and speaking to him as if they were long lost friends. The server walked to back to the kitchen and returned with a fresh éclair on a small paper plate. I thanked her, offered three quarters, which she waved off and went back to serving lunches.

As I handed Sebastian the paper plate with the fresh éclair on it, I asked what had happened. Where was Frankie?

"I made him an offer he couldn't refuse," was all Sebastian said.

"What offer?" But Sebastian had nothing else to say about it. He merely shrugged and began to sloppily munch into his éclair. After a moment, I shrugged as well and began to munch on mine.

Sebastian may have sorted things out but Frankie wasn't finished with me that day.

After school let out, I walked with Sebastian to his van. It had snowed the night before, around six inches, but not quite enough to require our superintendent of schools to cancel school. During the day, it had snowed another four inches or so and the temperature had dipped to something like twenty-five degrees. Therefore, by the time classes let out, the lawns were covered by a velvety, white blanket of wet snow that still gave kids my age thrilling thoughts of building six foot snowmen, sledding down steep hills, hitting tree trunks or sides of house or faces of other kids with icy snowballs or better yet, starting vicious team snowball fights involving ten or more kids.

"See you tonight, right Seb?" I asked.

"Yeah, sure," he told me.

Aunt Dottie gave me a kindly look and patted me on the head as she closed the door. She asked me if I wanted to come over for dinner, and I said I'd have to ask my mom. She nodded and thanked me again, for something like the hundredth time, for being such a good friend to Sebastian. I responded with a sheepish shrug and, after a wink, she got into the van and drove off.

I was halfway up the sidewalk to the bus stops near the front of the school when I saw Frankie Nytz and his toadies huddled together another twenty yards up, and blocking my path. As I approached, Frankie strode forward, "Giving your little lady a goodbye kiss, Greenfag?"

I looked up at him and, out of the corner of my left eye, to my horror, I saw that Molly Scott and several of her friends, had stopped short to watch another Frankie Nytz spectacle.

"Come on, Frankie," I said, "it's too cold and snowy out here for your nonsense. And we should be getting to our buses."

Frankie stepped forward and poked me in the chest. "You got a smart mouth, Greengay. You know that?"

"Well, I'd rather have my smart mouth, Frankie, than your..." I sighed, trying to restrain myself, "...dumb one."

As the import of what I had just said sunk in, Frankie's eyes got mean and dark. He grabbed me by the shoulders and dragged me toward the leafless oak tree where, on warmer days, he liked to stand in the morning like the class tyrant waiting for the school late bell to ring. Finally, he stopped right below the heaviest branch of the tree and proceeded to give me a hard push. I slipped momentarily and fell backwards onto my behind. Naturally, Frankie's toadies guffawed.

"Why don't you pick on someone your own size, Frankie

Nytz?" said a girl's voice from behind the immediate circle of Frankie and his toadies. To my deepest chagrin, I realized that the girl protesting my treatment was none other than Molly Scott.

I pushed my ungloved hands on the snow-covered ground in an attempt to get back onto my feet and saw right then that the snow into which I had nearly stuck my left hand was dull yellow like a lemon slushie gone bad. Jerry Burton, the nearest thing to Frankie's best friend, saw this as well and starting pointing and laughing.

"Look," he said, still laughing, "Greengay wants a taste of yellow snow."

It occurred to me right then that some idiot dog had selected the spot under the oak tree, right next to where my left hand now rested, to lift a leg and take a doggie leak. I immediately jerked my hand away and jumped to my feet.

But Frankie stepped forward and grabbed me by my slim shoulders with this powerful right hand.

"You like eating yellow, dog pissy snow," Frankie said. "Don't you, Greenpisseater?"

He forced me down to my knees and shoved my head toward the patch of yellow dog piss snow.

"So be my guest," he said, "and take a gulp of a doggie slushie."

But just as Frankie's right hand and body tensed about to send my face into the yellow mush, I heard a loud crack above us. And then, there was a whoosh and an instant later, a hollow thunk. What I later learned was that the large branch of the oak tree over which this drama had been unfolding had snapped in the wind and snow and come crashing down straight onto Frankie Nytz's head.

"Frankie! Frankie!" Jerry Burton was shouting. He had knelt down at Frankie's side and, after a time, turned him over. Then, Jerry looked up at the rest of us with fear in his eyes and said, "He looks dead! Somebody call an ambulance!"

I arrived home that dark, snowy afternoon, an hour or so later than usual, with my mother frantically waiting by the front door for me and the snow still piling up on the porch. I immediately called Sebastian.

"Thanks," I said.

"Thanks for what?"

"For making that oak branch fall on old stupid Frankie Nytz' head," I told him. "For saving me from eating yellow snow. But you may also have killed Frankie."

"I have no idea what you're talking about," Sebastian said.

"You mean, it wasn't you?" I asked after a time.

"It wasn't me what? What are you talking about, Henry?"

I told him the whole story, start to finish, from the time I saw him leave in his special van, to the time I saw Frankie's face in the yellow snow.

"How is he?" Sebastian asked. "Frankie?"

"I'm have no idea," I said. "They took him away in an ambulance."

"Poor Frankie," he said.

"Poor Frankie?" I was incredulous at Sebastian's now inexplicable level of sympathy for that old, stupid bully. "What about poor me? I nearly got a mouthful of a dog pee slushie."

Sebastian had no answer for that.

"So if it wasn't you who made the branch break off, " I finally asked him, "who do you think did it? Who caused the branch to crack off and fall right on top of Frankie Nytz's head? Who?"

"Maybe it was just the wind and snow," he said. "An act of God." He sighed. "Or maybe it was you."

"No," I said.

And then I remembered a dream I had some time ago, murky in my recollection, but there it was. About a tree falling down and crashing onto someone's head, rescuing me from harm. And in the dream from months ago was a pretty girl. Now I knew who the girl was.

"No," I repeated, firm in my opinion. "It wasn't natural what happened. And it wasn't me."

I nodded to myself with certainty. "It was Molly," I told Sebastian. "Molly Scott."

# Chapter Eleven
## The Parsifal Effect

Nothing much else happened the week before Christmas break after the tree limb fell onto Frankie's head. He had ended up in the hospital with his toadies mulling around the school hopelessly abandoned. For reasons I couldn't figure out, I didn't get around to asking Molly Scott to the Holiday Ball and I didn't even attend the dance. Then, school was done for two full weeks and off we went with my classmates happily anticipating Christmas presents and family gatherings. For me, it was fairly boring because in our house we neither celebrated Christmas nor had much in the way of family. But then, in the midst of this lack of revelry, around 7:00pm on December 27th, our doorbell rang.

Sipping his second after dinner cocktail while stretched out on his favorite easy chair, my dad had been grumbling to himself as he read some article in the newspaper sprawled across his lap. I was sitting cross-legged on the couch across from him reading a hardcover book Sebastian had lent me titled *Psi-Warriors* by retired Army Colonel Max Drummond, chronicling the bizarre doings related to psychic experiments conducted by the U.S. Army and CIA in an underground military base in the mid to late 1990s under the name 'Project Mind Bloom'. That's where they must have gotten the name from for the video game, *Psi Wars!—Project Mind Bloom*.

According to Colonel Drummond, he commanded a group of fifteen officers and enlisted soldiers selected to participate in the project based upon their innate psychic abilities identified through various psychological and intelligence tests. He further claimed that in the four years during which the project operated, this platoon of 'psi-warriors' succeeded in proving that psi powers do indeed exist and have great potential military application. Though Colonel Drummond's book never mentioned Colonel Peter Drake, Sebastian assured me that his father was among the men selected for Project Mind Bloom and took over command of the project with Colonel Zebb after Colonel Drummond abruptly resigned and then retired from the Army.

Without independent evidence to prove any of his claims, Colonel Drummond provided numerous anecdotes in which psi-warriors performed wondrous psychic feats such as bending metal objects, including rifle barrels (his particular specialty) and tank guns. They could also read minds, view distant locations and past times, control the minds of animals and even, supposedly, other humans, stop and speed up clocks, walk through walls, teleport to distant locations, and conjure creatures directly from their minds.

Colonel Drummond said he quit the project after two years, claiming, without much elaboration, that his superiors and colleagues had lost control over the use of the very psychic powers being studied and enhanced. It was like letting the genie out of a bottle. He also expressed grave concern over the research and development and most of all, use, of a drug that could supposedly enhance psychic powers. I would later learn that drug was called, 'Boost.'

Drummond stated he had written this book to reveal the dangers that the continued secret development of psi powers by our military and intelligence agencies, not to mention those of our enemies, posed for mankind. He especially feared the develop-ment of rogue elements commanded by maniacal, megalo-maniacal leaders (I had to look up the word, 'megalomaniac' and found that it meant a person who was power mad), that might attempt to employ advanced psychic abilities to take control over the world. Colonel Drummond's book, in short, was a warning to his fellow man.

According to Sebastian, after the book came out, more than fifteen years ago, Colonel Drummond seemed to have fallen off the face of the earth. He published no subsequent books and there were no references to him on the Internet or anywhere else for that matter. He didn't have a personal web page, no social media presence, and no addresses listed under his name anywhere in the world. His book had gone out of print some years ago and, as we found via an email exchange, the publisher of *Psi-Warriors* had no idea where he had gone.

After the second doorbell chime, my father barked for me to answer the 'damn' door. I put the book down, pushed myself off the couch and trotted over to the entrance foyer. By the time I got there, the doorbell had chimed for a third time.

"I said get the door, Henry!"

"I am," I yelled back as I opened it.

Scowling down at me on the front porch on that dark cold night were two soldiers. They were dressed identically, in brown leather aviator jackets, khaki pants and state trooper sunglasses. In fact the one to my left looked exactly like Major Tom from the NDMAA test.

"Henry?" he said. "Henry Greenberg?"

"Who is it Henry?" my father yelled from the living room.

"Yes," I told the soldier. "I'm Henry Greenberg."

"Henry!" shouted my father.

A moment later, my mother was standing behind me.

"Can I help you gentlemen?" she asked.

The soldier to the left removed his khaki hat and bowed his head, then introduced himself as Major Aldous Tomelanos. He introduced the soldier to his right as Captain Daniel Stanwyck. With a smile, Major Tomelanos asked my mother to call him

Major Tom for short. He quickly added that they had come to talk with her and Mr. Greenberg about me.

"Is somebody going to tell me who the heck is at the front door?" my father yelled from the living room.

"About Henry?" my mother asked and gave me a worried glance. "What's he done?"

"Oh, he's done nothing bad," Major Tom said. "In fact, it's quite good."

Now she was frowning and the frown intensified when from the living room, my father screamed, "Who the hell is at the damn front door?"

My mother ushered Major Tom and Captain Stanwyck into the living room before my dad could let out another yelp. When he saw the two soldiers, he stood, tossed the newspaper to the carpet, dusted himself off, and after a sip of his drink, put it back down on the coaster on the table next to the recliner. He squinted as Major Tom and Captain Stanwyck introduced themselves. As they sat down on the couch across from his chair, my father sat back in his recliner and mother took the love seat next to the couch and I had to sit cross-legged on the floor.

"So what is this about, Sirs?" my father asked most deferentially.

My father had pulled a stint in the Army way back, in the early '80s between the Vietnam and Desert Storm wars, when not much was going on: three long, awful years he described it as. He had been a lowly enlisted man who fixed jeeps, or something, at what he always called 'an ugly desolate base' in the Midwest, Fort Podunk, Kansas, he called it. Still, despite his supposed loathing of military service, he always stood at attention and took his hat off during the playing of the national anthem, and right now, he seemed genuinely awestruck in the presence of the officers.

"We represent the National Defense Special Student Project," Major Tom began. "It was established for the purpose of identifying boys and girls in their early teens with above average psychic abilities. Once identified, they are invited to attend a newly established academy for the teenage students where those powers can be further studied and possibly enhanced."

Major Tom stopped a moment and looked at my parents.

"Do you know what I mean by this?" he asked. "Psychic powers?"

My father looked at my mother, shrugged.

"Yeah, sure," he said, "I think, like, powers of the mind. Like mind reading, bending spoons. That sort of thing. Right?"

"Well, yes," Major Tom said, "that sort of thing."

"Psychic powers are real?" My father asked. "They exist?"

"Well, all I can tell you," Major Tom said, "is that they've been found to be real enough that the United States government spends a portion of its defense budget studying them for possible application in the real world."

My father turned and squinted at me a moment, then looked back at Major Tom.

"Are you telling me that our Henry here has been identified with that?" he asked. "Psychic powers?" Then he looked back at me. "Mind reading?"

My father turned to my mother as if to say 'see, I told you so! Our boy is definitely weird. And now the United States Army says so too'.

"Yes, Mr. Greenberg, that is exactly what I am telling you," said Major Tom.

My eyes nearly bugged out.

"About a month and a half ago, in early November," he went on, "Henry and his fellow ninth-graders at Colonel J. B. Weber High School, as well as thousands of other ninth-graders across the United States, were administered a kind of psychic powers aptitude test. This test has helped us identify those gifted students who are now being invited to attend the first-ever class of a special Academy where the powers of these students can be developed and enhanced.

"So," Major Tom continued, surprising me by finally removing his sunglasses as he leaned forward and looked at my parents with his intense, deep blue eyes, "we've stopped by your home this evening to offer your son Henry the opportunity of attending that Academy."

"It's like a school or something?" my father asked.

"Yes," Major Tom said. "A kind of boarding school. To attend, Henry will have to leave home and live there, at the Academy. Of course, in addition to developing his psychic powers, he'll receive a top-notch education in each of the classical areas of study; mathematics, science, literature, as well as two foreign languages.

"I am also permitted to tell you that the gifted students who accept this invitation and successfully graduate, after only a two year course of study, will be guaranteed acceptance into any college of their choosing, tuition free. And, yes, we are talking Harvard, Yale, Princeton, Stanford or MIT."

My mother and father turned to each other with pleasantly surprised expressions.

"So when would it start?" I asked from my seat on the floor. "This…Academy?"

Major Tom looked down at me. "Next semester, January 3rd."

"Where is it?" my mother asked. "This school?"

Major Tom turned to her. "Well, the location of the Academy is top-secret. Of course, you'll be able to contact Henry whenever you want…although Sunday evenings are normally set aside for the boys and girls to call their parents. There is also a secure software program enabling such communications through Internet video. And, during the summer, we offer parents the opportunity of coming to stay at a lodge near the school for a week-long visit. We also allow the student a week off at Christmas, when he or she is allowed to come home."

I swallowed. This opportunity was promising to become dramatically life-changing. I suddenly wasn't sure if I was up for it. Who would be? A boarding school run by the Army at a distant, secret location with no summer vacation to speak of, except a week spent with one's parents. What would I be getting myself into?

Not that I had any great affection for continuing my education at Colonel J. B. Weber High or drifting along under the present yoke of my parents who had no idea what kind of kid I was or person I wanted to become. I had no real friends at school, or elsewhere for that matter, except Sebastian of course.

"What's the point of all this?" my father asked, suddenly doubtful. "I mean, why's the Army recruiting kids Henry's age to teach them special powers at a special school? Sounds a little strange to me."

"First off, it's a matter of national defense," Major Tom answered. "You see, it's come to our attention that certain of our nation's well, antagonists around the world, have developed programs similar to this one, involving the enhancement of psychic powers in teenage boys and girls that might have possible application in, well, military operations." He laughed. "Not that we'd be sending children Henry's age to war or anything like that. We just want to offer some of them an opportunity to increase their mental powers just to keep up with these other nations, that sort of thing. What the Army is doing is merely applying the age-old principle that it's better to be safe than sorry."

"But why kids Henry's age?" my father asked. "Why not use real soldiers?"

"Because of what's called the *Parsifal Effect*," Major Tom said.

"The Parsifal Effect?"

"Yes," he said. "You see, it's been found that over time, soldiers trained in using psychic powers, who we call psi-warriors, develop something of a block to their effective use.

It's been theorized that this lessening of psychic ability over time is due to a loss of naivety."

"Naivety?" I could tell my father was having a difficult time following what Major Tom was saying, as was I, to be frank.

"Innocence," Major Tom answered.

He sighed and scratched his chin a moment, seeming to be at somewhat of a loss himself as to how best explain what he meant.

"It's like the phenomenon of beginner's luck," he continued, and now his quizzical look had morphed into a frown. "It's a misnomer, actually. People are sometimes good at something the first time out not because of luck, but because they approached the task freely, without a preconception or expectation. But when they try it again, they have gained too much knowledge and they try too hard. Their mind has gotten cluttered with expectation, and so, they don't do it as well. It works the same with using one's psychic powers. If you approach it freely, with naivety, with innocence, like the mythical medieval knight, Parsifal, did in his pursuit of the Holy Grail, you obtain access to it."

"And this also explains, we think," he went on, "why children are better able to learn a new language than adults. The Parsifal Effect explains why. Their minds are free from clutter, and it takes longer for that clutter to build, unlike soldiers who have become cluttered or hardened by the experience of life." Major Tom sighed again and thought a moment. "Anyway, it's been found that, for whatever reason, children Henry's age are more amenable to enhancement of their innate psychic powers than adults and, once enhanced, better able to retain them."

"Make sense?" Major Tom asked.

My father shrugged. I could see in his eyes, he really didn't get it. But I did or at least I was starting to. However, I made a mental note to look up 'Parsifal' on the Internet.

"Other studies have also found that while all of us are born with some innate level of psychic ability, some people inherit more of it, kind of like intelligence. Some people have higher psychic IQs than others.

"So, the idea is," Major Tom continues, "if we could identify those stable and well-adjusted young teens at the highest psychic IQ levels, and then enhance those levels using proven methods for doing so, we could create a regiment, if you will, of potential psychic soldiers who could counteract and protect the rest of us from harm. I mean, in theory, and only just in case, mind you, in the remote possibility that in some future time, a country unfriendly to our principles, tries to use psychic powers to destroy or disrupt our way of life."

Major Tom smiled. "Not that we ever truly expect that to happen."

"Has anyone else from Colonel J. B. Weber been selected?" I suddenly asked from my spot on the floor. "Besides me?"

"As a matter of fact," he said as he looked down at me, "yes. I understand one of them is a good friend of yours. Sebastian Drake."

My heart lifted. But then, in the next moment, it almost seemed too good to be true. Like my father, I suddenly had reservations about what Major Tom was peddling at our house that evening. There seemed something amiss about the whole thing.

"And one other student," Major Tom added. "A girl. Molly Scott."

My mouth fell open upon hearing her name. Molly Scott. The yellow snow incident was still fresh in my mind. I could still hear the sound of that branch cracking before it fell on Frankie Nytz.

The meeting in our living room ended as Major Tom abruptly stood, followed stiffly by Captain Stanwyck, who had said nothing the whole time. The point of his presence had never been made clear, except perhaps to somehow enhance Major Tom's authority.

Standing before us in the middle of our living room, Major

Tom told my parents they had forty-eight hours to decide whether or not I would attend the first-ever Academy. Only thirty kids had been selected across the United States and there was a waiting list. Major Tom handed my father a card that was blank except for the 1-800 number emblazoned across the front of it in thick, black ink.

"Please call this number by 5:00pm, December 29th, and inform us of your decision," Major Tom said. "A simple yes or no will do. Failure to call will be taken as a no."

I got to my feet as my parents awkwardly shook hands with Major Tom and Captain Stanwyck and led them to the front door. As my father opened it for them, he asked, "So what's this place called, this Academy?"

"We simply call it," Major Tom said with an apologetic shrug, "the Psi Academy."

My father grunted and bid Major Tom and Captain Stanwyck goodbye.

After my father closed the door and we had returned to the living room, he turned to me.

"So, what's it going to be, Henry?" he asked in a harsh tone as if I had done something wrong. "You wanna go to this…Psi Academy? Though it sounds like the most ridiculous thing I ever heard, another terrible waste of taxpayers' money. But they sure sounded sincere about what it might mean for you, and us. Tuition paid for at a place like Harvard."

I thought a moment and shrugged. I really wasn't sure what I should do. As I said, by then I had a funny feeling about the whole thing. But if Sebastian and Molly Scott agreed to go, I probably would as well.

"Well?" My father's frown had transformed into a grimace. "Because God knows, without this, you certainly would never get into Harvard. And for that matter, you'll have a hard time getting in any decent college with your damn grades. And forget about a scholarship. College loans up the ying-yang is what you'll be paying."

"Why don't you call your friend Sebastian?" my mother suggested. "See what he's going to do."

My father agreed that this seemed like a good idea. I nodded and sheepishly asked for some privacy while I made the call.

My parents shrugged and left me alone in the living room. Using the cell phone, I tapped out the number to Sebastian's cell. He answered immediately and confirmed that he'd already been offered a spot at the Psi Academy.

"So, are you going?" I asked.

"Yes," he said at once, "Why wouldn't I?"

"I figured you'd say that," I said.

"What about you?" he said.

"Don't you think it's just a little weird, Seb?" I asked. "Teaching kids like us to become psi-warriors or wizards or whatever in a Psi Academy? Sounds awful Harry Potterish to me."

"Except it's real," Sebastian said. "They are promising to teach us how to develop our psychic abilities so that we can move objects through the air, read minds, control what people do, walk through walls, and other things that Colonel Drummond wrote about in his book. Not by casting corny spells or saying silly incantations, or using fake wands, but by proven methods backed by science."

"So what's it gonna be Henry?" Sebastian asked after a time

After thinking about it another thirty seconds or so, I said to him, "Can I ask you something, Seb?"

"Sure, shoot."

"How long have you known you're psychic? That you can read minds and bend spoons and all that?"

He didn't say anything for a while. "From before I ended up like this, a cripple in this chair," he finally said. "Though it's pretty vague, I can remember in bits and pieces my father teaching me some things. Like magic tricks, pulling a rabbit out of a hat, bending spoons. Or perhaps those were only in my dreams, wishful thinking on my part. Once I was put here, in this wheelchair, I've had plenty of time to remember and perfect whatever I was taught."

"So it was you who made the school bell ring early your first day that saved me from a beating from Frankie Nytz."

"Well," he said.

"And it was you who made Frankie piss his pants in the lunchroom; and, it was you who made the seagull crap on his head; and, those gusts of wind that came up out of nowhere knocking a football in his face and his goofy hat into Marsha Kendall's feet, preventing Frankie from beating me up, that was you, too."

"Well, yes," Sebastian said. "I did all that."

"But not that branch falling on Frankie Nytz's head?"

"I told you," he said, "I had nothing to do with that."

"Molly Scott did that."

"Yes," he said, "after today, I know it was Molly."

"Seb," I said, "I just want to know how it's done. Because no matter how well I did on that test, I can't do any of that stuff. I can't bend a blade of grass with my mind let alone a spoon."

"I don't know how it's done," he said. "All I know is that sometimes I can wish things into happening. And sometimes I can hear what people think. And sometimes when I try, I can bend spoons, or make a gust of wind come up from out of nowhere, or clocks slow down or speed up." He sighed and waited a time before telling me, "And I think, what you can do, Henry, is dream."

"Dream?"

"Yes, dream," he said. "Dream about the future. What's going to happen. Like when you told me about that dream, about a bird crapping on Frankie Nytz's head."

"But I think all that was just wishful thinking," I said. "After the fact, I seemed to recall dreaming that. A *deja vu* sort of feeling." I sighed. "And what the hell do all those dreams about some evil psi-warrior trying to kill you have to do with the future?"

"I have no idea, Henry," he said.

"Especially that one with Colonel Zebb, where he said you were the bad guy, not him," I said. "What the hell does that mean?"

"I don't know."

I thought a minute, and reached a decision. It really was a no-brainer. I nodded and smiled to myself. Sure, I thought, with some measure of pride: I was going to attend the Psi Academy and become a psi-warrior. Defend the country and maybe, save the world.

"Well, alright," I finally told him. "I'm going."

I heard a sigh of relief on the other end of the phone.

"And anyway," I said, "I think I've been dreaming of doing just that for years."

# Chapter Twelve
## Reforming Frankie Nytz

After the call, I told my parents I was going. My father smiled, pleased with me for perhaps the first time in his life. With my decision at least he didn't have to worry about college tuition. I had just saved him two hundred grand. But my mother frowned and made one of those worrisome pouts.

The following afternoon, my mother took me over to Sebastian's house.

"Are you sure about this, Henry?" Sebastian asked.

"Not really," I told him. "Like Princess Leah says to Hans Solo in *Star Wars,* I got a bad feeling about this."

"Me too," Sebastian said.

Aunt Dottie came into Sebastian's room with a snack around 3:00pm interrupting our *Psi Wars!* game. She looked down at me with a kindly smile and said she was so glad I'd be attending the Psi Academy with Sebastian and keep him company.

"Well, he'll be keeping me company too," I told her.

She patted me on my head and left us alone with a tray of crispy pizza rolls.

"Think she's going too?" I asked Sebastian. "Molly?"

"Yes, she is," he said and smiled. Then, he asked, "How do you feel about that?"

I frowned at him. "How am I supposed to feel?"

Sebastian said nothing. He knew, without resorting to mind reading that that Molly's attendance at the Psi Academy both bothered and thrilled me.

After telling my parents I wanted to attend the Psi Academy, my mother had called the 1-800 number and reported to the soldier answering the call that I was 'in'. He didn't have much to say except there'd be a van sent over to pick me up at around 0800 hours or, as he explained 'eight o'clock in the morning', on the following Tuesday, January 3rd.

As we finished off the last of the pizza rolls, Sebastian turned to me and said, "You know something? I think we should go visit Frankie Nytz. Poor kid missed Christmas."

"What?" I gave Sebastian a befuddled frown. "Frankie Nytz? In the hospital?"

"Yes," Sebastian said, "he's still there."

It had been a slow recovery for Frankie. The branch had almost killed him. Another inch to the left or right, who knows.

"Served him right, you ask me," I said. "For what he's been since kindergarten, a mean, rotten bully."

"And that's why I want to pay him a visit."

"Now, you're talking," I said. "You want to exact some revenge. A dish best served cold."

"No, that's not what I want at all, Henry," he said. "Just come with me."

Sebastian asked his aunt to drive us to the hospital. The tree branch had caused a major bump on his head, and he was out for something like two hours until he woke up in a semi-conscious state babbling nonsense about eating yellow snow. His doctor thought it best for him to remain hospitalized for observation until the swelling under his skull went down and the headaches stopped.

Aunt Dottie remained in the lobby while Sebastian and I got visitors' passes and took an elevator up to the pediatric ward on the fourth floor. Sebastian looked as if he belonged among the patients as he glided next to me along the shiny linoleum floors in the wide hallways of the ward that smelled a cross between Clorox and pee.

Finally, we came to Frankie's room and stood outside it for a time. Inside, a TV was blaring a Road Runner cartoon.

"Well, we really doing this?" I whispered. "We going in?"

Sebastian nodded confidently and wheeled into the room with me right behind him.

Frankie was propped on a pillow in bed, staring up at a small TV set on a shelf up along the wall in front of him. There was a middle-aged guy in a grimy jacket in a chair. He was snoring, fast asleep. Frankie's eyes widened when he saw Sebastian gliding into the room with me ambling awkwardly behind him.

"Drake?" he said, squinting at us. "Greenberg?"

It was the first time in all my life that the jerk had called me by my real name.

"How you feeling, Frankie?" Sebastian asked.

He shrugged and rubbed his forehead.

"Damn headaches won't quit," he said. He nodded to the sleeping, snoring guy on the chair in the shadows along the wall. He hadn't moved, and hadn't stopped snoring, despite our entrance. "And he doesn't help matters any."

"That your Dad?" I asked. I sniffed at the guy and smelled the faint aroma of sweat and booze.

"Yeah," he said with a scowl, "dear old Dad."

And in the next moment, Frankie Nytz's father began to stir. After a groan and cough, he lifted up and blinked at us for a time as if we were alien beings. There we were, a short, blond-haired geek and a deformed kid in a wheelchair visiting his bully-boy son.

"What you want?" he asked, almost growling at us, and all I could think of was the cruel Fagin from *Oliver Twist*.

"We just came to say hello to Frankie," Sebastian said.

Mr. Nytz squinted, scrutinizing Sebastian for a time as if he was lab specimen.

"You two friends with my Frankie?"

"Well, we're not exactly best friends," I said.

"May we have a word with you, Mr. Nytz?" Sebastian asked.

"A word with me?" Mr. Nytz frowned. He did a double-take as his gaze met Sebastian's.

"What do you want to talk to him about?" Frankie asked.

Sebastian ignored him. "Outside, Mr. Nytz."

I got the distinct impression at that moment, seeing the intensity in Sebastian's eyes, that this wasn't a request on his part, this was a demand.

"S-sure," Mr. Nytz mumbled. "Outside."

He stood, wavered a moment, then started out of the room with Sebastian on his heels, and me following. But after a moment, Sebastian stopped at the doorway, wheeled around and told me to stay in the room and keep Frankie company.

"What the hell are you doing, Drake?" Frankie whispered after us.

I returned to the room and sat on the chair next to Frankie's bed.

"What's he doing?" Frankie asked me. He scowled at the doorway. "Why's he wanna talk to that old drunk?" After another moment, he asked, "Huh, Greenberg?" And again I was surprised to hear my actual name coming out of his mouth.

"I have no idea, Frankie," I said.

A few minutes later, Sebastian glided back into the room.

"Where's my dad?" Frankie asked.

"He'll be back in a minute," Sebastian said. "He's, well, thinking things over."

I glanced at Sebastian and nothing in his face revealed what had happened out there.

Finally, after another few minutes, Mr. Nytz returned. He looked at Sebastian and nodded, then walked over to Frankie laying in his bed. He paused there a moment before leaning down to kiss Frankie on the forehead.

"I'm sorry, Frankie," he whispered. "For everything."

Then he stood, turned and left the room.

I had no idea what just happened. I gave Sebastian a curious, sideways glance. And in the next moment, I heard whimpering from Frankie's bed. I looked up and saw that Frankie Nytz was crying.

"So what just happened back there?" I asked Sebastian in the elevator on the way back down to the lobby.

"I don't think Frankie's dad is going to bother him anymore," he said. "And I don't think Frankie's going to be harassing any more kids either."

I frowned as the elevator stopped and the doors opened. I thought of us saying goodbye to Frankie and wishing him to get well soon after he was done crying. He smiled, shook hands with me, then Sebastian, and thanked us for coming.

"I will never forget this," he said, and from the look in his eyes, I thought he sincerely meant it.

When we were leaving, he even called me Greenberg one last time.

As we met Aunt Dottie in the lobby, she smiled and asked how our friend was doing.

"He's better," Sebastian said. "All better."

# Part 2
# The Psi Academy

# Chapter Thirteen
## Leaving Home

The next few days crawled by. Usually, Christmas vacation went by so fast that before I knew it, it was the day after New Year's Day and I was getting mentally ready to go back to school. But this year, I couldn't wait for the start of my new school at the Psi Academy that offered an escape from being a loner nobody to becoming someone special. It held the exciting promise of a new life.

Still, I was nagged by doubt. I was to be on my own in a challenging new environment, meeting and competing against kids like Sebastian with special talents and no doubt eccentric personalities. And Molly Scott was going as well. I would be soon riding in a van with her for however many hours it took us to get to wherever the Psi Academy was.

On New Year's Eve my mother let me stay up late and watch the ball drop in Times Square with her and my father as they drank cheap champagne and she even let me have a couple sips. On New Year's Day, we had a quiet dinner of lamb chops and the fixings and watched some boring college football bowl games droning on the TV.

On January 2nd, I spent the morning helping my mother pack my suitcase for my trip. The soldier at the 1-800 number had told her I should pack light as we'd be furnished with a special uniform and all the regular necessities at the Psi

Academy. For the trip itself, I should dress casual, jeans and a decent sweatshirt were fine. Still, my mother insisted on over-stuffing a suitcase with things I didn't need. I stopped protesting figuring doing that somehow made her feel better about my leaving home.

Finally, at 8:10am on January 3rd, with the sun just rising out of a leaden eastern sky, a long, black van with dark, tinted windows pulled into our driveway. A soldier exited the passenger side and strode up to the front door. He rang the doorbell and my mother quickly opened it.

Like Major Tom and Captain Stanwyck, he wore the characteristic psi-warrior uniform; a brown leather aviator jacket, khaki pants, an open collar khaki shirt, and state trooper sunglasses even though the sky was overcast and gray, with a steady, icy drizzle drifting down from it.

"Lieutenant Parker, Ma'am," he said. "I'm here for Henry."

She nodded, resigned now to losing her only son for the next few months, accepting it as for the best. I stood at her side, clutching the handle of my heavy, over-packed suitcase. My father stood behind us wearing his usual doubtful frown.

"He's all set," my mother said, her voice cracking.

Lieutenant Parker nodded and looked down at me.

"Well, Henry," he said. "You ready?"

I shrugged a weak affirmation. Right then, I really wasn't sure.

"Let's get going then," the psi-warrior said. "We have a long ride ahead of us."

My mother bent down and kissed the top of my head and as I lifted my suitcase and handed it to Lieutenant Parker, she started bawling into her slender hands.

"Rachel, he'll be fine," my father said as he took her into his arms. After a few moments, he moved her aside and looked down at me.

"You do your best, now, Henry," he said, "Alright. Your very best."

"I will, Dad," I said. And that was it. I was walking with Lieutenant Parker toward the van.

But before we got there, my mother called from the front door, "Lieutenant!" Lieutenant Parker turned. My father was with her, his arm still around her shoulders. "How long of a drive is it?" she asked. "Can you at least tell us that?"

"Sorry, Ma'am," he said. "Can't. He'll call you when he gets there." He shrugged. "That's the best I can do."

My mother nodded and turned her face into my father's shoulder.

At the van, I turned and gave a last, limp wave. My father nodded as my mother briefly waved, then she turned her face into my father's right shoulder. That almost made me cry, but I quickly turned away and stepped into the van and sat in the middle seat. Lieutenant Parker slid the side door shut with a hollow thud and got into the passenger seat. Feeling quite sad, I almost started crying as the van backed out of the driveway. But then, I turned and looked into the lovely blue eyes of Molly Scott.

She nodded, "Hi, Henry."

"Oh, hi, hi Molly," I stuttered like the lame idiot I was.

She looked away, cold as could be. She seemed mad at me and perhaps she should be. After the incident of the yellow snow and the branch conking Frankie Nytz on his head, I had never got around to asking her to the Holiday Ball. I never even went to the dance but stayed at home on a cold, snowy, lonely night, watching reruns of the *Twilight Zone* on Netflix. Perhaps, she thought I was the one who was stuck up, thinking myself too good for her. Sebastian had told me, flatly, that I'd been a fool and missed my chance. The girl's feelings toward me had turned negative, he said. She was convinced I was a loser. And that belief, he said, had nothing to do with mind reading. It was a fact of life concerning the relationships between boys and girls since time immemorial. Whatever that meant.

We drove over to Sebastian's house in cold, stone silence.

Finally, the van pulled into Sebastian's driveway and I was relieved to see him glide out his front door and down the special wooden ramp with his Aunt Dottie and Uncle Brad behind him. Lieutenant Parker, and the van's driver, Major Kaminski, also dressed in the same uniform as the lieutenant, loaded Sebastian and his wheelchair into the side of the van by a special lift much like the one on Aunt Dottie's van that transported him to and from school every day. Then, Aunt Dottie and his Uncle Brad waved goodbye from the front porch. Aunt Dottie had a sad look, like my mother's, as the van backed out the driveway.

"Well, here we go," Sebastian said with a smile as he looked over at me.

I nodded at him trying to match his enthusiasm. "Yep," I said with a nod. But I still had a bad feeling about the whole thing.

# Chapter Fourteen
## Grady O'Reilly

As we approached the entrance ramp to the New York State Thruway five minutes later, I asked the two psi-warriors just how long a ride was it.

Lieutenant Parker swiveled around and looked back at me with a smile.

"I'm sorry, Henry," he said. "As I told your parents, the location of the Psi Academy is top-secret. Giving out its whereabouts, even how long it would take us to drive there, is a serious breach of security that would get me court-martialed."

"But I don't understand why the need for secrecy should apply to us," I said. "After all, we're going there."

"If he can't," Molly broke in, "he can't. Leave the poor guy alone, Henry."

"How about this," Lieutenant Parker said. "We'll let you try and figure out where the Psi Academy is on your own. Using your talents that got you invited there."

"How?" I asked.

"By seeing it in your minds," Lieutenant Parker said. "Using a psychic ability known as remote viewing."

"But I can't do that," I protested. "I can't bend spoons or read minds or remote view. Isn't that what we're going to this school for—to learn how to do all that?"

Sebastian turned to me and smiled. "All you need is to believe, Henry," he said. "After all, you turned the screws."

"Turned the screws?" Molly had turned to us and laughed. "What does that mean?"

"In *Psi Wars!*" Sebastian told her. "It's a kind of video game we play. Henry unscrewed all the screws and escaped from a coffin."

"You guys played *Psi Wars!?*" Lieutenant Parker asked. "*The Psi Wars!?*"

"Don't you remember, Tim," said the driver, Lieutenant Kaminski. "The kid in the wheelchair is Sebastian Drake. His father was Colonel Peter Drake. He invented—"

"Yes, I know," Lieutenant Parker said. "He invented *Psi Wars!*"

Lieutenant Parker looked back at Sebastian.

"Did you guys known my father?" Sebastian asked.

"No, he was before our time," Lieutenant Parker said. "But we know of him."

"So have you played it?" Molly asked.

"Yes," he said, looking back at her. "We all have, every psi-warrior who ever lived, far as I know. It's part of our training."

"So," Molly asked, "did you unscrew the screws?"

"Wouldn't be here if I hadn't," he said with a smile.

Lieutenant Parker suggested that we concentrate our minds and remote view the appearance, physical setting and location of the Psi Academy. He took a legal pad from a briefcase at his feet and tore off three pages and handed them back to each of us.

"Take a few minutes," he said, "and draw what you see, best as you can, on those sheets of paper."

Like Molly and Sebastian, I closed my eyes and, as if I was playing *Psi Wars!*, I relaxed my mind and tried to see the Psi Academy, what it looked like, where it was. But for some reason, my mind kept drifting back to Hogwarts School from the Harry Potter books. I opened my eyes and tried to get the image out of my mind. But when I closed my eyes again, all I saw was Hogwarts. So, after a time, I decided that maybe the Psi Academy really did look like Hogwarts, a stone castle in the middle of a deep dark woods nestled among a row of black mountains.

After much concentration, I also saw somewhere deep underground, in the bowels of the Academy, deep in the basement, a dungeon. And I saw '13' and also in the dungeon, I saw a soldier. I drew that, too, or the best drawing of it I could make, not much more than a crooked room with a stick figure in it representing the soldier.

"When you're finished," said Lieutenant Parker, "hand what you drew to me."

I nodded, looked at my drawing and smiled as I handed it to Lieutenant Parker. He looked at it a moment, then frowned. Sebastian and Molly handed in their drawings and I wondered whether they saw the Hogwarts School as well.

By then, we were approaching Erie, Pennsylvania and soon after we were exiting the interstate.

"We're picking up another cadet," Lieutenant Parker told us.

We drove for some time down a long, winding state highway, up a hill and down another, until we made a left turn onto a side street and traversed a labyrinth of narrow roads in a residential neighborhood. At long last, we pulled into a driveway of a long, expensive colonial house. By now, it was almost 10:00am.

The kid we picked up was tall, thin and good looking with hair even blonder than mine. There was something cocky and devious in his grin that reminded me of Frankie Nytz. And so, I took an instant dislike to him. Another bully, I thought, sure as day. His parents, stalwart, upper middle class folks wearing strong, imitation smiles waved goodbye as their only child (I later learned) entered the van and joined our journey.

He confidently introduced himself, looking at Molly the whole time, as Grady O'Reilly.

"Welcome aboard, Grady," Sebastian said as Grady sat down on the seat in the back row next to Molly. "I'm Sebastian Drake."

After a moment, Grady glanced over at Sebastian with a dubious frown. He nodded and shrugged.

"Glad to know ya," he said.

"I'm Molly Scott," Molly said. Grady turned to her and they politely shook hands.

I said nothing, choosing instead to stare out the window as the van pulled out of the driveway of the expensive O'Reilly house to resume our trip to the secret whereabouts of Psi Academy.

"Aren't you gonna introduce yourself, Henry?" Molly called from the back row.

I swiveled around and looked at Grady.

"Yeah, sure," I said. "Name's Henry Greenberg."

I didn't stick out my hand or anything and Grady didn't offer his.

"Greenborg?" he asked.

"Greenberg, Greenberg," I said, thinking here we go again, more Frankie Nytz nonsense with my name. "Like the baseball player. Hank Greenberg."

"Never heard of him," Grady said with a shrug, "But, alright. Greenberk."

We were on the interstate again, heading south, still a couple hours north of Pittsburgh, when Lieutenant Parker handed Grady a sheet of paper and told him, like us, to remote view the Psi Academy and draw it. Grady nodded confidently and closed his eyes. After only a minute or so, he opened them and started to draw, then handed what he had drawn to Lieutenant Parker.

After that, he started laughing and I turned around to see what was so funny.

"Hogwarts, Greenbake? Really?" he said incredulously, and laughed again.

"What?" Molly asked. "Hogwarts?"

Somehow the creep had read my mind, and I suspected right then that I wasn't in the same psychic ability league as him or Molly and Sebastian. Or any of the other Psi Academy cadets for that matter and I began to wonder how I had ever been chosen in the first place.

"So what did we draw?" Molly asked Lieutenant Parker.

"When we get there," he said. "We'll see who won."

I looked forward and had to listen to Grady O'Reilly laugh to himself again.

"Hogwarts," he scoffed.

# Chapter Fifteen
## The Psi Cave

Near Morgantown, West Virginia, we stopped at a rest area along Interstate 79. Lieutenants Parker and Kaminski accompanied the three of us as we shivered from the parking lot to the restrooms. Upon our return, Lieutenant Kaminski fished out white lunch boxes from the rear compartment of the van. We had a choice of tuna salad, ham, bologna or peanut butter and jelly sandwiches, with a bag of potato chips, a large oatmeal cookie and a box of apple juice. We ate in the van to keep us on schedule, not to mention that there was no place to eat at the rest area that cold Tuesday afternoon.

After lunch, I fell asleep and woke up three hours later as we were entering a long tunnel southbound on Interstate 77 that cut through the East River Mountain, one of the Blue Ridge Mountains just south of Bluefield, Virginia. I was hungry again and grouchy after being cooped up all day in an uncomfortable van. We had long since escaped the mass of dreary, leaden clouds that had stretched from home to just past Pittsburgh. But with the sun so low in the sky that time of year, the day lacked any hint of warmth. Gloom seemed to have descended upon all of us as we rode in silence toward some unknown destination.

But not long after passing through a second tunnel, the Big Walker Mountain Tunnel, just north of Wytheville, Virginia, we exited Interstate 77. It appeared, now we were off the Interstates, that we were nearing the end of our long trip somewhere in the midst of the Blue Ridge Mountains.

We took a series of narrow, hilly, winding state and county roads until we came to an ominous, secluded turn-off onto an even narrower, unmarked road, shrouded by deep woods on both sides. Looming about half mile ahead of us was the sheer, steep side of one of the Blue Ridge Mountains. The dying light that January afternoon only enhanced the sense of foreboding and doom as we approached.

"This is it," Grady O'Reilly whispered from the seat behind me.

"Yes," Sebastian agreed.

Maybe we were going to a place like Hogwarts after all, I thought, a castle hidden in a thick primeval forest at the foothills of this sinister looking mountain.

But driving for another couple of minutes, we turned left onto a bumpy, gravel road. The road ended at a high stone archway jutting out from the granite bluff of the mountain. It was an entrance of some kind, with a metal door that was presently closed.

The van came to a stop before the archway and Lieutenant Parker turned and smiled back at us.

"Well, here we are, cadets," he said, "Welcome to the Psi Academy."

As if on cue, the metal door of the archway creaked and slowly lifted. Once it had risen sufficiently, Lieutenant Kaminski drove forward. I soon realized that we were driving into the mountain-side. The Psi Academy was nothing like Hogwarts. It was under a mountain.

As the van drove into the cave, I glanced out the window and thought I saw several smoky, black, ethereal shapes slinking among the deep brush and trees around us. And in that instant, I was reminded of the mind wraiths that Sebastian and I had generated in the *Psi Wars!* game.

I leaned toward Sebastian.

"Did you see them, Seb?" I whispered. "Mind wraiths!"

Sebastian smiled and nodded, but he didn't get to respond because Grady interrupted.

"Didn't see this coming, did you Greenbig?" Grady said with amusement in his voice.

"For the last time, it's Greenberg," I said and turned around to look at his annoying, grinning face. "And, no, I guess I didn't."

"You saw Hogwarts," he said and smiled derisively at me.

I frowned, wondering how the hell he knew that, and a little disturbed that he may have delved in and plucked that knowledge somewhere out of my mind.

"This is what you saw?" I asked. "All of you?"

Grady looked at Molly, then at Sebastian.

"Yes," Grady said. "We all did. Except you."

Nodding to Sebastian, Grady added, "And Drake here, son of the late Colonel Peter Drake, even guessed the exact place where the Psi Academy is located. By latitude and longitude, mind you. Latitude and longitude, for God's sake. That's how good he is." He turned to Sebastian. "Isn't that right, Drake?"

Sebastian shrugged.

"Yep," interrupted Lieutenant Parker. He turned and faced us again from the front passenger seat. "Molly and Grady drew the mountain and the door, and Grady even drew a fairly accurate depiction of the mess hall where you'll share meals with your classmates this very evening. But Sebastian got it exactly right, down to the latitudinal and longitudinal degrees and minutes. And he also drew a pretty good picture of what it looks like down there."

"And what about Henry here?" asked Grady, snickering. "What did he draw?"

"He didn't draw this place," Lieutenant Parker said, "but he did draw something that was equally impressive."

"Yeah, like what?" Grady wanted to know.

Lieutenant Parker ignored Grady's question and starting telling us instead about this place. He told us we were entering an abandoned, underground Army base that had been secretly constructed in the late 1960s during the height of the Cold War when the former Soviet Union, mostly what we call Russia today, and the good old USA, were locked in a secret battle for the hearts and minds of mankind. It had been used on and off at various times for various things, up until the early 1990s, when Psi Ops took it over and has been using it ever since. The unofficial name for it became The Psi Cave.

"Psi Ops?" I asked.

"Yeah," Lieutenant Parker said as he swung around to look at me. "Psi Ops. Something you and your fellow cadets of the Psi Academy are part of now. On your way to becoming psi-warriors, just like Lieutenant Kaminski and yours truly."

Psi-warriors, I thought to myself. Now, that had a good ring to it.

The van stopped seconds later in front of a huge stainless steel elevator door in the carved out cavern.

"Anyone claustrophobic yet?" Lieutenant Parker looked back at us.

I looked at my colleagues, Sebastian, who gave me a cheery wink, then Grady, who scowled at me, and finally, Molly, who stared forward. I had to admit that I was a tad bit squeamish now that we were fully engulfed within the dark, low bowels of a mountain. There were some large, dim bulbs along the low ceiling of the cavern but for the most part, this was a gloomy and closed-in place.

I kept my fears to myself.

"Good," Lieutenant Parker said, "but this is the easy part. We are about to go seven stories underground."

As we waited for the elevator doors to open, Grady asked Lieutenant Parker, "So, if I may ask again, sir, what did Cadet Greenberg draw that you found impressive?"

"He drew Colonel Zebb," Lieutenant Parker said, "inside Hogwarts."

"Who's Colonel Zebb?" Grady ask.

But in the next moment, the high, wide doors of the elevator opened.

# Chapter Sixteen
# **Guardian Angels**

Lieutenant Kaminski pulled the van into the cavernous elevator compartment and a moment later, the thick doors closed us inside. A moment after that there was a brief whoosh and with a barely discernible g-force, down we went. Seconds later, the elevator slowed and came to stop. The door opened and Lieutenant Kaminski backed the van into a small, dark parking garage with a low ceiling. He parked in a space next to several other identical vans.

Lieutenant Parker opened the side door and lowered Sebastian's wheelchair out onto the pavement. Molly squeezed past Grady and me, and on her way past, Grady gave her a favorable appraisal by raising an eyebrow and grinning mischievously. She jumped out of the van followed by Grady, then me. I was happy to be standing on solid ground after the nine hour road trip, even in a dingy parking garage.

"How far down are we?" I asked Lieutenant Parker.

He turned to me and smiled. "Like most things down here," he said, "that, too, is top-secret. Just know, you are damned far underground."

"So who, sir, is Colonel Zebb?" Grady asked.

"You'll learn that in due time," Lieutenant Parker told him, and then, to the rest of us said, "This way."

We followed him and Lieutenant Kaminski toward a door

along the far wall. As we approached it, Lieutenant Parker looked back over his shoulder at us.

"Guess we're not in Kansas anymore, eh cadets," he said with a wink. "Anybody want to go back home to Auntie Em?"

"Maybe Dorothy Greensleeves over there does," Grady said with a chuckle as he nodded at me.

"Screw off, jerk-face," I told him.

Lieutenant Parker ignored the banter and pushed open the door which lead into a narrow, bright corridor with white walls and a suspended white tile ceiling. We followed him and Lieutenant Kaminski until they stopped at a doorway at the other end of it. Lieutenant Parker knocked at the door and a woman's voice from inside gruffly said, "Come in."

Lieutenant Parker nodded for us to follow him into a wide office with a long modern desk with a glass top against the far, white wall. In addition to the desk, there was a leather couch against the side wall and a large modern, glass bookcase against the opposite one. Seated behind the desk was a slim woman wearing an aviator jacket and a khaki shirt. She looked to be around thirty, and was fairly attractive, although her good looks were diminished somewhat by the way she tied her short, dark hair tight above her head and by her rather severe expression. As we approached, she clasped her hands together on top of the desk and regarded us with a serious frown.

But what really got my attention as we stood before the lady psi-warrior were the four ethereal "beings" floating directly behind her. I recognized them at once as mind wraiths. The four before us, however, had a glowing, benevolent sheen, almost too bright to look at for any length of time. They were more like angels than wraiths.

Lieutenants Parker and Kaminski strode forward and came to sharp attention about five feet from the desk with us closely behind them. They gave crisp, simultaneous salutes and waited as the lady psi-warrior raised, then lowered, her own salute before they lowered theirs.

"Cadets Drake, O'Reilly, Scott and Greenberg delivered for duty, Ma'am," Lieutenant Parker stated in a formal, no nonsense tone.

"Thank you, Lieutenant," said the lady psi-warrior. "Job well done. You are dismissed."

Lieutenants Parker and Kaminski snapped to attention and again saluted the lady psi-warrior. After she returned the salute, they about-faced and strode out of the room without giving us another look.

By that point, I was seriously second-guessing my decision to attend the Psi Academy. Had I unwittingly enrolled myself into one of those stodgy, stuffy military schools with orders being constantly barked out? Waking up at 6:00am every morning for Physical Training; marching, push-ups, tasteless grub in the mess hall sitting with our backs so straight it hurt and eyes completely forward all the time and answering questions like, 'Cadet, you say you come from Buffalo, New York? Well, there are only two things that come from Buffalo, steers and queers. And I don't see no horns coming out of your head, boy, so which one are you?'

"Good evening cadets," the lady psi-warrior began in a soft, kindly voice, hardly the harsh bark I had expected would be her first order of business in order to put us in our place. "My name is Major Pamela Atkinson," she continued in a friendly tone. "I am the Principal of this Academy and I welcome you. After your long trip, my first order of business will be to get you settled in as quickly as possible. And I will do that with the help of these angels."

Smiling, she swiveled around to the four wraiths hovering patiently behind her.

"These are your guardian angels," Major Atkinson explained. "I have conjured them up and assigned one to each of you. But the assignment is only temporary. By this evening, you will have no further use for them and they will dissipate, fade into oblivion like a pleasant dream. But until then, they will

Vincent L. Scarsella

help you find your assigned quarters and otherwise assist you in your initial orientation to life here at the Psi Academy."

She flashed another kindly smile; it was the smile Glenda the Good Witch in the *Wizard of Oz* always gave Dorothy Gale.

Yep, Lieutenant Parker was certainly right. We weren't in Kansas anymore.

# Chapter Seventeen
## Casper

Major Atkinson told us that at 1900 hours, or 'seven o'clock' in civilian parlance, there would be a welcoming ceremony in the main mess hall. This would include a brief speech from the Psi Academy's Headmaster, Major General Grant 'Buzz' Bosworth, together with staff introductions and ending with a full four course gourmet dinner. Major Atkinson added with a smile that we shouldn't expect such gourmet fare each and every day. However, she promised that we'd find the Academy's food to be of the highest quality and healthy as well and certainly better than anything we were served in our cafeterias of our former public or private schools.

But before then, our assigned guardian angel would show us to our assigned quarters where we could freshen up with a hot shower or bath, glance through the Academy student handbook and curriculum guide that had been downloaded onto the tablet computers waiting for us in our rooms, and perhaps still have time for a quick nap.

Major Atkinson then told us that from this point, henceforth, we were to address our fellow cadets by their surname, preceded by the designation, Cadet. No more calling each other by our given names, like Sebastian, Henry, Molly or Grady, and certainly no more nicknames, derogatory or

Vincent L. Scarsella

otherwise. And we were to address all the Academy instructors and staff as either Sir or Ma'am.

"Well, then," Major Atkinson said with a sigh, "before you are dismissed to start your academic career at the Psi Academy, does anyone have any questions or concerns?"

I hesitated a moment, then sheepishly raised my hand.

"Yes, Cadet Greenberg," she said, squinting at me. Molly, Sebastian and Grady turned and squinted at me as well.

"Ma'am," I said. "I was wondering, were those black wraiths back there in the hills at the entrance to the Academy?"

She raised an eyebrow, then nodded and gave me another of her kindly smiles.

"Very observant of you, Cadet Greenberg," she said. "Yes, those were black wraiths, sometimes called, dark wraiths. Actually, the proper name is a McLeay projection, after the psi-warrior who, well, first invented them, that is, who conjured one up down here in this very facility in the late 1990s. The projections you saw guard the Academy grounds."

Molly glanced over and briefly nodded, seemingly impressed with me for a change. For his part, Grady gave me a cold stare.

"Anything else?" Major Atkinson asked and looked at each one of us a few moments. "As there are no further questions, you are dismissed."

She waved to the wraiths hovering behind her and each of them floated over to where we were standing. They nodded for us to follow them out of the office and, in awestruck silence, we obeyed and went out after them into the corridor. I stood out there for a time until my assigned wraith seemed to smile and pointed for me to come along.

"This way," I heard it say, more of a kindly whisper than a voice.

I nodded and started walking after it.

Sebastian had his wheelchair already in gear a few feet ahead of us and was following his wraith down the corridor and right behind him was Grady and his. Molly was nearest to me, also heading in the same direction. But each of us was focused upon our respective wraiths—the fantastically odd incarnations somehow evoked out of the brain of Major Atkinson. For the moment, the wonder of this made me forget my colleagues, even Sebastian.

Finally, as I focused on my surroundings, I realized that this place had little in common with the Hogwarts School of Wizardry and Witchcraft, except perhaps that it taught young teenage boys and girls how to develop their nascent, supernatural powers in order to become wizards and witches or in our parlance, 'psi-warriors', in order to supposedly serve and protect ordinary American citizens from evil psychic forces. (Unlike the fictitious Potterian universe, we had no cute special name for ordinary citizens like 'muggles').

In appearance, ambience and design, the Psi Academy could not have been more different than Hogwarts. Its underground corridors were white and antiseptic and smooth, all business, without hidden crevices and quaint, dark and mysterious or magical chambers haunting the place. Or it didn't appear so at first glance. It in itself was an Army operation, carefully constructed and rigidly tested, regulated and regimented. The only mystery of the place, at that point, was how many levels it had. From what little I could make out so far, the Psi Academy was located on the seventh level. But we had not been informed how many other levels there were in the Psi Cave, and what they were used for.

I followed my wraith down the long corridor until at last we made a left turn and proceeded down another corridor before turning right down yet another. Sebastian and Grady stopped about halfway down the second corridor and were shown their quarters and then, a few moments later, Molly was shown hers. At long last, at the far end of the second corridor, at a dead end, my wraith stopped at the second last door on the right-hand side. My quarters I presumed.

"Please look into the scanner," my wraith directed. "It will record you iris print."

There was a retinal scanner embedded in the door about a foot above the doorknob and I looked into it. A moment later, the door clicked unlocked.

"You may enter," said the wraith.

I turned a golden doorknob and stepped inside a small living room furnished with a modern looking blue cloth fabric couch with oak arms and a matching loveseat next to it. There was an oak coffee table set directly before the couch and a squat end table adjacent the love seat. In the corner or the room stood a tall metal lamp. I was pleased to note a fifty inch flat-screen television also hung on the wall across from the couch and loveseat. Finally, a small metal desk with a black vinyl swivel chair had been placed against the side wall.

I followed the wraith down a short hallway and he gestured to a narrow bathroom with a shower with frosted glass but no bathtub. Immediately past the bathroom was a bedroom with a full-sized bed, fairly large dresser, and a reading chair. The dresser was stocked with official Psi Academy issue skivvies and socks, red, white and blue plain tee shirts, gym shorts, and sweat suits. One of the top drawers contained two belts and various other accouterments.

A small closet in the corner of the room was crammed with five sets of the official Psi Academy uniform of plain khaki pants and khaki shirts. Sewn onto the left breast of each shirt was an insignia depicting the outline of a shadowy, androgynous psi-warrior's face, immersed in a hazy blue background. The psi-warrior was staring at something, slightly sideways, with a small circle of light blazoning from his forehead. I decided the insignia was quite cool.

The closet also contained what looked to be a dress uniform for official ceremonies; a navy sport coat with the same Psi Academy insignia and navy pants, as well as several regular civilian pants and shirts. However, I was immediately disappointed that the closet did not contain at least one brown aviator jacket. I supposed we'd be issued one, together with the state trooper sunglasses, upon graduation from the Psi Academy when we'd be certified as psi-warriors.

"Welcome to your quarters," said my guardian angel wraith in a soft, kindly voice. "Is it to your liking?"

"Yes," I said, looking around the place. "Very nice."

I didn't tell this to the wraith, but though it was nice, and seemed comfortable enough, it was still oppressively, solidly and inescapably underground. There was a claustrophobic feeling that could not quite be overcome. I yearned to be outside again, to smell fresh air, to look up into a clear blue sky.

"I suggest, sir, that you take a hot shower," said the wraith. "And while waiting for dinner, review the Psi Academy student guide on your tablet."

My wraith's mannerisms and gestures and even tenor of speech reminded me a little of Major Atkinson. And that was only logical; after all, it was a manifestation of her mind that she had somehow transformed into a physical being.

"A shower sounds great," I told the wraith and then, thinking a moment, frowned.

"What shall I call you?" I asked. "Your name?"

The wraith seemed amused by the inquiry.

"I don't have a name," the wraith said. "I am a mere hallucination, a temporary mirage."

"But everything deserves a name," I said.

I suddenly recalled a dream I had a few weeks back about, of all things, that cartoon, *Casper the Friendly Ghost*. That was all I could remember about the dream. Casper. "Casper," I blurted. "I shall call you Casper."

My wraith smiled benignly at me, seemingly pleased with the name.

# Chapter Eighteen
## Dexter Chumley

After a long, hot shower, in which I fell asleep standing up for about five minutes, I felt refreshed enough to skim through the Psi Academy student guide on the tablet that had been assigned to me. I sat at the desk in the living room and waited while Casper demonstrated how to power up the tablet and its uniquely designed operating system (as well as Kansas, we were not in the world of Microsoft or Apple anymore).

Once the machine had booted, Casper helped me open the browser, and obtain a user name: *Hammerin' Hank* and password: *Nytz*, enabling entrance into the secure, top-secret Army intelligence network available to Academy cadets, as well as psi-warriors and various other secret agents in the vast and strange world of military intelligence. From there, it was a relatively quick and easy process to navigate around the Academy website requiring little further help from Casper.

The logo for the Psi Academy site was the same as the insignia on our Psi Academy cadet uniform shirts of the anonymous, androgynous psi-warrior staring with a light emitting energy from his forehead. Casper clicked on a link on the left margin labeled 'Curriculum' and floated off to let me review its contents. I leaned back in the swivel chair and began to read.

*Overview: Mission*

The *mission of the Psi Academy is to enhance each cadet's innate psychic abilities through a regimen of intense instruction, competitive games, and mentoring. Through such training, mere potential shall be transformed into real life application in furtherance of the cadet's personal advancement and his country's defense. The mission of the Psi Academy is stated in its Latin motto: Extra mentum, salutem.* Beyond the mind, salvation.

I skimmed past another several paragraphs of self-congratulatory, introductory fluff to a listing of courses making up the odd Psi Academy curriculum meant to advance its lofty sounding mission.

*Core Curriculum*

*First Semester*

*101 The Nature and Historical Application of the Psychic Arts*

*102 Quantum Mechanical Theory as an Explanation for Psychic Phenomena I*

*103 Literature and Art from the Psychic Perspective I*

*104 Language Studies: English*

*105 General Development and Application of Psychic Abilities I:*

*Intuition; Healing; Telepathy; Astral Projection and Conjuration of Wraiths (Lab)*

*106 Mind Games I (Team Competition and Assessment of Abilities)*

*107 Psi Wars! I (Gameplay)*

*108 Physical and Psychic Training (PPT) I*

*Second Semester*

*201 Literature and Art from the Psychical Perspective II*

*202 Language Studies: Chinese*

*203 Quantum Mechanical Approach to Psychic Phenomenon II*

*204 Communications with the Spirit Realm: The Dark Arts Unveiled*

*205 General Development and Application of Psychic Abilities II:*

*Telekinesis, Teleportation, Mind Control*

*206 Mind Games II*

*206 Psi Wars! II*

*207 PPT II*

I was about to turn the page to see what other strange subjects were planned for instruction when I heard a thud against the far wall of the living room. A moment later, there was another.

I looked up from my tablet and asked Casper, "What's that?"

Casper had floated from the corner of the room to the wall, when the third thud shook it. After a moment, he turned to me with that eerie benevolent smile. Then there was a fourth.

"What is it?" I asked.

"It's your next door neighbor Dexter Chumley," Casper said. "He's a wall walker."

A fifth thud shook the wall between Dexter Chumley's room and mine.

"Hey!" I called out. "Stop it! My television's coming off the wall!"

The thudding stopped and I turned to Casper.

"A wall walker?"

"Yes, but he's supposed to walk through walls," Casper said with a laugh, "not into them."

Then there came a sixth and final thud.

"Hey!"

"Sorry!" called a high-pitched voice from the next room. Dexter Chumley I presumed. A few moments later, someone was knocking at my door. Casper answered it and let in Dexter Chumley.

"Sorry to have bothered you," Chumley said. "But as an old Indian chief once said, sometimes the magic works, and sometimes it doesn't." He sighed. "I had wanted to make well, a rather more dramatic entrance and introduction."

Chumley walked over and stuck out his right hand. I looked down at it a moment, then shook it.

"Dexter Chumley," he said.

"Pleased to meet you," I said. "I'm Henry Greenberg, like the ballplayer."

Dexter squinted at me, seeming not sure about the ballplayer part.

"Casper here says you walk through walls," I said and nodded back toward the wall with the TV set hanging on it. "Or try to."

Chumley's wraith sauntered into the room and nodded at Casper.

"Yes, try to," Chumley said with a sheepish shrug. "But as you see, usually without much success. Though I've done it on several occasions in the past, at least partially, sticking my hand through a wall, that sort of thing, that scares my mother half to death. But I haven't quite yet mastered the art of quantum tunneling sufficiently to enable me to walk through walls. Point of fact, my concentration, at the atomic level, at least, is not quite up to par, I'm embarrassed to say. That's what I've come here to learn. How to do it. But until then, I supposed I will continue to bang into walls instead of walking through them."

"Gentlemen," said Casper, "I do believe it's time to get into your dress uniforms and head to the dining hall."

# Chapter Nineteen
# **The Headmaster**

The corridor was crowded with our fellow students and their respective wraiths. Each of us, even the girls, looked stuffy and uncomfortable in our dress blue uniforms; the dark blue pants and sport jacket, an azure blue shirt, and a dark blue tie (which Casper had to help me tie and fasten securely under my Adam's apple). I sincerely wished that Psi Academy cadets could wear the comfortable looking khaki pants and shirt and aviator glasses that psi-warriors wore instead.

It was a somber stroll, as we were all somewhat apprehensive about the dramatic and difficult change to our lives that attending the Psi Academy was promising to be. We turned left, right, then left again down identical looking corridors until finally we arrived at a wide, open double metal door that led into a spacious hall that served as both the Psi Academy's mess hall and auditorium. There was a long stage, complete with a curtain and an area behind it with offices and dressing rooms. A podium had been positioned in the center of the stage and on the front of it a plate with the Psi Academy insignia had been attached. Some feet behind the podium a long row of folding chairs had been set up. They were empty as we entered the hall which, I later learned, had been named Drake Hall in honor of Sebastian's father.

Three long dining tables had been positioned perpendicular

to the stage. There were five chairs on each side of the tables, except for the table to the left of the stage which had only nine chairs, with five on one side and four on the other, leaving an open spot for Sebastian's wheelchair.

There were placards with names on them sitting on china plates at each place telling us where to sit. I had been assigned the seat next to Sebastian. Just like old times, I thought, as I remembered our daily lunches at Colonel J. B. Weber High that seemed now a million years ago.

As I took my seat, along with the other cadets, Casper looked at me with a kindly smile. That's when I realized that I would never see him, or it, again. He'd dissipate like a figment of Major Atkinson's imagination.

"Casper," I whispered as I looked back at him.

"Good luck, Cadet Greenberg," it said.

I had to take a gulp of air to stop myself from crying as Casper floated off to only God knows where. As I turned my gaze from him, I spotted Grady O'Reilly smiling at me as if to say what a sentimental fool I was. Looking away from him, I saw several other cadets, including Sebastian and Molly, similarly affected by the departure of their wraiths. I looked back at Grady with a scowl desperately wanting to learn how to block his mind from prying into mine.

By then, Major Atkinson had walked onto the stage and was now standing before us at the podium.

"Cadets!" she said in her chirpy way. The thirty Psi Academy cadets assembled at the three tables and looked up at her with rapt attention. It was truly, finally here; the official beginning of life at the Psi Academy.

"It is my pleasure," she began, "to introduce to you at this time your Psi Academy instructors."

From stage left, our stern faced instructors, wearing the distinctive psi-warrior khaki uniform without the Psi Academy insignia, and the aviator jacket and trooper sunglasses, marched single file across the stage and stood facing us at their assigned folding chairs. Major Atkinson then proceeded to introduce them, one by one, announcing their respective ranks and names. As she did so, each of them stepped forward and gave us a slight nod. The ones I remembered were three colonels with expressions hard as granite, including one, short, tough-looking woman named Colonel Bertha Beckwith. Next came Major Aldous Tomelanos, or 'Major Tom' as he prefers to be called and four other majors. She then introduced five captains, including Captain Stanwyck, and finally, Navy Commander James Marzo. In total, I counted fifteen instructors.

After the introductions, Major Atkinson turned to us and said, "I am quite certain that during your time at the Psi Academy, you will learn a great deal from these esteemed instructors about the psychic arts. And in the process, I am sure you will come to like, if not love, each and every one of them."

She looked back at the team of instructors and flashed a smile, then turned back to us.

"And now," Major Atkinson said, "it is my distinct and supreme honor and privilege to introduce the Headmaster of the Psi Academy, Major General Grant Buzz Bosworth."

General Bosworth entered from stage left and his tall, massive frame strode forward. He scowled as he glided toward the podium while Major Atkinson turned to us, gestured for us to stand and stated loudly, "Attention on deck!"

We jumped to our feet and came to attention and remained that way as the Headmaster approached Major Atkinson, so unlike the ninth-graders back at Colonel J. B. Weber High who lolled around waiting for the pledge of allegiance to end. When the Headmaster reached the podium, Major Atkinson gave him a sharp salute. He returned it with a sharp salute of his own. His height, all six foot five of him, dwarfed Major Atkinson's five foot seven inch, lean frame.

Like us, General Bosworth wore his dress uniform. Two silver stars on gold straps were on the wide shoulders of his dark blue jacket. The lid of his cap was decorated by a set of gold leaves. It was cocked slightly to the right on top of his impressive silver-haired head.

"At ease, Major," he said and nodded.

Major Atkinson stepped aside and relaxed by placing her arms behind her back and widened her stance. General Bosworth then stepped up to the podium, lifted the microphone up and glared out at us.

"First off," he began with a smooth and reassuring Texan drawl, "I'm pleased to welcome y'all to the first ever class of the Psi Academy." He glanced back and gestured to Major Atkinson standing behind him. "I want to take this opportunity to thank Major Atkinson for her superior efficiency in getting all of you here expeditiously and safe and sound, from the four corners of this great land of ours and getting y'all settled in so quickly.

"Well, now, the hard work begins. During your stay here we hope, with your help, to tap into your innate psychic talents and put them to use in service of this great country."

General Bosworth shuffled about on his feet and his eyes became intense. For a moment, I thought his eyes had settled directly on me and, to avoid any kind of further scrutiny, I quickly lowered my gaze to my feet.

"We expect that each of you will give one-hundred and ten percent at all times in realizing your maximum potential as a student of the psychic arts at this academy."

General Bosworth stepped back and his scowl melted into a kind of mischievous grin.

"But enough of that," he said. "It is only your first day, and I realize you are tired from your long trip. I sincerely and warmly welcome you the Psi Academy and trust that once you have completed your course of study, and have become psi-warriors, you will appreciate the highest sense of accomplishment and reward."

He gave us one last, long hard look.

"And now, cadets, enjoy your dinner."

And that was it. The General saluted Major Atkinson and upon her return salute, he turned left and strode off the stage without another look back.

# Chapter Twenty
## Grady's Claim

"Thank you, Major General Bosworth for such inspirational words," Major Atkinson said as she lowered the microphone, making it squeak. She glanced in the General's direction then looked back at the instructors patiently sitting behind her. She nodded and they rose in unison then turned sharply and marched off the stage.

"And now, cadets, if you would place your right hand over your heart and recite with me, the Pledge of Allegiance."

We recited it, some loudly, others, like me, mumbling, as if we were in the first grade reciting it for the first time.

"Please be seated," Major Atkinson told us. "Please note that you have been divided into three platoons; Platoon Drake," she pointed to the table where Sebastian and I were sitting, "Platoon McGoneagle…" pointing to the middle table. "…And Platoon Stubblebine," pointing to the table to her left where Grady O'Reilly and Molly Scott sat.

"And now, dinner will be served," she said. "After dinner, you will be dismissed to your quarters. Before going to bed, you should review the student guide and curriculum, as well as your class schedule. Formal instruction commences tomorrow morning at 0700 hours sharp in the main classrooms. They are right down the corridor and to the left from here. Breakfast is served in this mess hall from 0530 until 0645 hours."

I computed that, or tried to, and was frowning miserably when Sebastian leaned over and whispered, "That's 5:30am to 6:45," and I nodded glumly in reply.

An enlisted man brought our first course, a bowl of dark, somewhat salty soup—it was a kind of gourmet mushroom and lentil bisque. Though I had never cared for mushrooms, after I started spooning it into my mouth I couldn't stop and wanted to ask for another bowl.

The rest of the dinner was equally delicious. There was a crisp romaine salad in a large bowl with a choice of various, savory dressings accompanied by a dish of crusty French bread. For the main course, we had a choice of chicken picatta, beef wellington, or an Asian vegetable and tofu stir-fry for vegetarians, served with potatoes au-gratin or rice pilaf with a heaped plate of buttered vegetables. It had been hours since lunch and we were starving. Our hunger, together with the superb quality of the food, caused us to eat pretty much in silence, savoring every last bite, with the only sounds the clinking of stainless steel knives, forks and spoons against our china plates.

Following the main course, the enlisted servers wordlessly cleared our plates and offered us a choice of strawberry cheesecake, vanilla ice cream with dark fudge syrup, or a chocolate éclair. I selected the cheesecake.

While the desserts were being devoured, some of my classmates began to stir and started to move around. I sat, remaining somewhat shy in my new environment, occasionally nodding to Sebastian on my left with a favorable comment about the food. Sebastian smiled at me or nodded an agreement as he scooped another chuck of vanilla ice cream lathered in fudge syrup into his mouth and some of it dripped onto his bib. He seemed generally pleased by our state of affairs. The Psi Academy was turning out to be an obviously efficiently run, high-class facility.

With a bite or two left of my strawberry cheesecake, and Sebastian's bowl of ice cream melting into mush, Grady O'Reilly sauntered over from the Stubblebine table with a smart-alecky, crooked grin. He edged between Sebastian and me and lowered to one knee. Sebastian turned, frowning, and drip of vanilla and fudge saliva dripped down his chin to hang there a moment before falling like a raindrop to the napkin on his lap. I felt that I had taken a time machine back in time to Colonel J. B. Weber High School and was witnessing yet another of Frankie Nytz's tiresome, mean-spirited harassments.

"What do you want Grady?" I asked.

"It's Cadet O'Reilly, remember," he said.

"Alright, *Cadet O'Reilly*," I said. "What do you want?"

He kept smirking as he turned and cocked his head to me.

"What do I want, Mr. Greenliar?" he asked. "Let me tell you what I want—I want to ask you how it feels to be a fraud."

"What the hell are you talking about, Grady, ah, Cadet O'Reilly?"

By now, Molly Scott had sauntered over and was standing directly behind Grady. Her arms were crossed and she wore a sour expression as she looked down at him kneeling between Sebastian and me.

"Why don't you ask your best buddy, Sebastian, here," Grady said, "what I'm talking about."

"Ask him what?"

"Tell him Sebastian," Grady said. "Or I will. Tell Greenfibber what a fraud he is."

"What are you talking about? What makes me a fraud?"

Grady looked back at me without giving Sebastian a chance to speak.

"Because," he said, "you're not supposed to be here." He looked back at Sebastian. "Is he?"

"What is he talking about?" I asked Sebastian.

"You didn't pass the test, Greensham," Grady blurted out. "You demonstrated no innate psychic powers."

"So, so, why was I selected to come here?" I asked.

"Tell him," Grady said to Sebastian. "Tell him what I read

out of General Bosworth's mind. Tell him what Bosworth thought."

"How did you...I thought they blocked..."

"Well, he didn't block me," Grady said. "Somehow I slipped in."

"He thought," Sebastian said, "General Bosworth thought, 'there's the kid who didn't pass. Henry Greenberg. Like the baseball player. The little Jewish kid who doesn't really belong here'." He sighed and bowed his head. "I read that, too."

"What?" I said in a loud enough voice that drew some stares. "Is it true, Sebastian, what Grady is saying?"

"It's true, Geenfake," Grady said.

"Then, how? Why?"

"Tell him, Cadet Drake," Grady said.

Sebastian sighed. "Because I told them I wouldn't attend the Psi Academy unless you came too," he said. "But they're—"

"That's right," Grady said. "Cadet Drake here threw a sissy fit and said he wouldn't attend the Psi Academy unless his best friend, you, came along. Even though you demonstrated no innate psychic abilities, and a rather low IQ on top of that I might add."

"That's not quite true, Cadet O'Reilly," Sebastian said. "I suggest you leave it alone."

"I won't leave it alone," Grady said. He turned and glared at Sebastian.

"I think you've said enough," Molly said "You said your piece."

"No, I haven't," he said, looking back at her momentarily, then back to Sebastian.

"Know what your little sissy fit resulted in?" he said. "My best friend, Alan Stinson, a kid who does have psychic powers," Grady glanced at me before turning back to Sebastian, "A kid who passed the test, he got bumped from attending the Psi Academy at the last minute, because Mr. Green-phony here took his place. So he's back home twiddling his thumbs, wasting his talents, all because Cadet Drake, the obvious teacher's pet of this school, because of his heroic, dear, dead daddy, could get his way."

"That's really quite enough, Grady," Molly said.

"You have no idea what you're talking about," Sebastian said. "I suggest you return to your seat and finish your ice cream."

"Whatever," Grady said as he stood and took a step back before looking down at me. "Hope you're proud of yourself, Cadet Green-deceit. Hope you get a first class education here."

And with that, Grady strode back to the Stubblebine table.

I looked over at Sebastian with hurt in my eyes. My instincts had been right all along. I didn't belong here. Grady O'Reilly was right. I was a fraud.

# Chapter Twenty-One
## Sebastian's Rebuttal

After the enlisted servers had finished clearing our dessert plates, Major Atkinson returned to the podium.

"Attention, cadets!" her voice boomed from the microphone. "Cadets! Your attention, please! I have several important announcements!"

Finally, we quieted. Still stunned by Grady's allegations, I glared at Sebastian but he had turned his wheelchair around and now faced the stage.

"First of all, I want to again congratulate each of you for being selected," she said. "You are the *crème de le crème*, as they say. The best of the best."

"Now that your appetites have been, I would hope, satisfied," Major Atkinson continued, "I want to again strongly encourage you to review your student guides and course curriculum this evening before going to bed. Doing so will give you a basic understanding of the course of study at this academy upon which you are about to embark so you can, as they say, hit the ground running tomorrow.

"Finally, cadets," and now she beamed a smile, "I am most pleased to tell you about my favorite part of the Psi Academy curriculum which has been developed for you. The Mind Games."

A collective murmur rose up from the class. Mind games! How cool did they sound. What could they possibly entail?

"The Mind Games are competitions among the three platoons during your entire enrollment at the Psi Academy," Major Atkinson continued. "Based upon these competitions, a champion will be crowned each semester bestowing the winning platoon with great respect and honor, not only among their fellow classmates, but also among all future classes who are destined to attend this academy.

"Each semester, the platoon leading the Mind Game competitions will be awarded the Drake Cup and will retain it until, if and when, they are dethroned in a subsequent semester. It will be a supreme honor, of course, for the same platoon to retain the Drake Cup the entire six semesters of attendance here at the Psi Academy." Now, Major Atkinson smiled. "Though I think that is most unlikely."

Major Atkinson further explained that the Mind Games would be played using a kind of video game called, *Psi Wars!*. She added that the simulation had been developed and improved upon over the years by past and present psi-warriors as a way to further develop and enhance psychic skills with the express purpose of meeting a prospective enemy psi-warrior in battle.

"Finally, cadets," Major Atkinson continued, "we have a saying here at the Psi Academy: 'Keep the faith, cease all doubt.' What that means is that as you progress through your instruction and training, you must be diligent in both suspending all disbelief and skepticism, and come to accept that anything, and I mean, anything is possible."

"With that, cadets," Major Atkinson said, "you are now hereby dismissed. I leave you with our motto: *Extra mentum, salutem.* Beyond the mind, salvation."

It took some time for us to realize that we could leave the room after Major Atkinson had exited the stage. It was as if we weren't quite yet convinced of the reality of our situation.

Finally, we collectively stood and started shuffling out of the dining hall into the corridor leading to our respective quarters.

Some of my fellow platoon members started introducing themselves to each other. A pretty, blonde haired cadet stepped forward and stuck her right hand out at me. I shook it and she said she was from Boulder, Colorado. I shrugged, and though still bitterly distracted by Grady's allegations, told her my name and where I came from, and, after a few moments of silence, she shrugged and moved past me to introduce herself to Sebastian.

"So you are Cadet Drake," she marveled. "Son of Colonel Peter Drake."

Sebastian gave a sheepish nod and said, "Yes, I'm Cadet Drake."

I rolled my eyes by now having grown quite tired of the seemingly excessive, vicarious adoration for Sebastian solely because of his father's grand reputation. It was as if Colonel Drake had been a holy saint or something. There was a platoon named after him and a Cup and now even his crippled son was a local celebrity. I quickly moved away as Cadet Randolph fawned all over Sebastian while he glided forward with spittle drooling from his mouth.

With Grady's allegation still nagging at me, I hugged the wall on my way down the maze-like corridors back my quarters. Not to mention that I was also dead tired after the long day. I was also still angry with Sebastian for putting me in this situation— undeservedly admitted as a cadet to the Psi Academy upon his demand that had cost a deserving kid a chance to attend. The anger stayed with me after entering my quarters until, after ten minutes or so, I couldn't stand it anymore. I left my room and walked over to Sebastian's and banged several times onto his door. He opened it without saying a word, glided backwards and allowed me entrance into his quarters.

"Aren't you going to say something?" I asked after his front door closed behind me.

"I know you're angry, Henry," Sebastian said, his back

still to me. "And I would be, too, if I was you. But you have to believe that Grady wasn't quite right in what he said." He wheeled around and faced me. "You didn't fail the test. Not completely anyway. You do possess some level of psychic talent."

"But not high enough to earn a trip here," I said. "Grady was right about that, at least, that I'm here only because of you. They wanted you bad enough to take a psychic weakling along for the ride."

"Well," he said and looked down at his lap. "That much is true. They were not inclined to take you until I insisted." But as he looked up, there was a gleam in his eyes. "But, Henry, I didn't ask for you to be here merely because you are my best friend. You do possess a psychic power, Henry, an important power. Something that the Psi Academy needs very much. That's why I convinced the Army to take you."

I shook my head for a time before letting out a small laugh.

"I think you're full of crap, Seb," I said.

"No, Henry," he said, "I'm not."

"So what's my friggin' psychic talent?" I asked. "What could it possibly be? I can't bend spoons, read minds, remote view, or do any of the things the other cadets attending this nuthouse of a school can already do. What's my special talent?"

"Dreaming, Henry," he said. "It's your dreams. Remember? We talked about this. I think your dreams foretell the future. And there aren't many psychic talents better than that."

I shook my head dubiously but held onto Sebastian's claim. Yeah, I almost forgot. My dreams. Maybe I did have something special within me.

Maybe I was destined to be a psi-warrior after all.

# Chapter Twenty-Two
# **A Bad Dream**

After leaving Sebastian's room, I tried reading the student guide on my tablet but fell asleep after about five minutes— right there on my chair at the desk in the living room. At some point after that, I had the dream.

All of sudden, my subconscious mind was involved in a bizarre drama over which I had no control. And like any other dream, this particular drama was mixed up parts from various events in my life with a vague touch of pure fancy.

In the dream, I woke up in a kind of dark and gloomy fortress with gray stone walls, again reminding me of Hogwarts. I was somewhere deep inside the place, in a cramped, dark room with gray, wet stone walls. I suddenly realized that Sebastian was with me, only he wasn't in his wheelchair. He was standing next to me listening for something.

In the next scene a psi-warrior materialized out of nowhere and was standing in the room with us—it was none other than Colonel Zachariah Zebb. Just as in the video game, *Psi Wars!*, Zebb was a tall, fierce looking man with an intense dark scowl. He had a thick athletic build and imposing wide shoulders and he towered over both Sebastian and me. We'd certainly be no physical match for him. And just like in *Psi Wars!* his face was somewhat vague, nondescript.

*Well, well, well*, he said to our minds.

*How'd he get in here?* I asked and glanced over at Sebastian.

*I teleported in,* Colonel Zebb said and his mouth formed a wide v-shaped grin, like the Joker in *Batman.*

*What do you want?* I asked him.

*Well, I want Sebastian Drake most of all.*

*No.* Sebastian and I transmitted the same thought at once.

*I am afraid you have no choice in the matter,* he said, and in the next instant, we were surrounded by four ugly black wraiths wrapping their long boney looking smoky arms around us. Neither Sebastian nor I could move.

*No!* we telepathically shouted.

*Take them,* Zebb ordered the wraiths.

*No! Leave us alone!*

*You have nothing to fear from me,* Zebb said, *I'm one of the good guys.*

Suddenly, Zebb had morphed into someone else, a tall, friendly looking, gaunt figure, more like the actor Jimmy Stewart (you know, George Bailey from that Christmas movie) than some evil villain. I looked back at Zebb as the black wraiths dragged us out of the room and into the dark hallway. He was smiling, but it wasn't a mean or devious smile anymore. It was a kindly, caring smile; the kind of friendly smile an uncle might give.

*Stop struggling with them!* Zebb said. *We have to get you out of here. Now!* And then he looked at Sebastian. *And we still have to get your father.*

Then I woke up. My back felt stiff from having slept so long in the chair at my desk. I checked my watch and noted it was 12:47am. I had been asleep for over two hours. I closed my eyes and reviewed details of the dream and decided I'd better write it down.

After typing what I could remember into my tablet, I powered it off and crawled back into my bed and tried getting back to sleep. By now, the digital clock read 1:26am. But I couldn't fall asleep. All I could think of was the dream and

Colonel Zebb assuring us that he was a good guy, and that we needed to go with him. And his suggestion that Sebastian's father was not really dead.

After tossing and turning for another half hour or so, I got up and sat on the edge of the bed panicking over what to do. The Psi Academy student guide advised us that should anything amiss or strange happen at the school—even the slightest thing and seemingly insignificant at first blush—we should exercise caution and contact Major Atkinson. She'd determine whether we needed to be concerned. I thought the bad dream was reason enough to reach out to her, even at 2:00am.

I found my Psi Academy issue cell phone, usable only to make calls to other students and the Academy staff, and found Major Atkinson's number, simply a four digit code: 0001. After the second ring, Major Atkinson answered.

"Major Atkinson," she said as if she had been fully awake at the time of my call.

"I, I had a bad dream," I blurted and suddenly felt embarrassed, like a scared little boy away from home missing his mommy.

"It was about Colonel Zebb," I added. "He, he had broken into a fortress of some place, a castle, like Hogwarts in Harry Potter…" and, I had no idea why I had thought to add that "… and he kidnapped Sebastian and me."

"Did you write it down?" she asked. "Your dream?"

"Yes," I told her. "In my tablet."

"Good, email it to me. I'll send a wraith down to get you. We'll talk more about it in person in my office."

A minute or so later, there was a gentle rapping at my door. When I opened it, I let out a gasp. I had been expecting a white, benevolent wraith with an ever kindly smile like my late, Casper, but instead, a seemingly seven foot tall and nearly touching the corridor ceiling black wraith hovered like bad, factory smoke. For a moment, I feared the Grim Reaper had come to take me away to Nirvana.

"Come," it said and stuck out a bony looking, smoky finger gesturing for me to come with it.

I followed the wraith down the silent corridor, envious of my fellow students sleeping securely in the rooms as I passed. Finally, after traversing, in exact reverse, the same maze of corridors along which I had followed Casper earlier that day on the way to my quarters, we came to Major Atkinson's office.

Major Atkinson was in her crisp and clean psi-warrior khaki uniform as if she had never taken it off for bed. Looking up from her tablet as I entered she smiled and gestured to a black leather chair facing her desk. As I sat down, the black wraith floated to a position in the back of the room.

"Welcome, Cadet Greenberg," she said. "I just read your email, about your dream. And it disturbs me. It could mean that Colonel Zebb can breach the Psi Cave."

She told me I would learn more about Zebb in Major Tom's classes. The short, 2:00am, morning version was that Colonel Zebb was indeed a real person. He had been a psi-warrior who had trained with Colonel Drake at this very facility, and also co-commanded Project Mind Bloom. At some point, he had gone astray and convinced a number of other psi-warriors to rebel and apply their powers toward controlling the whole human race. In the process, the rebel group consolidated their abilities and became what is known as a z-Prime: a hive mind of super-enhanced psychic ability.

"So," Major Atkinson said, "your dream gives me cause for concern." She sighed. "We have always suspected you are a precog, Henry. You see, there is no real test for that. One's dreams cannot be tested."

"What's, what's a precog?" I asked.

"A precog is a person who can foretell the future," she said. "Usually this is done by dreaming about it. But we believe that it can be harnessed as well through trances and waking visions. We think a precog can be taught to project himself or herself into the future and report back what was seen; what the future holds. And perhaps, with this information, we can figure out what can be done to change it."

If I was, as Major Atkinson surmised, a precog, though I sincerely doubted it, then what future had I seen?

"So what could my dream mean?" I asked Major Atkinson. "For the future?"

"What I fear," she said, "is that Colonel Zebb has found a way to breach our security and will, at some point, enter the Psi Cave in pursuit of Sebastian Drake."

"How could he get down here, under all that rock?" I asked.

"A z-Prime can do a lot of things normal psi-warriors can't," she told me. "And Zebb was an accomplished psi-warrior to begin with. Teleportation would certainly not be beyond his powers. And there is a certain, well, mechanism that he may be using to enhance those powers further. Again, that is something I will leave to Major Tom's lectures."

She leaned forward and blinked at me, and for the first time, I saw strain in her. I noted dark circles and tight wrinkles at the corner of her eyes.

"Is it inevitable?" I asked. "What I saw?"

"I have no idea." Major Atkinson said. "Before today, I had never met a precog."

I was both elated and terrified at this turn of events. Grady O'Reilly was full of it. I did belong at the Psi Academy. But what Major Atkinson said had also frightened me. It meant that Sebastian and I were in danger, that we were central to the plans of the evil forces led by Colonel Zebb. And Colonel Zebb was not a fictional evil character in a video game, he was a living, breathing evil genius who had made grandiose plans whose purpose was to control mankind.

Still, I couldn't shake the idea that, in my dream, at least, Colonel Zebb hadn't seemed evil. In fact, part of me liked him. When I admitted this to Major Atkinson, she told me that was how he did it—that was in his bag of tricks. That was how he fooled people into following him and doing bad things in furtherance of his evil master plan.

"You mustn't believe a word of what he says to you," Major Atkinson admonished. As I followed Major Atkinson's black wraith back to my quarters, yawning several times along the way, I felt numb and energized all at once. But somehow, after I crawled back under the covers of my bed at what was by now almost 2:30am, I fell fast asleep.

And at 5:30am, when the buzzer went off on my Psi Academy issue alarm clock, I did not feel all that tired despite getting only three hours sleep. I was instantly alert and ready for my first day of school at the Psi Academy. All that knowledge of myself, what I really was kept me going. It made everything new and vibrant.

I sat down next to Sebastian at the Drake Platoon's assigned table and he gave me a double-take. "You look awful," he said.

I laughed for a time as he squinted at me with annoyance and concern before I finally told him about my bad dream.

# Chapter Twenty-Three
# The Nature and Historical Application of Psychic Phenomena

Breakfast at the Psi Academy on Wednesday, our first day of school, was family style, with heaping plates of fried and buttery scrambled eggs, toast, waffles, hash brown potatoes, fried sausage, bacon, ham, fresh fruit, cheddar cheese, bagels, an assortment of cereal boxes, and an assortment of fruit juices, milks - white, skim, low fat, chocolate. They were delivered to our tables by the unspeaking, somber enlisted servers.

"Wow!" I said with a laugh as the food kept coming. "Are we breaking the defense budget or what? And is this good or what?"

"It certainly is," said the cadet sitting to my right, a girl. She smiled shyly at me and said her name was Cadet Morgenstern. She bowed her head and told me her first name was Freda. I thought that an odd name, but kept it to myself. I told her my name was Cadet Greenberg, Henry, like the ballplayer, I added, but she gave me a blank stare. Freda Morgenstern was mousy girl with lots of freckles along her nose and long forehead. She had a long, horsey face and kept looking down at her lap as if she had dropped a hunk of scrambled egg on it. She was shy but seemed taken with me. She wasn't as pretty as Molly Scott, but with Molly's ogling of Grady O'Reilly every chance she got, I had all but given up any chance of romancing her.

Freda looked up at me with a sly smile and I hoped her particular psychic talent wasn't telepathy.

Moments later, at exactly 6:45am, a dull buzzer sounded from a set of speakers recessed somewhere in the ceiling dismissing us from breakfast. We were off to attend our first class at the Psi Academy. According to the schedule posted in the student curriculum on my tablet, the course was named *The Nature and Historical Application of Psychic Phenomena* and instructed by Major Aldous Tomelanos—the same Major Tom who had stopped by my house, now seemingly endless weeks ago, with Captain Stanwyck to recruit my attendance at the school.

With Sebastian gliding at my side and slightly behind me, I accompanied the other Drake Platoon members, each of us carrying our tablets, down the corridor. At the front of the classroom was a desk and sitting on top was a grinning, affable Major Tom. Behind him along the front wall was a large screen with the following PowerPoint slide projected upon it:

The Nature and Historical
Application of Psychic Phenomena
xxx
Unit One:
The Identified and Theoretical Types of
Human Psychic Powers
By
Major Aldous Tomalanos, US Army
xxx

"Come on in, don't be shy," Major Tom said, gesturing as we cautiously entered the classroom. "Welcome."

There were nine desks with the tops folded down, just like those in classes back at Colonel J. B. Weber High School, arranged in two neat rows near the front of the class. The first row had only four desks, with five in the second, leaving a space in the first for Sebastian's wheelchair.

Vincent L. Scarsella

"There's no assigned seating in my classroom, so find a seat, sit down, and get yourself comfortable," Major Tom said. "No time to waste."

Major Tom hopped off the desk and stretched his back as each of us found a desk and Sebastian settled into an empty slot along the front row. I ended up in a seat at the other end of that row and Freda Morgenstern gave me another shy smile as she sat down next to me. I was wondering if she might turn out to be my girlfriend at some point in the school year when I again realized that she could be reading my mind at that very moment. And, in the next moment, I thought of Molly and Grady in another classroom with the Stubblebine Platoon and wondered if she was still ogling after him.

With a sigh, like my classmates, I lowered the top of my desk, placed my tablet computer on top of it and waited for Major Tom to begin. I sighed, settling into the idea that the Psi Academy was just another school with loathsome rules and boring classes and teacher's dirty looks.

"Alright then, let's begin," Major Tom said. "As indicated by this introductory slide behind me, this course is going to cover the nature and historical application of psychic phenomena, a pretty extensive topic, to say the least."

He scanned the class but didn't give away whether he was impressed or put off by the array of eager faces staring back at him.

"Anyone have any idea what the psychic phenomena are?"

Cadet Curtis Sims, a tall kid with a long face and sad, droopy eyes, sheepishly raised his hand. "Powers of the mind?" he asked.

"Well, yes, Cadet Sims, something like that," said Major Tom and he scanned the rest of us. "Anybody else?"

Sebastian raised his arm.

"Cadet Drake?"

"An innate human mental ability," Sebastian answered, looking up as if remembering a definition from a book, "in

144

which brain energy is intentionally used to perform extra-sensory activities. It is an unused or under-used human attribute or talent."

Major Tom smiled.

"Very good, Cadet Drake," he said, and clicked the next PowerPoint slide:

xxx

What is a Psychic Power?

xxx

An innate human mental ability in which brain energy is intentionally used to perform extra-sensory activities. It is an unused or under-used human attribute or talent.

xxx

A murmur of amusement and amazement arose from the class in admiration of Sebastian's ability to know what the slide said before it was shown to us.

"Can anyone break it down further?" Major Tom asked, scanning the class again. "How about you, Cadet Greenberg? Want to elaborate, define it further for us?"

I sighed and thought a moment. I knew what the textbook said a psychic power was from my limited reading last night. But the definition seemed too rote, too, well, textbook.

"There is no definition for it," I said. "It just is."

Major Tom nodded, seemingly impressed by what I had said although I wasn't quite sure what it meant.

"Interesting insight, Cadet Greenberg." He looked around the class again. "What physical or bodily process is believed to cause it?"

Several hands popped up and he settled on the one offered by a cerebral looking kid with thick black-rimmed glasses in the second row.

"Yes, Cadet Palmer," said Major Tom.

Cadet Palmer answered, "Well, as the slide says, the brain is the cause of it. I would say that psychic powers are caused by chemical and electrical reactions within the brain."

"Well, that's getting fairly close," Major Tom said and after a sigh, began to pace the floor in front of his desk.

"Suffice it to say, for the purposes of this course, psychic powers have been found to be real, measurable forces—explainable, in theory anyway, by quantum mechanics. Such forces can even be written as mathematical equations. The quantum processes that seem to explain psychic powers will be discussed in greater detail in your next class by Commander Marzo. What I want you to take away from this lesson is that a psychic power is as tangible and real as sunlight, intelligence or consciousness and as difficult to explain as a concept by any language—mathematical or otherwise."

He stopped, turned and smiled uncomfortably as if he himself could not quite comprehend what he had just said. "What we do here at the Psi Academy," he continued, "is use an instructional process that enhances a person's innate psychic powers."

Major Tom looked out at us.

"Consider this," he said. "Pretend there is this kid, and pretend this kid has some artistic or athletic ability beyond his schoolmates. You know, he makes really good drawings or carries a musical note better than most. Or say, he can hit a baseball farther than the other kids on his team. When that talent, that gift, is recognized and improved upon, you know, taken to the next level, we say that the person has developed his art form, become an artist. The kid's talent has been magnified, by choice and practice, so that he or she can reach a higher potential, to make museum worthy paintings, to record smash hits, or to break baseball records.

"Intelligence is another example of what we want to do here at the Psi Academy," he went on. "Some kids are very intelligent, and some of them we'd call geniuses. But left alone and not exercised, whatever the intelligence the kid had might not help him or her learn anything and might not be put to proper use. His intelligence would go to waste.

"And like all the above examples, innate psychic talents can be developed and magnified, and made into something artistic and useful. Something that can benefit mankind. That is what we want—to teach our students how to develop to the best of their abilities."

Major Tom scanned our faces again, trying to determine, I guess, whether any of what he'd been saying was sinking in.

"However," he went on after that pause, "these special psychic talents can also be developed in a negative, dark way and put to evil purposes, just as intelligence can be put to evil uses. If a kid is programmed by his schooling or environment to think bad thoughts, he'll do bad things.

"And as you will learn all through history, psychic powers have been perverted to do evil things to the detriment of mankind. And as you will also learn, the unfortunate uses to which Colonel Zebb and his evil platoon have applied psychic powers is perhaps the most recent, modern example of this travesty."

Major Tom sighed. "But, I am far getting ahead of myself."

Colonel Zebb? There he was again, invading my dreams, and now my studies.

# Chapter Twenty-Four
# **The Known Psychic Powers**

Major Tom clicked the next slide.

Known Psychic Powers:
- Telepathy
- Remote Viewing
- Telekinesis or Psychokinesis
- Astral Projection
- Conjuration or Evocation
- Energy Healing
- Tele-Influencing
- Trans-tunneling
- Teleportation
- Invisibility
- Precognition
- Spirit Communication

Major Tom looked at the slide with admiration before turning to face us.

"Each of you has exhibited a proficiency in at least one of these powers," Major Tom said, reaching out his arms to highlight the wonder of that fact. "Some possess one, and others several, or perhaps all of them. However, we each have one power we are especially good at. That power is known as your dominant power. What we attempt to do here at the Psi Academy is enhance your dominant power and hopefully one or a few more of them."

I thought of my dominant power. *Precognition.*

"As I said, there are some people, very few and far between," Major Tom continued, "who are proficient in each and every one of the powers on that list. These are the most valuable, and most dangerous, people in the entire world. Colonel Zebb appears to be one of those people. There may be one or more of you among your classmates who are similarly blessed, or cursed."

I looked across the row at Sebastian and suspected that he was one of those most valuable, and dangerous, blessed or cursed, people in all the world.

"Now, that list behind me," Major Tom said, "may not be exhaustive. There are some psychic powers we only suspect, in theory anyway, that could exist, but they have not yet been mathematically demonstrated. An example is shape-shifting, which is the ability for a person to change his or her actual physical form or being, or, for them to somehow alter the atomic and molecular makeup of his or her being into something else." He shrugged. "There are a few more, but what I will be talking about this morning are those powers that have been at least demonstrated to exist, as I said, mathematically.

"With that said, let's review the known psychic powers. What they are. In the next series of slides, definitions are provided for each of them. However, I caution you that these definitions do not precisely describe them. Indeed, there is no known language, spoken, written, conceptual or mathematic, that adequately sets forth the underlying psychic and quantum processes representing these phenomena."

Major Tom then began the definitional slides.

xxx

Telepathy

xxx

The ability of one mind to communicate with, or receive information and communications from, another mind, via unilateral or mutual transmission of brain electricity.

*Xxx*

Remote Viewing

xxx

The ability of the mind to obtain impressions about or directly observe another spatial or temporal location outside the immediate presence of the seeker.

Xxx

Telekinesis or Psycho-kinesis

xxx

The ability to move objects through quantum or electrical forces emitted by the brain. Displays of such ability are diverse and include spoon bending, levitation, influencing the roll of dice, the play of cards, or even the direction of the wind in nearby areas.

Xxx

Conjuration or Evocation

xxx

The ability of a person to summon, call forth or create from the mind a spiritual form, such as a demon, wraith, vampire, zombie, orc, yeti, other supernatural or unnatural entity, monster or presence.

Xxx

Astral Projection

xxx

The ability of a person's spiritual being or essence to leave his or her physical body and travel to another spatial or temporal location. It is believed, though not proven, that a person may project one's present existence, or spirit, into another cosmic dimension or parallel universe, or in some cases, the afterlife or spirit dimension. States of projection are often achieved via dreaming, deep meditation or by using various techniques. The concept of astral projection has been practiced for thousands of years, dating back to ancient China.

Xxx

Tele-Influencing

xxx

The ability of a person to use his mental or brain energy or electricity to implant ideas or urges into the mind of another person that motivates, influences or controls the thoughts and actions of that person.

Xxx

Trans-tunneling or P-Quantum Tunneling

xxx

A quantum mechanical phenomenon in which a person reconfigures his or her atomic and molecular structure to enable him or her to pass through a physical barrier.

Xxx

Teleportation

xxx

The ability of a person to use brain energy or electricity to instantaneously, without any obvious means of locomotion, transport his or her body or the physical presence of another person, object or thing to another spatial or temporal location.

Xxx

Energy Healing or Anti-Healing

xxx

The ability of a person to channel his or her brain energy to effect the health and healing process of themselves or another. It may also have a negative component, like voodoo, when the healing ability is subverted to make another person ill.

Xxx

Invisibility

xxx

The ability to use brain energy to manipulate light photons so that such photons are bent or diverted around their target making the target unable to be seen. A target may be a person or thing, within the vicinity of the manipulator of light, including himself or herself.

Xxx

I sat up straight and leaned forward on my elbows when Major Tom's clicked forward to the next slide.

xxx

Precognition

xxx

The ability to see future events through extrasensory means, usually in dreams, but also through flashing thoughts, trance or meditation. The existence of this ability has been the subject of skepticism because it is not readily testable and has been for centuries a source of fraud. To some, it is considered to be a 'dark art' because the ability to see into the future implies a knowledge of things that should be kept unknown, such as the date of death of another. However, it has been theorized that future insight gained through the art of precognition is a vision of how things might be and not necessarily how they will be.

xxx

"Let me stop here a moment," said Major Tom after looking briefly back at the slide, "and add something about this power. Only two cadets have been identified as potential seers, or precogs. I say, potentially because, as the slide indicates, the power hasn't been proven to exist with any degree of scientific certainty.

"As you might expect, being a precog can be a troubling experience. Imagine being able to pinpoint the exact date and time of someone's death, someone you love, your mother or father, a brother or sister, for instance, not to mention yourself. But it cannot be stressed enough that, as the slide indicates, a precog only sees future events as they might be, not as they necessarily will be. Therefore, unlike the past, which cannot be changed (or so we think), it is believed that the future can be altered for the better, or for the worse."

Now, I felt even more special. I looked across at Sebastian

and knew he must be the other precog. I thought back to the time when we had the same dream about the evil clown who supposedly represented Colonel Zebb who was trying to kill him.

"And another thing about precogs," Major Tom said, "A person either is one, or isn't, and their method of seeing the future, foretelling event, which is usually by dreams, can't be changed."

Major Tom abruptly continued the topic by clicking to the next slide.

Xxx

Spirit Communication or Mediumship

xxx

Because of its supernatural and demonic implications, the ability to communicate with the spirits or souls of the deceased, or mediate such communications between the living and the dead, has been deemed to be a dark art. Like precognition, its practice has become suspect due to fraudulent claims on the part of many alleged mediums after séances became popular in the late 1800s. Nevertheless, several experiments have demonstrated the possible existence of mediumship.

xxx

"Spirit communication, also known as dead talking, is a so-called dark art similar to precognition," Major Tom said. "You either have it or you don't. It doesn't appear to be amenable to enhancement, and it can't be taught."

"And there you have it," said Major Tom, "the known psychic powers, in a nutshell."

He looked out at our bright, still eager faces. This was truly fascinating stuff.

"Well class, what are they again?" Major Tom asked.

"To start, telepathy. Popularly known as mind reading. For example," he looked around the class. "Cadet Norbert, I certainly agree with you—I do tend to drone on a bit too long and my hair is slightly askew this morning."

A buzz went through the class while Cadet Norbert went red and mumbled an apology of sorts.

"And then there is remote viewing: seeing places, objects or people from a distance."

Major Tom scanned the room again settling on the small (though taller than me) bright-eyed, dark-haired kid with the dusky complexion sitting next to me.

"Cadet Gallardo." He said. "I want you to close your eyes and see a place in your mind. The longitude and latitude for the place are as follows: *43-42'27" North* by *109-11'17" West.*"

Cadet Gallardo drew in a breath then closed his eyes. After only something like thirty seconds, he said "Yes, I see it."

"Open your eyes, Cadet Gallardo and tell me what you saw?"

Gallardo described a deep, rocky cavern at the bottom of which was a dark pool of water. He said there were sagebrush and other desert like vegetation along the surface of the cavern.

Major Tom opened a thin drawer in his desk. He took out an eight by ten photograph of some kind of landscape and held it up for us to see. It looked like what Gallardo had described.

"Is this what you saw, Cadet?" Major Tom asked.

"Yes sir," Gallardo said, nodding, "pretty much."

"Well," Major Tom said, "this is Devil's Hole, Wyoming. At the coordinates I indicated. Well done, Cadet Gallardo." Major Tom started clapping and we joined in.

"Thank you, sir," Gallardo said, beaming. Remote viewing was obviously his dominant physic power.

"The next power is telekinesis, or psychokinesis," Major Tom went on, "also known as spoon bending."

Major Tom stepped between the rows and reached out and lifted a ballpoint pen out of Cadet Palmer's shirt pocket. After a moment, it went limp like a boiled noodle. And then, in the next instant, it straightened and appeared undamaged as he returned the pen to Cadet Palmer's shirt pocket. We all *ooh'd* and *ah'd* at that as if we were among the audience of a magic show.

"That," Major Tom said, "was no magic trick. I actually bent the spoon. Don't ask me how, but somehow the energy waves emitting from my brain caused a total deconstruction, and then reconstruction, of Cadet Palmer's quite nice pen."

"Or there is this," he rose slowly from the floor and hovered at about the level of our heads as we gawked up at him. "Levitation, a sub-category of telekinesis."

Major Tom smiled as he lowered his two feet securely to the ground.

"A neat trick, isn't it?" he said, then frowned. "Only, it's no trick, although there are magicians out there who can simulate it, fake it. But what I just did was really, truly float."

He sighed and thought a moment while we continued to marvel at what we had just seen.

"So, after telekinesis, there is conjuration, also known as evocation. Which is making wraiths and other entities, including summoning a succubae; a pretty woman or handsome man from whom you might wish to receive a visit late at night." He grinned. "Although I warn you against doing such a thing."

Major Tom winked and raised an eyebrow. Then, in the next instant, forming next to him, literally out of thin air, was a beautiful, young woman in a short skirt. She smiled at us, curtsied, then nodded.

"That by the way," he said, "is Mrs. Tomelanos."

He clapped his hands and the wraith, his wife's ersatz doppelganger, dispersed like a puff of cigarette smoke into a shapeless gray cloud and then was gone. After a moment, we politely applauded the trick.

"Next, astral projection," he continued, "involving a whole assortment of mostly trance-induced, out-of-the-body experiences, which, I am not inclined to demonstrate for you at this very moment simply because there is not enough time left in this class for me to enter a trance enabling my spirit to leave my body and then return."

"And then there is tele-influencing, or mind control, or sometimes called, mind bending."

Major Tom looked around the room and settled his gaze on Cadet Jayne Browning, a tall, lean girl with a round, plain face and long sandy-blonde hair. After a moment, Cadet Browning yawned. As she yawned a second time, her eyes widened in sudden recognition that she no longer had control over her desire to yawn. After another moment, several more of us, including myself, yawned. As we continued to yawn, our other non-yawning classmates starting chucking until they too were yawning.

Major Tom let the class yawn for about a minute longer.

"I am boring you to death," he said and smiled. Then, he stopped his tele-influencing and the yawning stopped.

"Alright then, now that I have your full attention, let me tell you about trans-tunneling, your classic wall walking. It is something I don't do very well, so I don't intend to demonstrate it for you right now because it would likely only result in me being physically bruised and emotionally scarred." He sighed and thought a moment. "There is a boy in another platoon, Stubblebine, I think. His name is Dexter Chumley. I believe he is the only potential wall walker in the entire academy. And," he added with a laugh, "he too is somewhat bruised for all his efforts."

"He's got enough protection around the mid-section," Cadet Thurber mumbled from the second row and we all laughed.

Major Tom frowned, before continuing, "And then there is teleportation, the art of vanishing atom by atom from space A and materializing atom by atom in Space B, just like in *Star Trek* except you don't use a transporter, but your mind. Actually, teleportation is one of those powers, like precognition and spirit communication, that while theoretically possible, at least according to Commander Marzo, has never been demonstrated in actual practice."

He gazed out at the class. "It is my understanding that none of you has demonstrated the power of teleportation." He laughed. "Not yet anyway."

"Does anyone have a headache yet?" he asked. "Well, if so, I can employ the art of healing—or as it's known among your Psi Academy instructors, the power to cure the common cold so our students never miss a day of school."

There was a general, brief rumble of laughter among the platoon.

"Or, perhaps I can give you a headache if you start giving me one," he said. "That's known as anti-healing, or as a form of Voodoo in some circles. Actually, the Chinese have another version, *qigong* they call it, and supposedly, well, at least according to our intelligence guys, they have become quite good at giving their enemies headaches, both literally, and figuratively." Major Tom looked out at us. "But more of that later, I think."

"And then there is invisibility," he continued. "More commonly known as cloaking. It is similar to teleportation, only different."

He moved his arms above his head and brought them down around his body, and inch by inch, he literally disappeared from view.

"You can hear me," Major Tom's disembodied voice said as we tensed in our chairs, "but not see me. Why? Because I have bent light photons traveling from the source of light behind me, illuminating my presence, to your eyes." And then, after lingering as an invisible entity a few moments longer, he reversed the process, and his body was reconstituted, inch by inch, starting from the bottoms of his shoes until the top of his head became visible again.

"Next, precognition," Major Tom went on and seemed again to glance over at me, "another power I was not granted, thankfully, by the grace of God and nature. The ability to see the future, commonly known as fortune telling. There are psi-warriors who can tell us, supposedly, not only if, but when we will die in combat."

"I have been told, several of you have shown a flair for the power, most notably, Platoon Drake's very own—", and he reached out his hand as if to introduce me, "—Henry Greenberg."

I bowed my head briefly and smiled, glad to be recognized. My only regret was that Grady O'Reilly wasn't in the room to witness it.

After a sigh, Major Tom said, "And last but not least, my dear cadets, as alluded to earlier, we have the power of spirit communications, dead talking; a power in which those who are blessed with it dare mediate with the dead. We don't practice that art much down here at the Psi Academy, unless, of course, you want to."

"There is a rumor," he went on, "that Cadet Morgenstern shows a propensity toward the dark art of dead talking. Is that right, Cadet?"

Freda bowed her head and seemed embarrassed by the attention.

I closed my eyes and repeated to myself the popular names for the psychic powers from lesson: mind reading, spoon bending, conjuring, mind bending, wall walking, teleportation, healing, precognition, and dead talking. I sighed. That was quite some list. I saw how, equipped with these powers, evil minded people could take over the world.

"And that, cadets, is your lesson for today," he said.

In the next moment, as if right on cue, a buzzer sounded from the ceiling speakers, dismissing us to our next class.

# Chapter Twenty-Five
## Mind Games

The rest of our classes that first day were not quite as interesting as Major Tom's. There was, as promised, Commander Marzo's mostly incomprehensible lecture *Quantum Theory as an Explanation for Psychic Phenomena* that provided a quantum 'spin' (to use the Commander's admittedly bad pun aided by his crooked smile) or explanation for the existence of psychic powers. That mind-numbing hour was followed by Major J. Harry Whatley's opening lecture on *Literature and Art from the Psychical Perspective* and Captain Steven's lecture *Earth Science 1* after which we were dismissed to join the other two platoons at the mess hall for a much-needed lunch.

"So what did you think of our first morning?" I asked Sebastian.

"It was alright, I guess," he said without looking at me.

"What's wrong, Seb?"

"It's your dream about Colonel Zebb," he said as if he had been dwelling on it all morning. "It was a dream I should have had. After all, it foretold that my father is alive."

"I don't know what it foretold, Seb," I said. "Zebb told me he was a good guy in the dream, too." I sighed. "And like all bad buys, Zebb is a liar."

Sebastian looked away.

"What?" I asked him.

"Colonel Zebb has been in some of my dreams, too," he said. "Like that one we had together, back when we first met. You remember, when he was dressed in that silly clown suit, wearing that evil grin." He sighed. "But sometimes I wonder if that was really him."

"Well, if it wasn't him," I asked, "who was it?"

"I don't know," he said. "And Colonel Zebb's been good in some of my dreams, too. At least, he's told me that. Just like he told you last night."

"So which is he?" I asked. "Bad or good? And if he's good, then do you think that General Bosworth and Major Atkinson and the rest of them down here are lying to us? That they're involved in some kind of cover-up or something? That they're the bad guys?"

"No, I'm not saying that," Sebastian said. "I just think maybe someone could have fooled them. Maybe they've been duped and now the same people are trying to dupe us, too."

"Or maybe they're right and Colonel Zebb is bad, and is either lying to us in our dreams or somehow we're just interpreting the dreams wrong." I reached up and rubbed my temples with the palms of my hands. "My head is starting to hurt with all this."

"Mine, too," Sebastian said. "Still, I liked the dream you had last night because at least in that one, my father is alive."

The lunch bell sounded all too quickly and we were off for our afternoon classes. As we shuffled out of the mess hall, I spied Grady and Molly whispering and looking over at Sebastian and me. I sighed, thinking maybe I should think about Freda Morgenstern instead of Molly, when Freda took the empty chair next to me.

"So," she asked.

"What?"

"Are you going to think more about me instead?"

I sighed. She could read minds as well as talk to the dead.

"What do your dreams tell you about the two of us?" she asked.

I wished I could remember all my dreams. I wish I had known months and years ago that I sometimes dreamt about the future so I could have written them down.

"Nothing," I told her. "But when I have one about you and me, you'll be the first to know."

The afternoon was crammed with normal ninth grade studies such as *Fundamentals of Algebra and Geometry* (which after Commander Marzo's class seemed a bit lightweight), *Language Studies: English*, and *Essentials of World History*.

At around 4:00pm, we were herded into the mess hall for a mid-afternoon snack consisting of a nutritional power bar and a glass of fortified fruit or vegetable juice.

When we were seated Major Atkinson strode across the mess hall stage wearing her characteristic kindly smile. We all sat straight up and put down our snacks.

"So are you all enjoying your first day at the Psi Academy?" She asked chirpily into the microphone.

There were some general mumbles, shrugs, and reserved nods. Most of us were plain tired; me more than most after getting so little sleep last night.

"I think you will find that the best part of your first day at the Psi Academy is yet to come," she said. "After this snack break, you will be taken to the game rooms for your first round of Mind Games."

This was followed by a general murmur of polite assent.

"Once you assemble in the game room," Major Atkinson continued, "each platoon will elect a leader who will make important decisions for the platoon. If you don't like the way things are going for the platoon, you can always vote to change your platoon leader at any stage during the games." She took a deep breath and looked at us with expectant pleasure. "I am sure you all will do splendidly. Now, let the Mind Games begin!"

She stepped back, nodded briefly at us, holding her smile, then referred us to the three dark wraiths in the doorway to the mess hall. The wraith sent a thought wave into each of our minds like a whisper of wind that said: *Come now!* The sensation of a foreign whispered thought entering my mind from somewhere outside of it was the oddest thing, up to then, I had ever experienced. And this was coming from a wraith that was itself a conjuration of someone else's mind.

But I did not have time to dwell on that oddity very long before I was up shuffling off with the others following the dark wraiths to the game chambers. We took a left turn down the corridor past our classrooms and then a right turn down yet another corridor. I thought that if I was ever stranded alone in these maze of corridors, I would never find my way.

After walking almost the entire length of that third hallway, we came upon a nondescript, tan metal door that opened into a large room separated by three spacious glass chambers. A nameplate for each platoon had been attached to the glass doors of the respective chambers. While stepping through the door bearing the Drake Platoon nameplate, I glanced over at Molly and Grady as they entered their chamber. Molly gave me a smug look, knowing that I was watching her, thinking about her.

"Come on, Henry," said Freda Morgenstern as she slid her hand under my elbow and led me inside our chamber. "Let the games begin."

Our chamber was furnished with nine, wide black leather chairs, like those recliners in stores in the mall where customers sat getting massages. The chairs were arranged in a circle with a space left open for Sebastian's wheelchair. A black tray was attached to the left arm of each chair on top of which was a set of the same kind of black wireless VR goggles Sebastian and I had used to play *Psi Wars!*. Sebastian had been handed his pair of goggles already by the dark wraith.

The dark wraith had slithered to the head of the partition. *Elect a platoon leader.*

"You heard him," said Cadet Palmer. "We have to elect a platoon leader."

"I nominate Cadet Drake," Freda Morgenstern blurted out.

"I second that nomination," said Matt Thurber, "After all, the platoon is named after his dad."

*Any other nominations?*

Some seconds passed but there were none.

*Do you accept the honor, Cadet Drake?*

"I, I guess I do," Sebastian said.

*Alright then, put on your goggles and let the Mind Games begin.*

We put on our goggles and our wraith disappeared like a puff of smoke in a stiff, cold wind. The construct that had been programmed immersed each of us in a kind of suffocating, inky blackness and we began to get antsy waiting for something to happen. There was some shuffling and mumbling among the platoon, including me, when nothing happened. Several of our platoon-mates began to express concern.

"Patience," Sebastian said exercising his authority as platoon leader.

And finally the game began.

This time I didn't find myself stranded in a black dark coffin or tied to a pole in a dark, dank room with things slithering around my bare feet. Instead, I found myself in a large, medieval hall on an old armless chair, like out of the 14th Century or something, with Colonel Zebb—the same Colonel Zebb from the video game *Psi Wars!* sitting in a similar chair about fifty yards away on the other side of the hall. After a moment, he lifted his arm and waved at me and gave me a sickly grin. He looked exactly like the Colonel Zebb of my dreams, especially that bad dream last night. He was wearing the standard issue psi-warrior uniform; the khaki pants and shirt, a trim, though worn aviator jacket and the uniform sunglasses hiding his deep blue eyes. He was tall and lean and kindly looking now. More like a nice uncle than a murderous villain.

I wondered for a time what my classmates were seeing. Was it the same thing? Was Colonel Zebb sitting across from them, waving and grinning in the same friendly way he was waving and grinning at me?

*Do something, Henry!* It was Sebastian's urgent voice. Except that he wasn't using his voice. What he said was in my mind, like that dark wraith's voice. *Conjure up some wraiths, just like in the game. Attack him. Kill Colonel Zebb.*

"Hey, there's no reason to do that," Colonel Zebb called from across the room. He appeared to be speaking, using his vocal chords, and not his mind. He started walking across the great hall toward me.

"Hey, stop right there!" I yelled.

But Colonel Zebb kept coming.

*Conjure some wraiths, Henry! Do it!*

"There's no need to do that," Colonel Zebb was saying as he got ever closer, now half-way down the hall.

*Henry, don't listen to him. Conjure—*

"But there's no need, Henry…"

*—conjure—*

"I'm the…"

*—some wraiths.*

"…good guy."

Colonel Zebb kept walking forward casually with that nice, friendly grin.

*Summon some wraiths now, Henry. You're running out of—*

"Why am I having those dreams about you?" I demanded. "And where is Sebastian's father?"

*Too late.*

A gurgling, gotcha laugh came from somewhere deep within Colonel Zebb's gut and in the next moment, I was surrounded by dark, mirthless and faceless wraiths. They latched onto my shoulders and led me out of the great hall into a dark corridor.

*Too late.*

"I'm the good guy, Henry," Colonel Zebb laughed, mocking me from within the great hall.

And then there was a low mournful, almost mocking, air-out-of-the-balloon kind of reprise, the international sound for losing a video or arcade game. *Waa, waa, waa,* like it was a joke or something. My field of vision in the *Psi Wars!* goggles went black. A game's scoreboard box lit in the upper left corner and blinked my score in red digits. Zero. Nada.

I removed my goggles and looked about the game chamber. From the faces of my platoon-mates, I knew that I had let them down.

"Because of you," said Francis Palmer from across the room, "we lost the game."

Sebastian rolled up to my chair.

"You were the only one, Henry," he said, trying to act kind but I could see he was seething with anger and disappointment, "who did not conjure up any wraiths to fight Colonel Zebb."

"I know, but—"

"Sebastian summoned a mini-dragon, or whatever that creature was, and almost burned up Colonel Zebb," said Cadet Thurber. "But at the last minute, he got away."

"And that was because," Cadet Gallardo chimed in, "Cadet Drake had to spend his time trying to get you to do something. Didn't you hear him?"

I looked around at the forlorn faces of my classmates.

"I'm, I'm sorry," I told them. "But, but in my dreams—"

What else could I say? I had let the team down, simply because my dreams had raised a doubt in my mind that Colonel Zebb was a bad guy.

"What we have to do," Sebastian said, "is work together during these games. Join together as one mind, with one purpose. And that purpose has to be to win the game by destroying Colonel Zebb. Before he destroys us and everything that we love and hold dear." He turned to me. "That's what the object of the game, Henry. Not figuring out if he's the good guy."

The other members of the platoon nodded vigorously. I could only muster a sigh.

I still wondered if we might be killing the good guy.

# Chapter Twenty-Six
# **A Wraith Fart**

Heading to breakfast the following morning, the cumulative tally for the three platoons in the Mind Games competition was conspicuously posted on a large, portable whiteboard at the entrance to the dining hall. It indicating that the Drake Platoon was in last place. There was some grumbling among my platoon-mates as I sat down at our table. No doubt they still were miffed at me for registering zilch points for the team which was the primary reason we were in last place. I ignored the bad vibes as I solemnly ate my breakfast.

After a while, Sebastian turned to me.

"You sleep all right last night?" he asked. "No bad dreams?"

In fact, it had taken me quite some time to get to sleep despite the long day of classes, followed by Mind Games and PT, and then, all the reading we had been assigned. Letting the platoon down in our first competition for the Drake Cup had rekindled my doubt about my worthiness of being here. I had tossed and turned before finally falling into an agitated sleep.

And I had dreamt, but not about Colonel Zebb. In my dream last night, I was back at Colonel J. B. Weber High School and Frankie Nytz was there. But he wasn't giving me a load of grief. He was being nice, asking me as if he genuinely cared where'd I been the last few months.

"No," I answered with a shrug, "No bad dreams."

"Look," he said with a kindly look, "things will be better today. I promise you."

I nodded glumly and went about scooping up a forkful of ham and cheese omelet.

From the Psi Academy student guide I knew today we would be doing something called Psi enhancement labs or PELs. During these PELs a mentor who had been specifically assigned to each of us would assist in the enhancement process. From what I had read the labs were held in a narrow, dark room known as a PEL closet.

Right after breakfast, a dark wraith led me and my fellow cadets down another series of maze-like corridors to one where thirty PEL closets stretched out the length of it. It took a few moments, but finally I spotted my nameplate hung on the door of one of these rooms. From the student guide, I knew that upon entering the room, I should take a seat and patiently wait for my mentor to arrive.

After a breath, I entered the PEL closet and saw at once why it got that name. It was exactly that, no bigger than a closet, a dark, cramped space with two armless chairs roughly in the middle of it facing each other. As instructed, I sat in the chair facing the back wall and after a minute or so, had grown accustomed to the dark. I then waited expectantly for the door behind me to open and for my mentor to enter and start the mentoring process, whatever that might entail.

But the seconds became minutes and no one entered. Every few seconds, I turned and looked impatiently back at the door. And then, he was, just there. My mentor. Standing before me.

He was tall and thin, with a narrow, lean, sharp-edged face and he wore the standard issue psi-warrior uniform. He looked to be around thirty, no more than thirty-five.

"Good morning, Cadet Greenberg," he said with a slight bow.

His voice was smooth, lyrical, and seemed amused by

things. Despite the severe lines of his face, his eyes were bright and smiling as if he knew every secret of the world.

"How did you—"

"Get in here?" He laughed. "I walked in." He gestured with his thumb over his right shoulder. "Through the wall."

He was among other things no doubt a wall walker, like Dexter Chumley. Except he could do it at will.

The official name for wall walking, as Major Tom and Commander Marzo had told us, was quantum trans-tunneling, somewhat akin to teleporting. By focusing one's brain energy, a person was somehow able to widen or change the space between the atoms of the cells of his body so that the whole of himself could slip through the atoms of a solid wall, door or whatever. I thought back to the complex set of quantum equations for trans-tunneling that Commander Marzo had reviewed with us during his class yesterday morning which seemed so much gobble-de-gook then and now:

$$\frac{d^2}{dx^2}\Psi(x) = \frac{2m}{\hbar^2}M(x)\Psi(x) = -k^2\Psi(x), \quad \text{where} \quad k^2 = -\frac{2m}{\hbar^2}M.$$

$$\frac{d^2}{dx^2}\Psi(x) = \frac{2m}{\hbar^2}M(x)\Psi(x) = -k^2\Psi(x), \quad \text{where} \quad k^2 = -\frac{2m}{\hbar^2}M.$$

"My name's Captain Fabian," my mentor told me. "Lucius Fabian. I am officially, your mentor, at your service."

"Nice to meet you, Sir," I said.

"Pleasure's all mine," he said. "Though, after a few days, you may not consider it much of a pleasure at all. If after a few days, you can no longer stand me, you are free to submit a request and I will be replaced. Do you understand?"

"Oh, I don't think that will be necessary."

"Never say never." He sighed. "Well, then, shall we begin?"

"Yes, certainly."

I turned my head and regarded him for a time.

"What?" he asked.

"I didn't see you on the stage yesterday, among our instructors."

"You are a most observant young man." He sighed and peered up at the ceiling as if thinking up an explanation. "You see, they hide some of us psi-warriors on the levels below the Academy. We live down there. On Level Eight and Level Nine. We have lived down there for quite some time."

"How, how many levels are there in this place?"

"Now that is confidential. On a need to know basis, and you, my good fellow, have no need to know that, at least as of right now." He smiled. "I don't know the answer myself, you want to know the truth."

He squinted at me for a time. "Any further questions?"

I shrugged. I had more, but I wanted to get to what he was mentoring me about this morning.

"Very good. I think this morning we shall start with the conjuration of wraiths."

"Wraiths? But I can't do that, conjure up a wraith."

"Who said you could?" he laughed.

"My dominant power is precognition," I told him.

"Oh, yes," he said. "Fortune telling. As I have been informed." He raised his right eyebrow as if he doubted the veracity of that, then went on, "But just because conjuration is not your dominant power doesn't mean you can't learn how to do it. Any psychic power can be learned. You should repeat that axiom to yourself a thousand times, and then on a daily basis. *Any psychic power can be learned.* It has quite the ring to it, don't you think?"

He sighed, looked distracted for a moment, then continued, "And most anyone can learn how to concoct a wraith. It's one of the simplest psychic powers there is to teach. Not like wall walking or teleporting, which are in fact, damned hard to teach."

"Really," I said. "But isn't it conjure? You said concoct."

"Concoct, conjure, evoke, what's the difference. And I quite like the sound of that word, concoct." He stressed the "t" sound, clicked it, whenever he said the word. "In fact, if it was up to me," he went on, "I'd rename the power *concoction*."

He smiled slightly but then, in the next moment, he put the tips of his right and left index fingers to the corner of his mouth and used them to dramatically and intentionally widen his smile. I knew right then that my mentor, this Captain Fabian, was quite a character, an eccentric, a queer duck as my father might say.

"Ready?" he asked after lowering his arms.

"Ready for what?"

"Why, to concoct a wraith." His eyes widened and he appeared incredulous, but only momentarily. "Haven't you been listening?"

"Yes, but—"

"Well, then," he said, "Let's begin. The first thing you need to understand is the nature of a wraith. What makes it tick, so to speak. Is a wraith animal, vegetable, mineral or something in between? In short, what exactly is a wraith?"

I thought back to the wraiths I had seen—the dark, ominous looking ones lurking in the hills near the entrance to the Psi Academy, then, Casper my friendly wraith who had helped me get settled into the school and the other wraiths I had met since then to help us get around the Academy's underground corridors.

"Well, first of all, perhaps the question, 'what is a wraith?' should be asked this way 'What is a wraith *not*?' "

I shrugged. I had no idea.

"A wraith, first of all, is not real," he said. "Or perhaps that is overstating it."

And then, literally out of nothing, a cat appeared, a slender, totally black cat. The animal arched its back and then wound its way around Captain Fabian's legs, doing a figure eight as it brushed past mine. Of course, this cat was a wraith concocted for my benefit by Captain Fabian.

He reached down and stroked the glistening mane on the back of the animal and the cat meowed.

"Meow to you as well, Shadow," he said. Captain Fabian laughed to himself. "Shadow? Better name for a dog, I think, than a cat."

When I looked down to where Shadow had been, it was gone.

"So what was Shadow?" Captain Fabian asked. "Certainly, not a cat, at least not a real cat. So what was he, if he was not a real cat? A figment of mind, information energy made into matter? So if that is true, that he was a mere projection of mental energy, then each of us could be wraiths—thought projections from the mind of some god. Or, as one theory has it, we ourselves are demi-gods and have created the world around us for the purpose of playing a game—the human game." He stopped and sighed and looked at me. "Confused yet?"

I shrugged and tried to relax my intense frown.

"A wraith is," Major Tom continued, "a kind of holographic metaphor. It is plasma generated from brain energy, from thought—solid figments of forced imagination—photons of thought turned into particles of reality. I thought about a black cat, and the photon of the cat I imagined turned into Shadow."

And there Shadow was again, at my feet.

"But sorry to say. Shadow is not real, not really. Or maybe that is wrong, too. Maybe he is real."

Captain Fabian closed his eyes and poor Shadow faded again into nothingness.

"*Au revoir*, my dear Shadow," he said, with his eyes still closed. "Return to the nothingness of the collective subconscious from whence, it is theorized, you came."

At last, Captain Fabian opened his eyes.

"So what have we learned?" he asked. "First, that a wraith is a temporary holographic representation of brain energy, drawn from the collective subconscious, projected into and onto real time and real space. It can be anything the brain can think of making, animal, vegetable, mineral. It can be an animate, its usual form, or inanimate. And, did I mention that it is temporary, not a permanent thing? Even if, like Shadow, it is not intentionally deleted, all wraiths will fade over time. The thoughts creating them dissolve due to the nature of thought. Wraiths are the stuff of dreams. Like each of us."

"In short," Captain Fabian smiled, "a wraith is a temporary hologram of a thought." But then, he frowned. "Or is it better stated that a wraith is a hologram of a temporary thought?" He shrugged. "No matter, a wraith never lasts. And all of what I just said will be further explained, in more complex, rather incomprehensible detail, in your splendid course on the relationship between quantum mechanics and psychic phenomena.

"Now that you know what a wraith is, and is not," he continued, and laughed, again not missing a beat and barely taking a breath, "I suppose you will want to know what a wraith's motivation is; its purpose; its *raison d'etre*. Does it have thoughts, dreams, loves, hopes, joys, sorrows, memories, just like you and me? Or is it purely a thoughtless, dreamless, loveless, hopeless, sorrow-less, joyless ghostly automaton?"

Captain Fabian looked at me.

"Henry, any thoughts? It was not a rhetorical question."

I nodded as if someone had just nudged me from a nap. "Ah," I said, "are wraiths ghostly automaton, holographic robots?"

"Yes," Captain Fabian said, "that is the question. To be, or not to be."

"Well, I think they probably are what you called them," I said. "Automatons, generated for a particular purpose." Like dear, bygone Casper, I thought, and nodded to myself, pleased with my response.

"Well, you're wrong," he shot back. "I think wraiths are people too, so to speak. They are not mere ghostly automatons, or robots. Or any other insulting term you may want to call them."

"I didn't—"

"They are people, and there are even some amongst us who believe they have souls, because they come from the brain of a person who has a soul." He tapped the side of his head. "The wraiths are imbued with a soul in the process of their creation, like we were given souls when God created us in his own image, so it is said and was written. And like we are not mere automatons, neither are they." He sighed. "At least, that's one theory—one to which I espouse, being a tireless romantic. The more generally accepted theory, the one which you voiced, is they are essentially mindless, soulless robots, created out of our minds and programmed to think and do exactly as we see fit."

He sighed.

"So, want to make one?"

"What?"

"Your own wraith."

"How? I can't. I have the slightest idea how."

Captain Fabian smirked.

"Of course you can. Just close your eyes and think of one."

As if on cue, Captain Fabian closed his eyes.

"What, what kind of one?"

"Well, something small to start with," he said, with his eyes still closed. "Don't try and concoct Tyrannosaurus Rex for God's sake." He opened his left eye. "Think of a mouse or something, or better yet, a gecko." He sighed. "You haven't closed your eyes."

I closed my eyes. "Think of a mouse or a gecko and a wraith of one or the other will appear somewhere in this room. Yes?"

"Yep," he said, "that's all there is to it. Give it a try. What have you got to lose?"

I shrugged and closed my eyes and thought of a gecko, well, not really a gecko. It was a creature like that one in the

Geico television commercials; one of those funny little rubbery lizards like miniature dinosaurs I had seen hanging on the pool screens of the house my parents had rented during our summer vacation near Disney World. I had done some research on the Internet and think they were called anoles.

"Concentrate on the form of whatever creature you want to create," Captain Fabian said

For the next fifteen or twenty minutes, I focused on the little anole I had watched one afternoon during that Florida vacation while floating around in the pool. I called up the image of the lizard hanging on the screen, inactive mostly, then every now and then bobbing up and down as if doing lizard pushups while extending his orange colored dewlap.

"Well?" Captain Fabian finally said, interrupting my focus.

I opened my eyes. There was no anole wraith in the room.

"Sometimes the magic works," Captain Fabian said, "sometimes, it doesn't."

It only would get better from here, he assured me—failure breeds success. The key was to concentrate, to see the form of the entity you wanted to wraith in your mind and will it into existence. That's all you had to do. Takes time, though, he told me. And practice. Lots of practice. But like riding a bicycle, once you do it, you will never forget how.

I closed my eyes again and thought of that damned anole. Captain Fabian said nothing else and let me focus. The seconds and minutes passed and at long last, I seemed to enter a kind of dreamlike state, a trance, I guess, though I had never been in one to really know how it felt. I was beyond time and space in whatever realm into which I had gone, and I was still seeing that anole in the deepest part of my mind.

And then, after an indeterminable time, there was something. A spark of electricity, the smell of ozone, a low murmur like the distant buzz of an insect, or the patter of rain, coming from somewhere beyond the scope of my mental and physical dimensions.

Something had left the confines of my brain.
I opened my eyes and saw…a puff of smoke?
Captain Fabian laughed.
"Bravo!' he said and clapped. "Your first wraith fart!"

# Chapter Twenty-Seven
## A Sad Story

During the afternoon snack just before another round of Mind Games, I asked Sebastian about his mentor.

"He's okay," he said and shrugged. "A Marine Captain. Typical Marine, too, close-cropped hair, crisp uniform, in your face. How's yours?"

I thought a moment. How to describe Captain Fabian? He was no Marine that was for sure. And he didn't seem all that military to me.

"Well, let's just say he was a tad eccentric," I told Sebastian. "I like him, though."

"Yeah," Sebastian said. "I like mine, too." He sighed. "I think."

Grady O'Reilly was suddenly breathing down my neck.

"Heard you got the worst mentor here, Greenborg," he said.

"How would you know," I spat back. "And for the last time, the name's Greenberg. Cadet Greenberg to you."

"Very well, Cadet Greenboog."

I then employed the other thing Captain Fabian had taught me during our first session that morning, after conjuring a wraith fart—what he called a brain freeze. Captain Fabian said it would prevent mind stalkers, telepaths, or mind readers, like Grady, from probing your mind. He also said after a while I would learn how to install a brain freeze for my mind and keep it on automatic pilot. That made stalking pretty much useless down here, Captain Fabian had added. And that was why none of us, at least except for a couple of the stronger cadets (like Sebastian, perhaps), couldn't read what the instructors were thinking.

"So that's what your mentor taught you," he said, "how to block me. Well, my mentor told me there's a way around it. Double-reverse, they call it."

I shrugged. Grady had just violated a cardinal rule for mentors and their students, at least according Captain Fabian. You never told anyone what your mentor had taught or told you. And never meant never, to no one, not even to your best friend and not even the Headmaster or Major Atkinson.

"Well, I'm pretty sure most of us were taught how to conjure wraiths this morning," Grady went on. "And you should have seen the beautifully scary one I made."

"Sure, Grady," I said.

"It's Cadet O'Reilly, remember," he said. "So, Greensblurg, did your conjure a wraith this morning or not?"

"Yes," I told him. "It just so happens I did. I conjured up your mother, Grady. And she—"

Grady took an offensive stance waiting for me to finish the insult. And there I was, back at Colonel J. B. Weber High School, standing up to Frankie Nytz. But Sebastian wheeled between us preventing the altercation to escalate.

"Gentlemen, gentlemen," Sebastian said. "I suggest you stow it."

We had already drawn the attention of one of the wraiths conjured to monitor the snack break that afternoon. He skimmed toward us briefly, but when he saw that Grady and I had calmed down, he held back and resumed his position near the front of the dining hall.

I was beginning to grow wary of those wraiths. Rather than

help us, it seemed they had been conjured up purely to watch and control. And I didn't like that one bit.

Friday morning came around fast. I had slept reasonably well, better than the night before. I knew it was because of how I had played the Mind Games competition yesterday. I, like the rest my platoon, had taken Sebastian's lead, telepathically communicated, and joined with them to form a sort of z-Prime. Together our hive mind had conjured a formidable army of fierce orc-like wraiths to confront and battle the orc-like wraiths conjured up by the ersatz Colonel Zebb from his side of the same great hall from the same program the day before. We had soon had driven Zebb's out-numbered and overmatched orc army outside the hall and had them on the run down the dark hallway when the game ended and the image construct faded.

Having convincingly redeemed myself from yesterday's debacle, the Drake Platoon now tallied the most points for one day's play among the three platoons. Nevertheless, despite that good showing, we were still a distant second to Platoon Stubblebine. But the semester had just begun and we had Sebastian as our commander-in-chief. The future of Mind Games looked a whole lot brighter after only one day.

After breakfast I trudged along with my platoon-mates to Major Tom's classroom. During our first class two days ago, though it seemed like a century now, Major Tom had described the known psychic powers. Today, as indicated by the readings that he had assigned, he would cover the historical application of those powers, starting, interestingly enough, from the present and going backwards through history because, as he explained, he found it useless to study history the other way around. You had to learn where you are before you know where you've been, was the way he explained it, though I never quite figured out what that meant.

As we took our seats in his classroom that morning, we noted that Major Tom wore a grim expression. He waited for

Sebastian to situate himself at his spot before beginning the lecture by clicking a PowerPoint slide of a newspaper story onto the screen taking up almost the entire wall behind him.

The newspaper headline read: *High School Freshman Guns down 17 Classmates.*

"How many of you have heard about this tragedy?" Major Tom asked.

Six hands went up, including Sebastian's, but I had not. Upon returning to my room last night, I got right into the reading assignments and didn't bother to look at news on the Internet. I had not even turned on the TV before falling asleep at my desk at around 10:30pm and then shuffling off to bed.

The newspaper story reported the terrible things that had happened, almost too terrible to read or even think about. A freshman, a kid our age, from some high school in the Midwest, a kind of a loner the story claimed, had taken several of his father's automatic pistols the previous morning and, after using one of them to murder his parents and younger brother, had calmly finished his breakfast, taken the school bus just like he did every other day that semester, carrying the same backpack he carried every day, into which he had stuffed three of the automatic pistols. The kid then rode to school without a word to anyone, or any indication of the terrible crimes he had just committed and was planning to commit.

Some kids on the bus had said the kid had behaved normally; just sitting alone, saying nothing, staring out the window at the passing streets, like he always did every other day. And the kid continued to behave normally until the pep rally in the school gymnasium early that afternoon. The rally was to get the student body razzed about the big basketball game that night against the school's crosstown rival. The kid had carried the backpack into the gym and waited as the head basketball coach had finished introducing the team. Then the kid calmly stood up from his seat about halfway up the rolled out wooden stands and, without a word, pulled out one of the automatic pistols and started shooting the kids and teachers around him, firing randomly, at nobody in particular. One kid who had ducked just in the nick of time, allowing the bullet meant for him to strike the chest of the kid next to him, had told the police that the freshman shooter had a blank look in his eyes as he was shooting. 'Like a zombie' the kid had said.

Then, without any other warning and still with that zombie-like gaze, the shooter had ended the massacre by turning the pistol around and shooting himself in the head.

"Like a zombie," Major Tom repeated. "Does that description of the shooter give anyone pause?"

We looked around at each other, sickened by how something like this could have happened and how often it seemed to be happening lately, like an epidemic or something. How could someone, anyone, snap that badly, be so mentally deranged to kill his family and so many of his defenseless fellow classmates, and then so coolly kill himself. We were quite speechless.

"Zombies are what?" Major Tom said. "Cadet Greenberg."

"Ah, well," I said, thinking, and then came up with this, "mindless beings?"

"Very good," said Major Tom. "Mindless beings. What is another way of saying that?"

Major Tom pointed to Francis Palmer who had raised his right arm.

"True zombies," he said, "not the kind on TV shows and in movies, are brainwashed or programmed beings. It's a form of Voodoo, Haitian I think."

"Very good, Cadet Palmer," said Major Tom. "But, programmed beings. What does that mean?"

"Ah, it means, it means…" Cadet Palmer thought a while but when it was apparent he wasn't getting anywhere, Major Tom called on Freda Morgenstern, who had raised her arm.

"It means," she said confidently, like she always did, "that someone else has programmed them, is controlling them."

"Exactly," said Major Tom. "Controlling them."

Vincent L. Scarsella

Major Tom looked around the room. "So what could be the moral of this story?" he asked. He looked back at the screen and pointed. "This awful, disgusting story?"

"That the kid was controlled," Sebastian answered. "That some other force, or person, made him do what he did, using the psi-power of tele-influencing, also known as mind control." Sebastian paused a moment, then asked, "Some evil force?"

Major Tom nodded, still glum, much concerned.

"Exactly," he whispered. "Exactly. And that, boys and girls, is our problem now, isn't it? And *that* is the reason why all of you are here."

# Chapter Twenty-Eight
# Evil Eye, Stargate, and Mind Bloom

"We at the Psi Cave monitor this type of incident," Major Tom continued during that class. "When someone, without any prior indication of mental disease, commits such an atrocity, we get suspicious. Did someone make the shooter shoot?"

"And who, who do you think it may have been in this case, Sir?" Sebastian asked.

"Well, I am getting to that, Cadet Drake," Major Tom said. "That is what this lecture is about, the near, very near, history of the application of the psychic arts."

Major Tom used his clicker to advance to the next PowerPoint slide. On it, in bold deep, red letters was the term: PROJECT EVIL EYE.

"Can anyone tell me about Project Evil Eye?"

Everyone raised their hands. Project Evil Eye had been among the reading topics for this class. There was no textbook for this class, just a series of articles and websites that we were assigned to read before the lectures. Among the better articles was one titled *The History of Military Research and Development of Psychic Powers for Conflict and Clandestine Application during the Cold War* authored by General Saunders McGee.

Major Tom called on me.

"Evil Eye," I said, squinting a little, and I thought a moment more, "was one of the first military research projects to explore the use of psychic powers. I believe it began in the 1950s."

"Very good, Cadet Greenberg," said Major Tom.

Major Tom then went on, through his PowerPoint slides, to outline the various military, CIA and other obscure intelligence agency projects studying the application of psychic powers for military and clandestine use. The primary catalyst for such projects was the Cold War. We feared that the former Soviet Union's military and spy agency, the KGB, was developing both a psi-army and psi-spies and possibly already using psi-soldiers and spies in clandestine operations.

Project Evil Eye, whose name was quickly changed to The Orion Project, simply because no one liked the idea of belonging to something called 'evil' anything, was at first a rather humble affair. A partnership was formed with the paranormal research lab at a prestigious university and, after testing conducted by the lab, several military officers and CIA agents found to have innate psychic abilities became specimens in various experiments and studies. Although the results of the studies and enhancement exercises were mixed, they were good enough to convince certain military brass and CIA bigwigs that there was a future in Psi Ops.

This initial military and intelligence agency foray into paranormal research soon grew tentacles, resulting in several rather bizarre spin-off projects. There was MK-Ultra, the CIA's mind control project; the infamous Free Will Deactivation Initiative (FWDI), during which electronic pulses were secretly beamed by some kind of ray gun into an ordinary American town in an attempt to transform its inhabitants into zombie-like slaves; several covert UFO and alien search and capture operations; and, of course, the ill-fated, and little known, Tisdale Experiment, much like the Philadelphia Experiment conducted in 1943, in which cloaking or invisibility thought waves were applied in an attempt to make the tiny hamlet of Tisdale, Alabama, disappear. (General McGee described this experiment as 'ill-fated' because, not only did the town disappear, but it never re-appeared. It was simply, lost. Before a report of the incident was purportedly 'leaked,' the General stated that somehow, Army intelligence and the CIA were able to keep the matter quiet for over twenty years by various means, including pay-offs to relatives of the town's inhabitants.)

Like those spin-off projects, little is known, and much is denied, added Major Tom, regarding the achievements of the Orion Project and those projects succeeding it in the 1950s and '60s. Only rumor and speculation remain. Most of the records regarding those projects have gone missing, or been destroyed, so even the Freedom of Information Act has been of little use. Furthermore, the generals and other Army personnel and CIA agents who may have been involved in them, haven't talked. Many of them have long since passed away, or like Colonel Max Drummond—who had been in charge of Project Mind Bloom before Colonels Drake and Zebb, about which, Major Tom promised, he'd have more to say later—left for parts unknown.

Following the mixed results of these projects, the United States officially established *The Stargate Project*, not to be confused with the television series of the same name. Actually, it was not a project *per se*, but a code name for several projects that investigated a wide variety of psychic phenomena and looked for ways to develop their use in military conflict and spying. The focus of *The Stargate Project* was to use the psychic power of remote viewing to locate hostages and enemy spies and combatants.

"Did anyone see the movie, *The Men Who Stare at Goats?*" Major Tom asked.

Four hands went up, including mine.

"Anyone read the book?"

Two hands went up, but not mine.

"That pretty much tells the tale of the rather meager, and strange, results of Stargate," Major Tom said. "The point is, there were too many oddballs participating and running it.

Suffice to say," he went on, "the Stargate project was ended in the early 1990s based upon a CIA study, commissioned by Congress, falsely reporting that it was ineffective and that, furthermore, psychic powers were never shown to exist. So Congress cut funding for the project, around twenty million dollars a year, a mere drop in the bucket, and everyone involved in it at the time including Colonel Drummond, Majors Peter Drake and Zachariah Zebb, were cut free.

"The CIA's false report was intended to take Congress and the military out of the equation so all oversight for what it was now doing in the research and application of psychic abilities on its own, in secret, was removed. The CIA then promptly assembled a secret unit of agents and soldiers who had demonstrated superior psychic abilities. It called this unit, Sidekick, a play on the word, psychic, and its funding was obtained in the old fashioned way, by funneling money from other legitimate intelligence and defense projects.

"Somewhere along the way the CIA handlers of the unit lost interest in Sidekick, and in Psi Ops generally, now that the Russians were seemingly out of it. But Sidekick remained active, and saw fit even to hide itself deeper within the bureaucracy that had, for the most part, lost track of it, and, some say, used the powers of its members to obscure its existence even further and influence its support.

"And, thus, the Sidekick Unit became truly rogue.

"It started running the various psychic projects on its own under General Buzz Bosworth, presently our illustrious and beloved Headmaster. The first thing he did was find this pretty much abandoned underground base and un-moth-ball it. He moved Sidekick here and soon enough it was dubbed the Psi Cave.

"Once the Psi Cave became operational, General Bosworth came up with Project Mind Bloom, whose focus was research into the application of all varieties of psychic powers in Psi Ops. He brought Colonel Drummond in to run the day-today operation of the project. Drummond in turn recruited then Majors Drake and Zebb to help him establish a first-class operation. To supplement an already psychically gifted assortment of psi-warriors comprising Sidekick, they snatched up some top-notch soldiers, top guns, Navy Seals, and agents from the CIA, FBI and other intelligence agencies, who had had tested positive, like you cadets, for at least one dominant psychic power. With Sidekick fully manned and operational, the secret future of Psi Ops research and application was up and running.

"With tried and tested psi-mentors like Drummond, Drake and Zebb, what Sidekick accomplished from day one of Project Mind Bloom, circa 1996, was truly amazing. They were reading minds like circus acts, and bending spoons like over-cooked spaghetti noodles. They were conjuring wraiths, some of them quite unusual and scary (seven foot replicas of Howard Stern, for instance). Remoters were locating hostages, spies, missing children and murder victims in distance places. Still, others were controlling minds, making ordinary Joes out in the real world behave like idiots, like sheep. Two or three were getting quite adept at wall walking, and there was some suggestion that on one occasion, one soldier teleported himself from one room to another. Best of all, it was reported that one particular Sidekick member, Captain David Swartz, started communicating with the dead. So Cadet Morgenstern, you are not alone in the world in being a dead talker.

"But what we later found out about Project Mind Bloom's fantastic accomplishments was quite disturbing," Major Tom said as he began to pace the front of the classroom. "It was somewhat like finding out that the only reason Mark McGuire, Sammy Sosa, Barry Bonds, Alex Rodriquez and all those other guys hit so many home runs was that they were high on steroids. Juiced."

He stopped and turned to us.

"Because you see," he said, "the accomplishments of the

Sidekick psi-warriors during Project Mind Bloom was assisted by the drug, Boost."

# Chapter Twenty-Nine
## Boost

The next slide depicted a red, gelatinous pill.

"And there it is, cadets," Major Tom said. "Boost."

His gaze lingered on the slide for a time before he hopped onto the side of his desk.

"At first," he told us, "they considered Boost a miracle drug. A couple of neurologists, brain chemistry researchers, working in a lab in the bowels of the Psi Cave invented it. And like its name advertises, it boosted, that is to say, artificially enhanced, the already enhanced psychic powers of every psi-warrior who took it."

Major Tom told us Boost was a kind of potion made from natural and synthetic brain energy enhancing compounds (and so was almost called 'Enhance' or 'Hance' which it sometimes still was). It was made from a combination of ingredients; a particular mushroom known for its psychoactive alkaloid compounds of psilocybin, psilocin, and musimol; a man-made compound that was distant cousin of LSD; the mushroom flower, peyote and several other hallucinogenic flowers; and the compound, MDMA, more popularly known as Ecstasy. This odd recipe of ingredients was cooked together to form the gelatinous pill depicted on the slide. It was then administered, on an experimental, carefully controlled basis, to a select group of psi-warriors, including, at that point in time, recently promoted Colonels Zachariah Zebb and Peter Drake.

What Boost did, according to Major Tom, was dramatically enhance the energy of the brain such that it 'leapt' into a connection with the cosmic life force, or what the near eastern mystics called, the *kundalini*, or coiled power, a kind of supernatural energy that rises from the base of the spine to the brain and is transmitted it into the domain of heaven.

"And what it also did, unexpectedly, I might add," he then went on, "is to facilitate what is known as mind melding, the combination of brain energies of two or more minds into a hive mind. Down here in the Psi Cave, we call such an amalgam of psi-warriors a z-Prime. I will leave the possibilities of that to your imaginations."

He hopped off the desk, stood before us and sighed.

"But, and there is always a 'but'," he said, "like most wonder drugs, Boost had some unforeseen and unfortunate side effects."

He looked around the room at our blank faces, as if to purposefully build the suspense.

"It drove some of its users power mad and made them into megalomaniacs."

Sebastian raised his hand.

"Did a z-Prime ever arise, sir?" he asked. "Does one exist?"

"Unfortunately, yes," Major Tom said. "And the dominant force guiding this particular entity is none other than Colonel Zachariah Zebb." Major Tom sighed. "You see, Colonel Drake came to recognize the dangers posed by Boost. He feared that all mankind might be at risk, especially if a demented, that is to say, megalomaniac, z-Prime was formed. Therefore, the good Colonel immediately stopped using Boost and pleaded with Colonel Zebb and other psi-warriors to do likewise.

"But by then, Colonel Zebb was too far gone, too driven by his thirst for power. He refused to listen and instead, so the story goes, became convinced that Colonel Drake was out to destroy him. With some fellow psi-warriors, Zebb used Boost to form a powerful z-Prime with him in control. And it was that z-Prime that mutinied and, well, killed Colonel Drake."

Major Tom turned to Sebastian and gave him a sympathetic nod.

"How did they kill him?" Sebastian blurted. "How did my father die?"

"Sorry to say," Major Tom answered "The details are sketchy on that point. So, I really don't know. What I do know, is that it wasn't a fair fight. And what I also know is that Colonel Drake fought them off gallantly."

Sebastian bowed his head and appeared to sadly accept that explanation, though I was still curious as to the actual psychic method used by the Zebb z-Prime to kill Sebastian's father. Was Colonel Drake overwhelmed and torn to pieces by vicious, salivating dog wraiths? Was he telekinetically run through by a dozen, sharp daggers? Was he at last driven to suicidal madness by a tele-influenced onslaught of mind-crumbling, depressing z-Prime thoughts? And why were the details 'sketchy' about such an important event in the history of psychic warfare in this very Psi Cave?

"As far as we know, once Zebb's z-Prime escaped the Psi Cave, it disappeared. We have no idea where it went or what it's doing. Not even our best remote viewers can locate its whereabouts. All we know is that it's out there lurking about, doing bad things, the kinds of things I mentioned before. Entering people's minds and turning them into vicious, cruel zombie killers."

"So you think the Zebb, ah, z-Prime," Sebastian asked, "had something to do with the school shootings? They took over that kid's mind?"

"Well, we have no direct proof," Major Tom said, "but it is exactly something an evil z-Prime might do.

"And so," he went on with a sigh, "that's exactly why we need you cadets. Because, as you know, due to something called the Parsifal effect, it's easier to teach kids your age, young teens, the psychic arts necessary to help defend ourselves and America from the evil Zebb z-Primes of the world."

"So there are more of them?" Sebastian asked. "Other z-Primes beside Zebb's."

"Unfortunately, yes, Cadet Drake," he said. "We think there are rogue, or not so rogue, z-Primes created by the Chinese, Russians, or possibly terrorist groups."

"Anyway, that's the sad story," Major Tom said after a time. "The recent, sorry history of the application of psychic powers in the real world. What we have is one or more evil z-Primes out there and our job is to figure out a way to defend ourselves, and the American people, against them. So far, we haven't done that."

The bell rang ending the class on that rather somber note.

I sat down at the mess hall table during lunch and looked over at Sebastian.

"You alright?" I asked.

He bowed his head and gave me a half nod. Platters loaded with grill cheese sandwiches on thick doughy bread were being delivered by enlisted servers.

"That had to be rough. Hearing about your dad, as part of a history lesson."

"I don't believe it," Sebastian said.

"What?"

"Not a doggone word."

"What are you talking about?"

Sebastian looked at me. I noticed a line of spittle thin as a thread falling from his chin.

"I tried to read him, you know," he said, "Major Tom's thoughts, when he was teaching us all that, how Colonel Zebb and his men became a z-Prime and killed my father. For most of the time, he was able to block me. But I was able to sneak in there, snatch glimpses of some synapses in his brain. And what I saw was not the truth."

"What are you talking about, Seb?" I asked. "Major Tom was lying to us?"

"No, not really," he said. "Not intentionally. But Major Tom did not quite believe the story either. Not one hundred percent. I could see it in the part of his brain I was able to break into. There was doubt in the shadowy parts of his mind."

"Doubt?" I asked. "What did he doubt?"

"Everything," Sebastian said. "That my father is really dead, for one thing. And that the Zebb z-Prime had killed him."

"So Colonel Zebb might really not be a bad guy?" I asked. "Just like he says in my dreams? Is that what you think?"

Sebastian sighed. He looked worried and, for the first time since I had met him, unhappy.

"Do you really think it's possible Zebb's a good guy?"

"I don't know," he said, looking straight into my eyes. "I just don't know."

Neither one of us ate much of our grilled cheese sandwiches.

# Chapter Thirty
# **Kelly's Folly**

The next few weeks at the Psi Academy flew by.

During those weeks, 'Where does the time go', or 'Wish we had another few hours in the day', or simply, the short-cut, 'Already?', followed by a laugh, were common refrains among my fellow cadets, and even our instructors.

Our comprehensive regiment of classes and other activities relating to the development of our psi powers and general academic advancement was followed by evenings crammed with an almost overwhelming assortment and quantity of reading and challenging homework assignments. The most difficult of those assignments required us to decipher Commander Marzo's incomprehensible equations and proofs mathematically describing psychic phenomena, such as this one for entanglement-assisted trans-teleportation:

$$|\Phi^+\rangle_{AC} \otimes (\alpha|0\rangle_B + \beta|1\rangle_B)$$

$$|\Phi^-\rangle_{AC} \otimes (\alpha|0\rangle_B - \beta|1\rangle_B)$$

$$|\Psi^+\rangle_{AC} \otimes (\beta|0\rangle_B + \alpha|1\rangle_B)$$

$$|\Psi^-\rangle_{AC} \otimes (\beta|0\rangle_B - \alpha|1\rangle_B)$$

And, as we learned, the expression for the success criterion for teleportation is:

$$\sum_i \text{Tr} \, (\rho \otimes \omega)(F_i \otimes \Psi_i^*(O)) = \text{Tr} \, \rho \cdot O.$$

For our course in *Literature and Art from the Psychical Perspective*, there were naturally, novels and short stories and poems to read and dissect. Included among those readings, in the first three weeks of the course, were all seven volumes of J. K. Rowling's chronicle of the adventures of the kid wizard Harry Potter.

Our instructor for this course, Major Whatley, suggested that if we delved deeply enough into the Potter books, we might find helpful hints regarding the development and ultimate use of our own psychic wizardry. He also opined that the Potter series hinted, to him anyway, that Great Britain may have a Psi Academy of its own, perhaps code-named Hogwarts. Indeed, at times, I did find myself nodding my head while reading a certain passage in a particular volume that gave me pause because it truly seemed to mirror the trials and tribulations of us cadets attending the Psi Academy.

Weekends at the Academy were no less busy. Every Saturday and Sunday, each cadet was assigned guard duty consisting of watches stretching three hours long, during which we'd have to stand around and make sure there were no unauthorized personnel or 'entities' (wraiths, I supposed) in the corridors, mess hall, common areas or classrooms. In addition to that, every five weeks, we had to spend the entire weekend as the Academy's Command Duty Office and it was our job to oversee the cadets on guard duty and monitor other matters of general security.

Still, our time at the Psi Academy was not completely devoid of fun. A period of time each day, and more of it on weekends, was set aside for recreational and social activities, as well as just plain leisure time, during which we were free to do just about whatever we wanted to do, or absolutely nothing at all.

When not on guard duty Saturday or Sunday, we cadets could usually be found in a cavernous hall that had been dug out of the granite mountain at the end of yet another long, wide corridor. It had a surprisingly high, rough ceiling that was illuminated, intentionally it seemed, by mellow, soft light. It turned out that this place was a kind of underground amusement park and mini-mall for our entertainment every Thursday evening, and all day Saturday and Sunday, provided we didn't have guard duty.

The hall had been separated by tinted glass partitions into various shops. There was also an arcade filled with all sorts of things; video games, pinball machines, race car, space ship and roller coaster simulators, a miniature bowling machine with rubber balls, and various other gaming devices. There was even a small movie theatre, an impressive, winding miniature golf layout, and last, but not least, several rides, including one actual, full-size, bitching roller coaster.

The coaster, named appropriately enough 'The Psychokinetic Rant' or what we called 'The Rant' for short, did not have a particularly steep opening rise or drop, as its tracks were laid out high up along the walls of the hall and disappeared at times within narrow tubes built into those same black granite walls. The one-seat cars were in the shape of brains which made every one of us laugh until our sides split the first time we saw them. But we stopped laughing when we took our first ride. After jettisoning us into a dark tunnel, it whizzed and whirled almost silently as it turned and jerked up and around and upside down and inside the dark mountain wall, at times at speeds so fast that I worried how my car could possibly stay on the track. Plus, in the dark, it was impossible to anticipate the fast, sharp turns and loops—which made them all the more unexpected, thrilling and spectacular.

The last partitioned room in the amusement hall contained several *Psi Wars!* game chambers for individual play. A digital scoreboard attached to the top of the far wall indicated the current leading scorer. Not surprisingly, that first Saturday, Sebastian held the lead.

It was rumored that the mini-mall and amusement park was named 'Kelly's Folly' after Dr. Thaddeus Kelly, a paranormal researcher who had worked in relative obscurity years ago at an underfunded lab at some unremarkable private college. He conducted several studies in the late 1970s that, he claimed at least, conclusively demonstrated that fun and games and riding roller coasters, and shopping, of course, enhanced psychic performance. Naturally, because of the seeming absurdity of that, the nickname for the Psi Academy's amusement hall became Kelly's Folly or simply, 'The Folly'. Whenever we went there, we'd tell our classmates that we were off to The Folly.

# Chapter Thirty-One
## Sebastian's Choice

After several weeks at the Academy our Mind Games format changed. The games went from general competing against Colonel Zebb and his army to platoon against platoon. By now, after that horrid start because of my blunder, the Drake Platoon had crawled out of last place and we were a scant two points behind the Stubblebine Platoon, the one to which Grady O'Reilly, Molly Scott and my next door neighbor, wall walker, Dexter Chumley belonged. And, as it turned out, the Stubblebine Platoon was to be our first match in the teams' competitions while the McGoneagles had the bye.

Not surprisingly, the first team match scheduled for Tuesday during the fourth week of school was the source of much anticipation among the platoons. All that preceding weekend, as we strolled The Folly, or struggled with our homework assignments in the common library, some members of the Drakes and Stubblebines exchanged basic trash talk, including boasts, insults and predictions about our upcoming match. The most vicious exchange occurred between our very own, Francis Palmer, and the Stubblebines' leader, Grady O'Reilly.

Even our instructors and Major Atkinson seemed jazzed up about the scheduled match. During her routine announcement to the platoons before dinner on the eve of the match that Monday, she said, "I'd like us to wish good luck to the Drakes and Stubblebines tomorrow, and my hope for a fair and challenging match between them, in the first of the Mind Games team competitions. I understand first place for the Drake Cup is at stake. Therefore, this will make the contest the biggest competition in the history of the Psi Academy."

This amused me because the history of the Psi Academy was only a handful of weeks old.

Sebastian had called a platoon meeting for Monday night at 9:00pm in one of the lounges down the corridor from the mess hall. Once we had crowded in and sat down, he wheeled to the front of the room and looked us over.

"You guys ready?" he asked.

"Yeah!" we cheered in unison.

"Remember," Sebastian said, "we need to work together as one mind like we've been doing. Think as one, act as one, become one. That's how we'll get the Stubblebines. They have too many individual egos."

"Yeah," said Palmer, "especially that Grady O'Reilly."

I glanced over and gave him a nod.

"One thing though, Cadet Palmer, it was a mistake to have gotten into an argument with him Saturday," Sebastian said. "It's far better not to let them know what you are feeling."

"But I couldn't just stand there and let him insult us," he said. He nodded to me. "He kept messing up Cadet Greenberg's name, and called Cadet Morgenstern, freckle face. He even called you handicapped."

"Well, I am handicapped," Sebastian said, "And when you get emotional like that, you let your guard down, without even realizing it. You see, I was able to read what you were thinking while you were going at it with him. I picked up how we played the games the last three weeks, our tactics, our strategies. And if I could, so could he, or any other Stubblebine mind reader for that matter."

"But I was blocking him the whole time," Palmer argued, but then hung his head and nodded. "At least, I thought I was."

"But what about Grady's mind?" I asked Sebastian. "Were you able to read what he was thinking, what the Stubblebines' strategy is?"

"No," Sebastian said, and glanced again briefly at Palmer. "I tried. And though he may have seemed angry, it was cold as ice inside his mind, solid as an ice cube. His blocking wall was up, and it was thick and impenetrable." He sighed. "Cadet O'Reilly is quite clever, let's not underestimate him because he plays the part of an arrogant and ignorant bully."

"Well, then," Freda Morgenstern asked, "what's our strategy, Cadet Drake? How are we going to defeat the Stubblebines? They have some pretty good players."

"Like I said, by doing what we've been doing," he told us, "the amalgam method. We combine, mix our minds. We become a z-Prime."

By the end of classes on Tuesday, our tension about the upcoming match against the Stubblebines was intensified by the constant mention of it by Major Tom, and the rest of our teachers throughout the day. They wished us good luck and told us they really had no idea who would win.

Not surprisingly, the day dragged. But, at long last, the buzzer sounded dismissing us from our last class and we hurried off to the Mind Games chambers. The members of the McGoneagle Platoon were already up in the oval gallery that overlooked the chambers like the observation deck of a hospital operating room. They were champing at the bit themselves, scheduled to play us in Thursday's game when the Stubblebines would have the bye.

Major Atkinson, various Academy instructors, and other psi-warriors we had never seen before soon joined the McGoneagles. And, as if there wasn't already enough riding on this contest, Headmaster Bosworth himself waltzed in a minute or so before it was scheduled to start. Major Atkinson and the other psi-warriors rose and saluted in unison as he strode into the gallery and took his assigned seat along the front row.

"Cadets," said the dark wraith in a voice that hissed like steam. "Take your positions within your game chambers. Cadet Drake, representing the Drake Platoon, and Cadet O'Reilly, representing the Stubblebine Platoon, approach."

We entered our respective game chambers while Grady O'Reilly and Sebastian approached the wraith. The wraith turned over his smoky, skeletal hand, palm up revealing a large, gold coin. On the head of the coin was the mystical symbol for infinity: a sideways eight. The wraith picked up the coin and with its long fingers, turned it over. On its tail was a pentagram, the symbol for the five earth elements.

"Platoon Stubblebine," said the wraith, his voice low and gravely, "as you presently occupy first place after the preliminary round, you have the honor of the call."

"Heads," Grady O'Reilly said without hesitation, then clarified, "Infinity."

"It's going to be tails," I thought to myself, suddenly remembering a dream in which an identical coin had been tossed and come up tails. I could not recall who or what had tossed the coin or what otherwise the dream had been about.

After a solemn nod, the wraith tossed the coin into the air and it rose for what seemed like an eternity until it dropped with a metallic clank to the floor. It landed on its side and spun and rolled on its side for a time, and finally, it fell. And as I had dreamed, the pentagram was showing. It was tails.

The wraith turned to Sebastian.

"For whom do you fight?" he asked. "The Psi Academy or Colonel Zebb?"

So that was it? A platoon was given the choice of fighting for either the Psi Academy or Colonel Zebb. What sense did that make? What kind of amoral fool would choose to fight for Colonel Zebb, our arch enemy, the murderer of the heroic Colonel Peter Drake? (Later I would learn that the designers of the Psi Academy curriculum thought it important that occasionally, its cadets see things from the enemy's perspective.)

Sebastian said, "We fight for Zebb."

Grady O'Reilly blinked and a murmur of disbelief and objection rose up from the gallery. Sebastian had done the unthinkable. I held back my condemnation and scorn for the time being, knowing that Sebastian's selection must be motivated by the will to win. If he had selected Zebb as our ally, there must be some advantage in terms of playing the game.

"Very well," said the wraith with a hint of surprise. "Platoon Drake shall fight for Colonel Zebb. Platoon Stubblebine shall fight for the Psi Academy." He nodded to both Sebastian and Grady O'Reilly.

"*Pugnare parabis.*" it hissed. In Latin that meant, prepare to fight.

Sebastian wheeled into our game chamber and nodded for each of us to be seated and to put on our VR goggles. Francis Palmer glared at Sebastian from his chair.

"You chose Zebb?"

Sebastian glared back at him as he put on his goggles and made a cutting motion with his hand. "Put on your goggles," he said and after a moment Palmer obeyed.

With our goggles in place, we were thrust into the game. The next thing we knew, our avatars were together in a dark, formless hall that seemed to stretch on into infinity.

"Go Drake!" I shouted as we waited for our enemy, the Headmaster, to appear in the game construct.

From somewhere out there I heard the distant shout, "Go Stubblebine!"

It was Molly Scott.

# Chapter Thirty-Two
# **Amalgam Man**

"So this is what I dreamt about?"

I whispered this to no one in particular the moment the game started. Standing before us in a stark white room was none other than Colonel Zebb, this time, an exact replica from my dreams. He had that same square, handsome face, thick hair tinted with gray at the temples and an affable favorite uncle smile that could put anyone who came across him at ease.

"Nothing to fear from me, cadets," he said with that smile as he sauntered over to where we stood in the construct. "I'm the good guy."

To see him saying that, sent a shiver down my spine and caused the downy hair to stand up on my arms. So, did that mean the future I had seen in my dreams had involved nothing more momentous than fighting for an imaginary Colonel Zebb in a game of *Psi Wars!* against the Stubblebine Platoon?

But there was no time to think about that because an instant later, I heard Sebastian's voice in my head.

*Form the amalgam* he commanded.

I focused on being one with the others, and then found myself being sucked up into a vortex of a single mind that seemed to whirl upwards and then, all at once, spoke with a singular voice. I had become part of one mind, one being. We were a lithe, strong dude (but to be honest, it could have been a dude-ess as well), seven feet tall, with x-ray vision and superhuman strength. The Amalgam Man was wearing a tight red rubbery leotard showing off ripped pectorals and muscled arms just like some Hollywood movie superhero.

"Impressive," commented Colonel Zebb. "Now what?"

"Now we fight," said the Amalgam Man, his voice an overpowering, metallic echo.

"Look," Colonel Zebb said as a vision of the amalgam representing Platoon Stubblebine popped into our collective minds. It looked like our seven foot tall twin of ourselves except it was wearing a blue, skin tight rubbery leotard. So that's what it was going to be, blue versus red. And even more bizarre than that was seeing the Headmaster's construct standing next to the Stubblebine Amalgam.

Sebastian sent a thought into each of our minds telling us that the amalgamation of the Stubblebines was most likely Francis Palmer's fault. With his stupid trash talk, he had allowed Grady O'Reilly to enter a crack in his mind and read what our plan might be. But there was no time to dwell on that. Our advantage lost, Sebastian had to come up with a new plan.

"I can gladly help you with that," said Colonel Zebb. He held up a red gelatinous pill, the same pill depicted in the slide during Major Tom's lecture a few days back.

*Boost!* We exclaimed as one.

*Yes, Boost.* Colonel Zebb told us. He waved the pill at us and said, *A little dab'll do ya.*

There was a moment of indecision on the part of our group mind. Sebastian had the lead in any event. Whatever he thought, we'd do.

And then there came a roar from the Stubblebines' Amalgam, a horrendous, baritone scream that immediately grabbed deep within us, to the pit of our stomachs, to our souls. Behind it, General Bosworth pointed at us and gave the command to charge.

Rip-raw! Rip-raw! Rip-raw!

The Stubblebines' Amalgam was running toward us in full battle throttle.

*Sebastian?* Several voices, mine included, begged for direction.

The Amalgam Man strode forward and took the small, red pill from Colonel Zebb's outstretched palm. We held it a moment, staring at it. Finally, with one swift jerk, at Sebastian's command, we tossed the pill down Amalgam Man's throat.

When the Stubblebines' Amalgam had reached within twenty yards of us, we took a defensive stance and slowed, then finally stopping it. It was a seven foot tall beast, its face contorted into a mask of hate and menace, nostrils flaring, eyes narrow, eyebrows slanted down. It finally stopped within six or so feet of us and settled into a defensive, karate stance of its own. I felt a tingling in my mind as the Stubblebines tried to invade and feel our minds for the weakest link; the Amalgam Man brooded and pranced before us.

In the next moment, the Boost kicked in and with a telekinetic onslaught as if a hurricane wind had come up, and was driving off everything in its path, we sent the Stubblebines' Amalgam hurtling backwards.

"NO!" shouted Grady O'Reilly as he realized that the collective psychic powers of the Drake Amalgam had been dramatically enhanced by Boost.

"Unfair, illegal! Cheaters!"

And farther down the hall, the Headmaster had held up an arm to his face fight off the teeth of the wind.

But there was nothing anyone could do about it. In the next instant, the Stubblebines' Amalgam was smashed against the far wall and slumped next to General Bosworth on the ground, dazed, confused and out of breath. Within seconds, we were at its throat. The Amalgam Man's granite hands were unstoppable, choking, throttling it. In short order, the Stubblebines' Amalgam stopped fighting and lay motionless on the ground before us.

It was over. The Stubblebines' Amalgam and the Headmaster's construct disappeared.

"Bravo!" I heard someone say from somewhere behind us and soon realized it was Colonel Zebb. He was grinning, clapping his hands, applauding our victory.

"Bravo!" he repeated. "Bravo!"

Platoon Drake was now in first place!

But we emerged from the game chamber to silence.

No one cheered us, no one hailed our victory. In fact, the only thing I was able to read on the faces in the gallery above us was abhorrence and shock. We had helped the evil Colonel Zebb defeat the Headmaster and the forces of the Psi Academy. Even in simulation, that seemed wrong.

The other thing I noticed looking up at the gallery was that the Headmaster was gone.

# Chapter Thirty-Three
## Post-Game Analysis

We gathered in the lounge next to the Mind Games chamber for post-game analysis. But we were joyless, without cheer or even a hint of bravado despite our big win.

"What just happened back there?" Francis Palmer wanted to know.

Silence hung among us in the lounge for a time.

Finally, Freda Morgenstern said, "We won."

"Yeah," another of our platoon-mates said, "we won."

"Did you see how everyone looked at us?" Palmer asked. When no one in the game room answered him, he said, "And know why? It wasn't only because we fought for Colonel Zebb, but because we won for him by cheating. We took Boost. And it was Zebb, the good guy, according to himself, who gave it to us. Our victory is tainted."

"Clam up, Palmer," I said, sick of his whining. "Yeah, we won. We won. That's all they have to know, and who cares how we did it? In a war, how you win doesn't matter. So put a sock in it already." But, in truth, I wasn't a hundred per cent sure of that. Even in war, some limits must be set. "And I bet in our next game if the McGoneagles win the toss, they'll fight for Zebb. And they'll take the Boost and not think twice about it."

Sebastian sighed. His eyes had this tired, worn look and I could tell that the whole event bothered him immensely. After all, he had sided with the man who had supposedly killed his father.

No one seemed to want to say anything further anyway so Sebastian closed the post-game meeting. We had to get to the mess hall for dinner anyway, and we had a full evening of homework assignments after that. I sighed, thinking about all that.

As we walked into the mess hall the other two platoons regarded us coldly.

"Screw you," I mumbled to myself and glared at the other platoons as I walked past their disapproving stares on my way to our table.

Somebody mumbled something derogatory that stopped me cold. I thought I had heard the word Jew attached to whatever nasty thing was said and I glared right into the middle of my fellow classmates. I went to my usual seat next to Sebastian.

"Bastards" I grumbled.

Sebastian didn't respond. He seemed distracted that evening, in his own dark place. I noticed a change in him lately, a gloomier side, and wondered about it. Was it the enhancement exercises— giving him too much a sense of power? We were told to guard against that—absolute power corrupting *absolutely*, that sort of thing.

It was Chinese Tuesday, and there were plates of delicious Cantonese and Szechuan entrees spread across the table fresh out of the giant woks back in the kitchen with still more being brought by the enlisted servers. I filled my plate with *Moo Goo Gai Pan, Steak Kew* and pork fried rice. After that long, anxious day, I was extra hungry. Next to me, Sebastian was more civilized and gentlemanly in eating his meal although he could not help rice kernels and spittle falling onto his lap.

After a time, he turned and said, "Thanks, Henry. For backing me up today."

I sighed. "What else did you expect? But you know, I'm

still not sure where you are going with this. I mean fighting for Colonel Zebb—was that really necessary?"

I shoveled more *Moo Goo Gai Pan* into my mouth and chewed for a while.

"It worked, didn't it?"

I shrugged. He had me there. "I just want to fight for the right side," I said. "The good guys."

"I thought we did," he said with a shrug and then turned to me and smiled. "Like your dream predicted."

"Yeah," I said. "Like my dream. So that is all what my dream was about? A video game Colonel Zebb?"

"But you still dreamt it," Sebastian said. "And it was about the future, just not a real life one."

After a time, I nodded. Yeah, no matter what, whether in real life or in a psi game, I had dreamt that Colonel Zebb was in it, and that part had come true.

But I felt deep inside that was not all of it. My dreams meant more than that. I was sure they foretold more than how the Drake Platoon would do in a video game contest for the Drake Cup.

# Chapter Thirty-Four
## My First Wraith

During my PEL lab the next morning, Captain Fabian asked if I was ready to concoct my first wraith.

I shrugged.

"Did you at least practice trying to concoct something over the weekend?" he asked.

I shook my head and looked down at the floor of the PEL closet. It was dark in there and hot, and I was angry at myself for spending too much time during the weekend thinking about our Mind Game competition and doing other things.

"I managed a couple more wraith farts," I told him.

"You have to practice at this, Cadet Greenberg. All your powers," he said, almost scolding me, "including seeing the future. You must work on it in your spare time. Like I told you."

He had told me to mediate, think of a river flowing down a valley, into the future. Pretty soon, he promised, I'd be in some future time and place, seeing the possibilities.

But there seemed so little real free time to work on our powers. With guard duty, homework, and spending time with Sebastian and some of my classmates at The Folly, there was truly no time left over for anything at all.

"I know, I know," Captain Fabian said after I complained about the lack of free time. "They are intent at keeping you boys and girls busy. Not a moment's rest, despite what we mentors tell them." He sighed. "So we will have to do a better job here, work on your techniques, start seeing something more than wraith farts."

I sighed, feeling let down by my lack of initiative. Some of my classmates had reported great strides with their extra psychic power enhancement work. Freda Morgenstern, for instance, had boasted the other day in PT class, waiting for a telekinetic dodge-ball game to begin, that she had dead-talked with some unknown spirit on Sunday evening after making some headway with it during her last mentoring session.

"I understand," Captain Fabian said, "congratulations are in order. You defeated Platoon Stubblebine yesterday and now hold the lead for the Drake Cup."

"Yes," I said. "I wish I could dream up the final outcome, who wins the Drake Cup. Then, maybe I could sleep better at night and wouldn't worry so much about the games."

Captain Fabian laughed.

"Mediate on it," he said. "You might just surprise yourself."

I nodded and again regretted how lax I had been in attempting to develop my precog power on my own time.

"We should have some time to work on it today," he said, "but first, I think you need to concoct your first wraith."

I drew in a breath. I had come so close our last session. Smoke had arisen from somewhere, out of thin air it seemed, and hovered for a time behind my chair, but the wraith I had been conjuring in my mind never materialized. After a time, I could no longer hold onto the thought and the electricity behind my conjuration, and the misshapen smoke it had produced, had finally, woefully and mercifully dissipated.

The result was, as Captain Fabian had so dourly put it immediately afterward 'another in the long generations of mutant, degenerate Greenberg wraith farts'.

"So let's get to it," Captain Fabian said. "Concoct me up your first wraith."

I closed my eyes and, after a sigh, performed the concentration exercises he had taught me, meditating while mumbling the mantra, the Devanagari that supposedly fostered the psychic forces behind the conjuration of a mind wraith.

ॐ असतोमा सद्गमय ।
तमसोमा ज्योतिर् गमय ।
मृत्योर्मामृतं गमय ॥
ॐ शान्ति शान्ति शान्तिः ॥

This Devanagari chant was a kind of prayer, invoking my brain's connection with the subconscious realm, which meant, more or less, I think, 'lead me from ignorance to truth'. Commander Marzo had shown us the quantum equation for it. In addition to whispering the mantra over and over, you had to 'really see' as Captain Fabian stressed 'really, really see' the form of the wraith you were trying to create completely and firmly in your mind. You had to have an example of something; a person, a being, a monster, a thing.

From his chair only a couple feet across from me, I heard Captain Fabian mumbling his own Devanagari prayer.

At first nothing much happened; but after a few seconds, a mist of energy formed to my right. It was what Grady O'Reilly and some other of my classmates called 'wraith spunk'. It was from that initial charge, transmitted from my brain that a mind wraith would form into an actual being. All one had to do was concentrate, really concentrate, and finish the work.

The form that had popped into my mind that morning had been none other than Harry Potter. I quickly chased the thought. The last thing I needed was to conjure the famous boy wizard. Then I thought of Hank Greenberg, the old Hall of Famer. That would be fun. But then, for some reason, the image of Frankie Nytz popped into my head.

And in the next moment, poof, there he was—friggin' Frankie Nytz, a dark wraith, floating next to me, seven feet tall. I gawked at what had been brought forth, on my own, out of the depths of my mind. Frankie looked at me and scowled. It was the complete Frankie, too, his mouth twitching sideways and his aggressive stance, which I now knew was a subconscious response caused by years fending off an alcoholic father.

"What are you looking at Greenbum?" he asked derisively, exactly like the real Frankie would have.

Then he turned and looked at Captain Fabian.

"And who's this squirrel?"

Captain Fabian frowned. "Pleasant fellow."

The Frankie Nytz wraith hovered over and bent down to get a sniff of the Captain.

"What did you just say?" the Frankie Nytz wraith asked him. "You a wise guy?"

Captain Fabian sighed. He closed his eyes and in the next moment, the Frankie Nytz wraith dissipated in a puff of smoke.

"Exactly my sentiment," I said. "I can't believe I conjured him, Frankie Nytz, of all people."

"Well," said Captain Fabian, "at least you didn't eat the yellow snow."

I laughed, knowing that my mentor had surveyed the recesses of my mind and found all the old, nasty Frankie Nytz memories.

"But the point is," he went on and clapped his hands for a time, "you did it! You concocted a wraith, a bad one, but a wraith nevertheless. Bravo! Congratulations!"

"Let's do another," he said, "then work on your dreams."

This time I decided, what the heck, and conjured up the wizard, Harry Potter. Captain Fabian laughed, and laughed even harder when he started flying around the room on a broomstick looking for a Quidditch game.

"Bravo once again, my star pupil!" Captain Fabian said. "Now, wish him away," he added with a long sigh. "I hate those Harry Potter books."

# Chapter Thirty-Five
## Perchance to Dream

After helping me dissipate the Harry Potter wraith, Captain Fabian spent the rest of that session providing insight and methods for enhancing my precognitive dreaming. He specified certain mantras and concentration exercises that were helpful and then taught me how to lucid dream—that is, how to wake up in the dream you are having and then interact within the dream; ask questions of the people in the dream all without waking up from it. Not waking up was the hard part, because once you were alerted to the fact that you are dreaming, your mind tends to want to awaken from it. There were ways of avoiding waking and staying in the dream which Captain Fabian called 'dream tricks' and he tried helping me understand what they were and how to perform them.

"The best precogs," he told me, "are the guys who can do that. Wake up in a dream about the future and interact with it. And in that way, they themselves can affect the future."

That night, I chanted the mantras and performed the concentration exercises that Captain Fabian had taught me but when I slept, I did not dream about Zebb. I had various other strange visions and a vivid dream about being chased by strange, silver, flying insects. I ran with Captain Fabian and a pretty female Army officer of undetermined rank in a jig-jag pattern through a deep, dark forest. I was breathing hard, legs hurting all in order to avoid the heat ray blasts being shot at us from the flying bugs. Why they were chasing us, where we were and how we got there, I had no idea. The dream started with the three of us running scared.

And the next night, I had the very same dream.

I told Captain Fabian about the two nights of strange dreams during our next mentoring session.

"They weren't flying bugs," he said. "They were drones."

"Drones?"

"Yes," he said, "like the kind the military uses in the Middle East wars, Afghanistan and Iraq."

Yes, that's what the flying bugs were, I nodded. Drones.

"They were being guided," he went on, "by a mind pilot."

I sighed. That sounded ominous.

"A good mind pilot will sense the location of prey," he said. "Feel the fear, hear its thoughts. Even sniff it out."

"Well, that certainly doesn't sound like a future I want to get to," I said.

"Did you become lucid?" Captain Fabian asked after a time. "Did you try and wake up in those dreams?"

I sighed and shook my head. The thought of doing that had never occurred to me. I was locked within the dream and, like most dreams, it seemed like real life.

"Next time," he said, "try it. What you dreamt is something that is going to happen in the future."

"And then what?" I asked. "When I wake up in my dream? What should I do?"

"Help us escape," he said.

And that's exactly what I did that very night. I had the same dream again with me and Captain Fabian and the pretty Lieutenant running through a dark forest trying to escape an air force of drone insects. But this time I forced myself to wake up into it and led them to an outcropping of solid rock where we found a slit that led into a narrow cave where we hid.

And then I woke up.

# Chapter Thirty-Six
## Within a Dream

We played Platoon McGoneagle to a tie on Thursday following our controversial and, to some, disagreeable, win over the Stubblebines the previous Tuesday and so had retained first place. In that game, as we expected, the McGoneagles' Platoon Leader, Cadet Sarah Lloyd, had chosen to fight for Colonel Zebb and shortly after the game commenced, the McGoneagles' Amalgam had taken a dose of Boost. Still, by the end of a final battle between the two platoons, in a cavernous foyer leading out of the Psi Cave constructed for us by the game, we each had two wraiths left. They were gigantic, fire-breathing dragons—ours red and the McGoneagles' black. They flew around the granite ceiling of the cavern for a time trying to find an opening before it was determined using some mathematical calculation, that there was no way for either team to win.

And then after a much needed bye the following Tuesday, we had another big game against the Stubblebines that Thursday afternoon. Sebastian lost the toss and Grady O'Reilly chose to fight for Colonel Zebb. The Stubblebines took Boost and had us on the run the whole game. Our poor Amalgam Man ran down dark corridor after dark corridor and tried every psychic trick in the book but to no avail. At one point, the Stubblebine Amalgam tele-influenced our Amalgam Man to kneel down and bang his head against the stone floor of the game construct until it was bloody and delirious.

The game turned off and we had lost by thirty points—a shameful effort.

To his dejected platoon-mates in the briefing after the game, all Sebastian had to say was, "Well, tomorrow's another day."

We played the McGoneagles next Tuesday and if things kept going like today, they'd drop us into the last place.

"We've still got a lot of semester left," Sebastian added.

After a minute or so of glum silence, Francis Palmer suggested, "Maybe it's time for a new leader."

Sebastian shrugged and wheeled out of the room.

I had no clue what was bothering him, but Palmer seemed right for a change. Sebastian seemed to have lost his edge.

Still, I stuck up for him. "Just like true sunshine fans," I said. "Players play like crap, blame the coach."

I got up and walked out the room and shuffled down to the gym for PT.

That night, I finally dreamt of Colonel Zebb again. All of sudden, there he was standing before me. I said the mantra to allow me to enter the dream, to perceive it, to interact intelligently with it and to be aware within it, and I was there. Awake within the dream.

I smiled.

*Captain Fabian is a fine mentor,* Colonel Zebb said. *A tad eccentric, perhaps, but good. You are fortunate.*

*Yes, I know,* I said. I sighed and focused on the dream visage of Colonel Zebb. *Is that all I have been seeing in these dreams—you in the game?*

*The game was yesterday,* he said, *and tomorrow is tomorrow.*

*So are you coming into the Psi Academy to take Sebastian and me away with you?*

*You're dreaming exactly that, aren't you?* He said

*Please stop answering a question with a question and answer my question.*

*Alright, Henry,* he said. *Ask me a question, and I will try and answer it.*

*You're still the good guy?*

*Yes, I'm the good guy. I have always been the good guy. Don't believe so easily everything you are told. Especially by teachers.*

*But they say you're the bad guy,* I said, *and that you did and do bad things.*

*I told you before, Henry,* he said, because *they believe it, doesn't make it true.*

*Who are the bad guys then?* I asked.

*I'm not entirely sure,* Colonel Zebb said. *But it's one powerful z-Prime. So powerful, I would characterize it as a capital Z, Z-Prime.*

*Aren't you a z-Prime?* I asked. *An Amalgam of evil psi-warriors?*

*No, I am not a z-Prime. It's damned hard to form a z-Prime, Henry. With Boost, as you have seen from the Mind Games, it's easier. But don't get me wrong, if I could become one, I would. Because I'd like to get my hands on that Headmaster of yours. Bosworth. Now, he might very well be a bad guy.*

"General Bosworth? A bad guy? How's that?"

"*Stop being so naïve,* Colonel Zebb said.

I stood there looking at him, knowing he was just a dream, representing a *possible* future. But I also knew my interaction with him had changed the nature of it.

*That's exactly what it means, Henry. You can interact and change whatever future that you dream.*

*How will I know what to change, and what not to change?*

*I have no answer for that.*

There was a pause between us, as if waiting for the dream cameras to start rolling again.

*You were thinking of Colonel Drake.*

*Yes, is he really alive?*

*Colonel Drake lives.*

*He's somewhere in Psi Cave?*

*Yes.* Colonel Zebb sighed. *But somehow, his powers have been taken from him—neutralized.*

*How? I asked.*

*Another thing, Henry,* he went on without answering. *Sebastian, your friend, is not all that he seems.*

I thought about that for a time. *What do you mean?*

*I'm not sure myself,* he said. *That thought just came to me.*

*But you're only a dream.*

Colonel Zebb nodded. *Yes, I am,* he said, *but we're all just living a dream within a dream within a dream.*

He gave me a kindly smile, waved a hand at me and I woke up.

I immediately took the journal on the night stand on my bed and wrote down every detail, every statement, that I could remember from the dream. And after jotting all that down, I called Sebastian.

# Chapter Thirty-Seven
## Dead Talking

After the third ring, Sebastian answered his cell phone.

"You dreamt about Zebb," he said right off, without even saying hello.

"Yes."

"And he talked about my father?"

"Yes."

"He's alive?"

"That's what Zebb said, yes," I said, "in my dream."

Sebastian fell silent.

"Sebastian?"

Sebastian said nothing. I thought of what Zebb had also told me, that Sebastian wasn't what he seemed, whatever that meant, which even Zebb didn't profess to know. I didn't tell Sebastian that, but I knew he might have entered my mind and learned it anyway.

*Zebb's a liar!* Someone whispered in my brain. *A liar!*

"Sebastian?"

"I think it's time we went and found him," he said.

"Who?"

"My father."

"Your father?"

"Yes," he said. "Dead or alive. Can you come over?"

"Now? It's three o'clock in the morning."

"Yes, now," he said. "I have an idea."

I quickly changed into jeans and a tee shirt and stalked like a thief along the wall next door to Sebastian's quarters. He opened the door and I followed him into the living room and sat down on his couch while he wheeled to a spot in the middle of the room.

"So what's your idea?" I asked him.

Not a moment later, someone was knocking at his door.

"Who's that?" I asked as Sebastian wheeled over to answer it.

He opened the door and in walked Freda Morgenstern.

"Why's she here?" I asked.

"Why's he here?" Freda asked Sebastian as she glared at me.

Sebastian glided back to his spot in the middle of the room. "I asked her here to dead talk."

"Dead talk?" I said, laughing. "Spirit communication's a myth."

"And so is fortune telling," Freda said.

"Look, let's get started," Sebastian said and pivoted around to face Freda, who was still standing just inside the doorway.

"How does it work?" he asked. "What do you need to do to dead talk?"

"The best way," she said and then looked around the room, "is turn the lights off, keep quiet, and let me meditate, go into a trance."

"This is hokum," I said.

I had chosen to believe that dead talking was nonsense. Perhaps, all along, it was just that I was afraid of it. Imagine, to be able to talk to a dead person. Someone from beyond that veil between life and death.

"And dreaming about the future isn't hokum?" Freda shot back.

"Enough bickering," Sebastian scolded us and his scowl

told me to keep quiet and I shrugged. Then, he looked back at Freda.

"Please, sit down and let's get started," he said.

Freda sat on the chair across from me and waited for Sebastian to turn out the lights. Once we were sitting in darkness, she told us to close our eyes and concentrate. I wanted to say, 'Hokum' again, but because of Sebastian, I kept my mouth shut and waited.

I heard Freda humming some kind of mantra to herself as she fell into a trance. I opened one eye and looked across at her, but it was too dark to see much of anything.

I waited in the darkness, listening to Freda's murmuring.

"What's happening?" I whispered to Sebastian. "What's she doing? It's hokum, I tell you. Pure hokum. Like a carnival sideshow."

"Sh!"

I held my tongue and waited for a time.

*"Peter's not here."*

It was Freda speaking, a low grumble, but it didn't sound like her voice. It was an older woman's voice. But not too old, more like Major Atkinson's age, around thirty-five. And she spoke with an angelic, Irish brogue.

"Who's that?" I whispered.

*"You are wasting your time."*

"Who is it, Freda?" I asked. "You?"

*"I'm Sarah Drake."*

I gulped and looked at Sebastian. Sarah Drake was his mother's name. His dead mother.

"What do you mean?" I turned to Freda and asked.

Sebastian turned to me. He had gone limp and his eyes stared forward. He looked about to cry.

*"Peter Drake, my husband, is not here."*

From what I knew of Sebastian's mother, other than the sad fact that she had died in the same car wreck that left him a cripple when he was five years old, Sarah Drake had been born in

Ireland as Sarah Patricia O'Halloran and Sebastian's father had met her while on some secret mission overseas. She had been a scientist studying psychic phenomena at a hidden military base in the far north of England. Aunt Dottie had told Sebastian that his mother had been very beautiful and intelligent, with flaming red hair, intense emerald eyes, and a wide, loving smile. And of course, there was her effecting Irish brogue.

"You're Sebastian Drake's mother?" I asked.

*"Yes, I am. And thank you for being such a good friend to Sebastian."* Then, the voice whispered, *"Ask your questions."*

"What color is your hair?" I asked.

I still doubted whether Freda was really communicating with Sebastian's dead mother, that she was truly dead talking.

*"Red, my dear."*

I looked more closely at Freda. She still appeared out of it, in a trance. And it was funny to hear a mature Irish lass' brogue coming out of her mouth.

But guessing red hair, that wasn't so much.

"And where we you born?"

*"You are a doubting Thomas."*

"Where?"

*Why, Ireland. Well, we call it Eire.*

"Where in Ireland?"

*"Tralee in County Kerry."*

"Mother." Sebastian had finally broken down, convinced by these answers, the brogue of her voice, that this was truly the spirit of his dead mother, speaking with him through Freda Morgenstern, from the hereafter. He had slumped over and was gently sobbing into his hands.

But I remained skeptical. Freda could be merely reading Sebastian's mind, or perhaps she had already done so to know these answers. But wouldn't Sebastian have sensed that?

"How did you die?" I asked, really getting into it now.

"Stop it, Henry," Sebastian said. "She's my mother. I am sure of it."

*"I died in a car accident. Five years and two weeks after giving birth to Sebastian. So we shared the world together for only five years and two wonderful weeks."*

I heard Sebastian draw in a breath, almost lose it again, then suddenly compose himself.

"You say father's not with you," Sebastian said. "He's not dead?"

*"You father is not here. He remains with you, among the living."*

"Where is he?"

*"I don't know exactly, Sebastian. But he is somewhere down in the cave with you. Close by."*

And then all at once, his mother said, *"Goodbye, Sebastian. I love you. I will always love you."*

"No, mother," he cried out. "Mom!"

But that was it. Freda was stirring, mumbling gibberish. She shifted around on her seat on the couch, sat straight up, and rubbed her eyes.

"Did, did it work?" she asked. "Did I dead talk?"

I got up and switched on the light. I checked my cell phone. It was nearly 3:00am.

"Did it? Did it work?" She looked over at Sebastian, studied his worn, distracted stare, and then looked over at me.

"Yeah," I told her. "It worked."

I was about to tell her more when Dexter Chumley entered the room. Only, he didn't use the front door—he walked in through a wall.

# Chapter Thirty-Eight
## Disappearing Act

Chumley stood before us with an elated grin stretching halfway across his face.

"I did it!' he said. "A second time, I did it!"

What he was so elated about, was that he had walked through the wall of his room into the corridor, then walked from the corridor through the wall into Sebastian's room.

"Where'd the Irish lady go?" he asked after a moment, looking about.

It was still funny to think of chubby Dexter Chumley walking through walls, but I had just seen him do it with my own two eyes.

When no one said anything, he said, "I heard her. An Irish lady. Where'd she go?"

"That was Sebastian's Mom," I said.

"His mom?"

"Never mind," Sebastian said. He had sat up in his wheelchair and seemed himself again. Determined, in charge.

"Want to join us in a little adventure?" he asked Chumley. "An adventure where your wall walking will come in handy?"

"What adventure?" asked Freda Morgenstern.

I glared at Sebastian, thinking, yeah, what adventure? It was 3:00am for gripe-sakes.

"Follow me," he said, offering nothing else by way of

explanation. He wheeled to the front door of his quarters and looked back at Chumley. "I'll go through the door, if that's okay with you?"

"Sure," Chumley said. "I don't want to show off. Or press my luck."

After negotiating several corridors, we approached the wide door of the main elevator to the various levels of the Psi Cave that, we had been told, were strictly off-limits. Sebastian brought his wheelchair to a stop and waited for us to circle around him.

"What's your plan, Seb?" I asked. "Where are we going?"

"To find my father," he said. "My mother said he's somewhere inside the Psi Cave."

"Psi Cave's a big place, Seb," I said. "And I don't think we're supposed to be exploring much of it."

I gestured to the sign above the elevator door:

OFF-LIMITS: AUTHORIZED PERSONNEL ONLY

There were no up and down buttons next to the elevator doors, just a slot for a key card.

"How are we supposed to open the doors?" Freda asked. "We don't have a key."

"Even if we did have a key," I said, "we shouldn't do this. We'll be—"

"Expelled?" Sebastian asked. "So let them. I'm trying to save my father."

Sebastian turned to Chumley.

"Can you walk through those doors?" he asked.

Chumley sighed and scratched his beefy jowls.

"They're pretty thick," he said and sighed. "Pure steel."

"I'm asking you to try," Sebastian said. "I'd do it myself, except for this wheelchair."

Chumley looked down at the wheelchair and then at the wide, thick elevator doors, and gave his jowls another long scratch.

"I don't think he should try it, Sebastian," Freda Morgenstern said. "What if he gets stuck?"

And then it came to me, a dream I had a couple nights back. Dexter Chumley had walked into an elevator. I had thought nothing of it at the time.

"He can do it," I told Freda, and the rest of them turned and looked at me. I nodded to the elevator. "He will do it. I already saw him."

"Then go," Sebastian said to Chumley. "That was the future Henry saw. You doing it."

Chumley took a breath, then stepped forward until his nose was flush against the cold, steel door. His breath formed a mist. He closed his eyes, took a deep breath and stepped forward and, as in my dream, I saw his chubby frame meld into the hard, cold steel. He was sucked in and disappeared. Hopefully, he had walked through to the other side and was now standing in the elevator. I was stunned for a time to see a human body fuse like that into a solid object, becoming part of it for a time, and then disappear. And then, in the next moment, I grew fearful that he had walked through and fallen down an empty shaft because I had no memory of what happened to Chumley in my dream after he had walked through the elevator door.

But in the next moment, I heard Chumley's high pitched voice.

"Hey, guys?" he said. "Now what?"

"Open the doors," Sebastian said. "Open them."

And then, the elevator doors opened.

Sebastian immediately wheeled inside and turned around to face us.

"Well, come in," he said.

Freda and I looked at each other a moment, then, after a breath, we stepped inside.

Chumley stepped forward and looked at the large silver panel before him on the right side of the elevator door. It had a series of numbers, one to thirteen, signifying the levels of the

Psi Cave I supposed, with large, round buttons next to each number.

Chumley turned to Sebastian and asked, "Which one?"

"Thirteen," he told Chumley. "The very bottom seems as good a place to start as any."

Chumley shrugged and pressed the button labeled '13.' The elevator door closed and in the next instant, there was a whoosh as we descended. After mere seconds, the elevator stopped and the doors opened. The corridor before us was completely dark and silent.

"Now what?" I asked.

Sebastian glided out into the dark corridor.

"Where you going, Seb?" I whispered harshly after him. "Where you going?" I stumbled out after him with Freda and Chumley right behind me. "Sebastian," I called, but he kept going somewhere down the corridor.

"He's down here," he said. "I feel it now. This way."

By the time we caught to him, I saw that his eyes were closed and I knew he was remote viewing into the room he had stopped in front of.

*He's a liar!* A chorus of voices whispered in my mind. *Sebastian is not what he seems.*

"Sebastian," I said. "Why did you stop? We need to get out of here."

I checked my watch. It was 3:30am.

"I think Henry's right," Chumley said, "time to go back. We can ask Major Atkinson about this tomorrow."

"No," Sebastian whispered curtly. He was tired like the rest of us, and confused. He had dead talked with his mother, or thought he had, just minutes ago. A mother he could barely remember and now knew only from photographs, videos, and the recollections of Aunt Dottie and Uncle Brad.

Sebastian turned to the door and glided his wheelchair right up next to it.

"He's in here," he whispered. "I know it."

229

"Your dad?" I asked. "In, in there?"

"Yes," he hissed. He turned to Chumley. "You have to walk through it."

"Into there?" Chumley asked. "That, that room." He backed away a step. "No way."

"Chumley, please," Sebastian said. "Just do it."

But Chumley stood his ground, too scared and worried to blindly walk into a dark room from a dark corridor in a place they shouldn't be.

"If your dad's in there," I said, "why doesn't he just open the door and come out himself? Why do you need Chumley here to go in and get him? I don't get it?"

"Because my father's being held prisoner in this room," Sebastian said. "There's a chamber inside it, made out of lead. I think my father's in that lead chamber, a room within a room. So that's why I need Chumley to go inside." He turned again to Chumley. "So Chumley," he said. "Go!"

But by then it was too late. A hot wind had blown from down the other end of the corridor. Each of us turned that way. And in that moment, we saw the figures, a group of them. Seven foot dark wraiths slithering toward us.

"We're doomed," Chumley said.

We were quickly surrounded by faceless, dark wraiths. They hovered over us for a time before one of them, the leader, I supposed, pointed his boney arm and long, skeletal index finger down the corridor from which they had come.

And then I saw the wraith look down at Sebastian, or at the wheelchair in which he had just been sitting. But Sebastian was no longer in it.

"Where the heck is he?" Chumley said.

"Sh!" I hissed.

But then, the wraith pointed his boney arm and index finger a second time down the corridor and, in the next moment, we were being hustled down towards the elevator. And Sebastian's wheelchair had been left behind.

# Chapter Thirty-Nine
## The X Squad

A platoon of psi-warriors I had never seen before was waiting for us at the elevator. The leader was a square-jawed, narrow-eyed Captain together with six or seven mean faced Sergeants.

Once we were in the platoon's custody, the dark wraiths dissipated.

"Who are you?" I asked.

The Captain turned to me with a frown.

"The X Squad," he told me. "And you, cadet, are in a world of crap."

We were hustled inside the elevator and taken back to the Psi Academy on Level Seven. After the elevator doors opened, we were double-timed through several corridors before finally stopping.

"Where are we?" Freda asked.

But no one answered. I noticed that there were four doors. Four separate rooms for each of us, except that Sebastian was no longer with us. Two sergeants led me by my shoulders into a small conference room. One of them was a dark-skinned, bald, scowling Master Sergeant with deep, hard lines etched on his dark fudge-colored forehead. The other was stern-faced with short-cropped hair who looked every bit Marine Corps.

"Sit down," the dark-skinned Master Sergeant barked. He

pointed to an armless chair at a table. As I sat down on it, I noticed an ID badge above the shirt pocket of his khaki psi-warrior uniform indicating the name 'MSgt. Reedy.' Below it were several rows of variously colored bars signifying medals he had been awarded over his undoubtedly long, impressive and honorable Army career.

The other psi-warrior was Gunnery Sergeant named Olson. He didn't have as many rows of medals as Master Sergeant Reedy, but he had enough. He walked over to the far corner of the room and stood there scowling at me with his arms crossed.

Master Sergeant Reedy circled my chair for a time before finally stopping in the front of it and glaring down at me.

"So what the hell were you cadets doing down there?" he asked. He put his hands on his thick thighs and bent down almost level to within about an inch or two of my face. "You want to tell me that, Cadet Greenberg?"

I closed my eyes and tried to think, figure out how this night had turned into such a disaster.

"Cadet Greenberg," stated Master Sergeant Reedy, "I asked you a question."

I reached a quick decision. Telling the truth was the best option. And really, what was there to hide?

I opened my eyes and looked at him.

"We were looking for Colonel Drake," I said. "The kid in the wheelchair's father."

Master Sergeant Reedy stood up and continued glaring down at me.

"The kid in the wheelchair's father," he repeated.

"Yes, sir," I said.

"Well, where the hell is he?" he asked. "The kid in the wheelchair? All we found was his wheelchair."

"I, I don't know," I said and shrugged. "He disappeared."

From the corner of the room, the Gunnery Sergeant said, "We know he disappeared, cadet. The point is, where did he disappear to?"

"I have no idea, Sir."

Master Sergeant Reedy glanced back at his partner with what appeared to be mild annoyance, then turned back to me. "You know all the decks above and below the Academy are off limits," he said. "You know that, right Cadet Greenberg?"

"Yes, sir," I said glumly. "I know that."

"So you intentionally violated school regulations, is that what you're telling me, Cadet?"

I bowed my head. I could not believe that I had been, that we had been, so stupid as to have probably earned our expulsion from the Psi Academy. My father would be furious. And I couldn't blame him.

"Yes, sir," I said. "I did. But, but—"

"But what, Cadet?" the Master Sergeant bellowed. "There are no buts when it comes to regulations. You either obey them, or you don't. You do, we maybe win the war. You don't, we definitely don't." He bent down close to me again. "You understand that, Cadet?"

I wondered what 'war' he was talking about. "Yes, sir. But, we thought we were helping win the war by finding Colonel Drake."

Master Sergeant Reedy stood and looked back at the Gunnery Sergeant still standing in the right corner of the room. After a time, he turned back to me.

"So that's it," he said. "That's all you got to say?"

"Yes, sir," I said. "That's it."

"And the other cadet," he said, "the one who disappeared. You have no idea what happened to him?"

"No, sir," I said.

He nodded and after gesturing to Gunnery Sergeant Olson, they left me alone in the dark, cramped room. After five minutes or so contemplating my expulsion from the Psi Academy, about how my life was ruined and still wondering what happened to Sebastian, Master Sergeant Reedy returned.

"Come with me," he said from the doorway as he waved his right hand.

I stood. My legs were wobbly, weak. It was almost 5:30am.

I walked behind Master Sergeant Reedy and Gunnery Sergeant Olson down the corridor, past our living quarters and soon realized we were headed to Major Atkinson's office.

As Master Sergeant Reedy knocked at the office door, I stood at attention, fearing the worst. And then, there was Sebastian gliding toward us with a couple sergeants from the X Squad walking beside him.

"Where the heck you been?" I whispered as he took the spot next to me.

But there wasn't time for an explanation. Master Sergeant Reedy had opened the door and was gesturing for Sebastian and me to enter.

"They're waiting for you," he said.

They? I wondered. Who's they?

Soon enough I found out. After walking under the stern gaze of the Master Sergeant with Sebastian right behind me, I first spotted Major Atkinson, not behind her desk, but standing stiff and straight at the side of it. Behind her desk, with an imperious gaze, sat the Headmaster, Major General Buzz Bosworth himself.

Seeing him, I knew definitely this spelled the end of the road for us. I would be out on my ear, shipped back home in the next available government van. No going to Harvard now.

"Come on in, Cadets Greenberg, Drake," the Headmaster said in an affable, kindly, grandfatherly kind of voice. He waved a hand, gesturing us forward. "Come in."

I wanted to run, but instead I took a deep breath. I looked at Sebastian, who remained expressionless. Finally, we strode forward to within three or four feet of General Bosworth. We both saluted and stood at attention.

"At ease, Cadets," General Bosworth said. There was an unlit cigar lodged in the corner of his mouth.

He leaned forward and regarded each of us menacingly for a time. Then, he turned to Sebastian

"Why the hell did you go down to Level Thirteen, a restricted area?"

"To find my father," Sebastian blurted out. "Why are you holding him prisoner down there?"

Major Atkinson gave the General a worried glance and General Bosworth sighed and seemed to go limp as he leaned back in this chair.

"What makes you think that, Cadet Drake?" He asked.

Sebastian hesitated a moment before telling the Headmaster everything. And then he told them what I didn't know. After the wraiths had interrupted our mission he had slithered out of this wheelchair and wall crawled inside the room and seen the lead container, and knew that his father was in there. Then, his powers were suddenly gone, and the next thing he knew, the X Squad soldiers burst into the room and brought him here.

"I can appreciate you motivations, Cadet Sebastian," the Headmaster said. "But why didn't you come to Major Atkinson with your suspicions?"

"I have to admit, Sir," Sebastian said as he sheepishly looked down at his lap. "And I don't think you could blame me." He looked up. "But I'm not sure if I can trust you or Major Atkinson. Maybe Cadet Greenberg's dreams are true and Zebb is not a bad guy, he's a good guy. That means the real bad guys are you and Major Atkinson."

"Cadet Drake," hissed Major Atkinson, "such insubordination will not be tolerated!"

General Bosworth waved his right hand at her, telling her to back off.

"I'm afraid, you've been misled, Cadet Drake," General Bosworth said. "There's nothing in that room. But you are right, once it did hold Colonel Drake. Zebb stuffed him in there after he went z-Prime and was going AWOL. But the lead container couldn't hold him and he escaped. And, that's when the Zebb z-Prime..." the General hesitated a long moment, "...that's when Zebb's z-Prime killed your father."

"And ever since then," he went on, "Level Thirteen has been empty and the room you found, left just as it was as a reminder of that terrible day when the Psi Wars began."

"But, sir," I piped up, "what about what Sebastian's, I mean Cadet Drake's Mom, what the spirit of his mom I mean, told us. That his father was not in the spirit realm, but was still alive, and that he was being held prisoner somewhere in the Psi Cave."

"Spirit communication," General Bosworth said, "is an inexact psychic art. The spirits who are contacted play games with dead talkers. And sometimes, the spirit who is summoned by a dead talker's power is not the spirit whom that spirit professes to be."

"But I felt my father in that container in that room, General Bosworth," Sebastian said. "I felt that he was there."

"As I told you," said General Bosworth, "he was there, or had been. That is what you felt. His emotional and spiritual residue. Psychics who are employed by the police on murder cases do that all the time—feel the presence of a victim, and even feel how the victim was murdered."

Sebastian sighed. It seemed the General had an answer for everything. It was indeed either true, or just the statements of a practiced liar.

"No, Cadet Greenberg," Major Atkinson said and glared at me. "He is not lying."

"That's quite alright, Major Atkinson," said the General. "I don't blame them one bit for being suspicious, after what they've been through. I want you to take them back down there and show them. Open up every room on Level Thirteen and show them."

"That won't be necessary, Sir," Sebastian said. "I—I believe you."

"Sebastian?" I asked, incredulous how easy he'd caved.

General Bosworth nodded and seemed gratified.

"The question now," the Headmaster said, "is what to do about your breach of regulations."

"Well," Sebastian said, "if you do anything, you should do it to me. I was the ringleader. I talked the others into it."

The Headmaster seemed to relax. He crossed his legs as he leaned far back in Major Atkinson's black leather chair and rolled the unlit cigar around his mouth for a time.

"Rest easy, boys," he said. "I've decided to give you another chance, considering your honorable motivations. You've been granted a reprieve."

# Chapter Forty
## The Tesla Field

It was 6:00am by the time I got back to my room. I dropped onto my bed and dozed but thankfully woke up with a start after only a few minutes. In light of the reprieve granted by the Headmaster, the last thing I needed was to fall into a deep sleep and be AWOL for my first class that morning.

I sat up on the edge of my bed, yawned, stretched and rubbed my tired eyes. It was going to be a long day. Fortunately, it was Friday and thus only a half day of classes. After taking a quick shower and getting into my Psi Academy uniform, I found my cell phone and called Sebastian. There were still a lot of unanswered questions, like for instance why his powers had gone limp in the room on Level Thirteen in which his father, I still believed, was being held prisoner.

"Do you really believe that stuff the Headmaster told us?" I asked. "That what you felt was your father's residue?"

Sebastian sighed, himself beat after a long sleepless night.

"I don't know what to think," he said. "My probe of the minds of the Headmaster and Major Atkinson didn't help."

"Of course not," I said, "they blocked you."

"Major Atkinson tried," he said, "but I got in. And General Bosworth has no powers to speak of. He administers the Psi Cave and is the liaison with the highest military and intelligence powers, but he's not himself a psi-warrior. His attempt to block is amateurish, fairly easy to break through even for a novice. And this time, he didn't even try.

"Point is," he went on, "what they told us is what they were thinking. What I had perceived when I was in that room was my father's residue."

"I just don't know," Sebastian said with a sigh. "Maybe Freda was duped by a rogue spirit. Maybe all I sensed was my father's residue."

It was my turn to sigh.

"Want to tell me the whole story?" I asked. "What the heck happened down there? After the wraiths came. That was some disappearing act on your part."

"Once I became invisible," he said, "I wall-walked into the chamber. Or rather, I wall crawled. On my belly."

I tried to imagine that—poor Sebastian crawling like a worm into the room.

"As I told the Headmaster," he went on, "there was a large metal container in the middle of the room. A room within a room."

"So?" I asked. "What was in it, the room within the room?"

"I don't know for sure if anything was in it," Sebastian said. "As I said, I sensed my father, or maybe, like the Headmaster said, his residue."

"Or it really was him," I said. "And if it is him, just like the spirit of your mom says, and just like Zebb in my dreams says, the question is why has he been kept down there all this time—and, why hasn't he used his psychic powers to get out?"

"I don't know," Sebastian said. "As for his powers, the only thing I can think of that could have neutralized them, and mine as well after I entered the room, is a reverse Tesla Field."

"A Teslak Field?" I asked. "What's that?"

"Not Teslak, Tesla," he corrected. "A Tesla Field, named after its inventor, Nikolai Tesla. He invented it to enhance the energy used for generating psychic powers. But when reversed, a Tesla Field can neutralize psychic powers." He sighed. "Theoretically, at least. It's never been proven to exist. I read about it somewhere. I just can't recall where. Maybe it's something Major Tom knows something about."

"No, it wasn't theoretical," I said. "It worked on you. It neutralized your powers."

"I'm not sure of anything anymore," Sebastian said. "Maybe I simply went limp and passed out because I was tired, or overcome by the emotion of seeing and hearing my mother's spirit and trying to rescue my father—even if all of it was fake."

"So now what?" I asked.

"Now, we wait,"

"Wait for what?"

"Why," he said, and glanced at me with a wink, "For your dreams to come true."

# Chapter Forty-One
# **The Kinsman Dreams**

After that wild night, the next three weeks at the Psi Academy were rather dull even though there was never nothing to do. We had classes, mentoring, Mind Games, PT, homework, breakfast, lunch and dinner, and on weekends, guard duty and hanging out at The Folly which occupied virtually every waking moment. Not to mention that that on most weekday evenings and weekends, we were encouraged to join intramural leagues for table tennis, bowling, miniature golf, badminton, shuffle board, and any other odd sport that more than one student was interested in playing. Thus, there was not much time for a Psi Academy student to get into trouble.

For most of those weeks following our near expulsion, Sebastian and I didn't talk much about the room on Level Thirteen. And despite extensive Internet research by both of us, we weren't able to find a single link to an article or other reference to a Tesla Field even on the most bizarre sites about psychic phenomena. Sebastian had no explanation for this. He was sure he had come across an article or something on the subject at some time in the past.

But when I questioned Major Tom about it during class, he frowned, put a finger to his chin, screwed his head around and finally, shrugged.

"A Tesla Field?" he said. "Hm." After a few more moments

he looked at me and said, "I've heard of Nikolai Tesla, the inventor of the AC current, and after that, some other bizarre things based upon his study of electricity, including wireless transmitters and the ray gun, but I can't recall anything about a field that enhances or neutralizes psi powers."

Sebastian had turned to me with a scowl after Major Tom's response. During lunch that day, he shook his head and said, "I think he knows more about it than he's saying."

"You read that?" I asked.

"No," he said. "He was blocking me. But I feel it in my gut."

But that was all Sebastian cared to say. He grew silent, probably mulling over what it all meant. Like Sebastian, I knew that there were three possibilities, none of them particularly good. First, that what General Bosworth had told us was true, that the Zebb z-Prime had imprisoned his father down in that room and during his escape, killed him; or second, that his father was indeed being held prisoner down there because Colonel Drake was truly a bad guy who needed to be locked up; or third, that Colonel Drake was imprisoned down there because he was a good guy, meaning that those running the Psi Cave, and by extension, the Psi Academy, were bad guys. Or perhaps, something else entirely.

Troubling, too, was that not even Captain Fabian wanted to talk about it. Did he know anything about what was down in that room within a room? Was it at all within the realm of possibility that the Colonel Drake might be imprisoned with his psi powers silenced by a reverse Tesla Field? In fact, had he even ever heard of such a thing, a Tesla Field, let alone a reverse one?

"Just leave it alone, Henry," he had told me one mentoring session after I had raised these very questions. Then, he had laughed, "But a reverse Tesla Field. Really, Henry, what comic books have you been reading?" He gave me a sympathetic look. "Just pretend the whole thing never happened, your little soirée down there. Forgot, for the time being anyway, that the room exists, or for that matter, that Level Thirteen exists."

Then, late one night, the quandary started bugging me again. I had finished my homework, struggling mightily over another of Commander Marzo's quantum proofs, this one for teleportation, when it hit me. We had been down there, we hadn't dreamed it. And General Bosworth's story seemed too neat, a contrivance if there ever was one.

I started pacing my quarters, walking from room to room, contemplating what it all meant. Finally, I couldn't stand it any longer. I needed to talk to Sebastian about it. I bolted over to his room just a few minutes before the annoying lights out warning bell would ring.

"We gonna talk about it or what?"

"Talk about what?" he asked.

"You know what, Seb," I said. "Your father. Is he really locked up down there or not? Are General Bosworth and Major Atkinson on the level or full of it? Is a Tesla Field real and is it being used to neutralize your father's powers. Your alive father's powers?"

Sebastian wheeled away from me.

"I don't know for sure what's down there, Henry," he said. Then, he turned and faced me. "Haven't we talked this to death already? Maybe General Bosworth was right. Maybe it was your dreams about Colonel Zebb, his good guy stuff, and telling us we have to find my father, that caused me to dream up the whole thing."

"Maybe," I said. "And maybe not."

"Well, there isn't much we can do about it," he said. "What are your dreams telling you lately, Henry? What's going to happen next?"

"I wish I knew," I said. "I haven't had a Zebb dream in a while. Ever since we went down there, Colonel Zebb has once again abandoned me. The only dreams I'm having lately involve our old friend, Frankie Nytz. Only he's a nice guy now

Vincent L. Scarsella

and not the jerk he was." I sighed. "That, and a recurring one that, well…"

"That well, what?" Sebastian asked.

"That well, disturbs me," I said.

"What's it about?"

"A guy with a wide smile who keeps saying he's my next of kin," I said, remembering the disquieting, almost clownish grin of that guy. "And then, he's chasing us, you and me, with an axe or a cleaver or a steak knife raised up in his hands, like some kind of deranged B-grade movie serial killer."

Sebastian suddenly frowned.

"Sebastian? What?"

"Oh, nothing," he said. "Except I had a dream something like that, too. Something about, about, yeah, that was it, a kinsman?"

"Kinsman?"

Sebastian let go of a sigh and wheeled around again to face me.

"Yeah," he said with a shrug, "That's what he said. Next of kin…kinsman." He sighed and threw up his arms. "Geez. I don't know. Dreams."

He drifted off a moment, mulling it over, then looked back at me.

"So what do you think we should do, Henry?" he asked. "What's your plan?"

"I think we should sneak back down there," I said, "and find out for ourselves if we've been fed a load of bull. See for ourselves whether your father is being held prisoner, and if he is, find out why."

"What about the reverse Tesla Field?" Sebastian asked. "How do we get by that—if it exists, that is?"

And with that, the lights out alarm sounded three short bleats. I had to leave.

"I don't have an answer to that yet," I said.

But a couple days later, Sebastian did.

244

# Chapter Forty-Two
# **Where Dreams Come True**

At breakfast two days later, Sebastian spoke into my mind—in a low whisper that only vaguely sounded like his voice.

*Henry. Don't say a thing.*

I looked up and over at him with a quizzical frown, then nodded.

*How did you get past my block?*

*I'm getting better at breaking through. I practice a lot. But that doesn't matter. I need to tell you. I found out about the Tesla Field.*

*How? How did you find out? On the Internet?*

*No. As I said, I'm getting better at breaking down blocks. And there are some psi-warriors down here, in the Psi Cave, who aren't all that careful or aren't all that good with their blocking. Best of all, from them, I think I've figured out what to do about the Tesla Field.*

When Sebastian didn't say anything for a time, I thought, *Well, what?*

*We have to reverse the reverse Tesla Field.*

I thought a moment, trying to get straight what he was talking about.

*How does one reverse the reverse Tesla Field?*

*With a Tesla Wand.*

*What the heck's a Tesla Wand?* I asked.

Sebastian proceeded to tell me what he had learned in his mind probing exploits. A Tesla Wand had been patented by

Nikolai Tesla in the early 1940s. It was a device, supposedly, capable of focusing a Tesla Field. The user of this Tesla Wand, theoretically at least, would increase the output of his or her brain energy and thus enhance his psychic powers. And according to Sebastian, it could be used to negate a reverse Tesla Field—to reverse a reverse Tesla Field. Thus, if we could get it into that room on Level Thirteen we just might be able to restore Colonel Drake's psychic powers and then, break him out.

Then, after looking momentarily right and left, Sebastian pulled out from under his butt a short, thin metal stick. It looked like a pointer used during PowerPoint presentations.

*This,* he whispered, *is a Tesla Wand.*

*Where the heck did you get it?*

*Let's just say,* Sebastian said, *there are some weak-minded psi-warriors down here who are easily influenced. Who can…be talked into things.*

Mind-controlled into doing things they might not otherwise do, he meant of course.

I nodded, most impressed. Sebastian had somehow tele-influenced a psi-warrior to provide him with a Tesla Wand.

*So what's the plan?* I asked.

*Tonight, we go back down to Level Thirteen.*

During our late afternoon snack period we approached Dexter Chumley about helping us. Despite his initial protests, he agreed to meet us at Sebastian's room after lights out.

"This'll get us expelled for sure if we get caught," he said. "Or worse."

"You got that right, Dexter," I said.

Sebastian had also suggested we enlist Freda Morgenstern and to my question, why, he answered, "Just in case."

"Just in case what?" I asked.

"Just in case we need my mother," Sebastian said.

A few minutes after lights out at 11:00pm, we gathered again in the living room of Sebastian's quarters. And not long after that, Molly Scott showed up.

*Why's she here?* I shot into Sebastian's mind.

*In addition to bending spoons,* Sebastian told me, and *causing tree limbs to fall on bullies heads, she has mastered the art of tele-influencing. Better even than me. And we may need to control a few minds along the way.*

Sebastian explained to us the logistics of the plan. This time, we were not going to take the elevator, because doing so last time had triggered an alarm that had alerted the X Squad. This time we were going to walk down the main escape staircase.

"All that way?" I asked and looked at Sebastian in his wheelchair. "How are you going to walk down those stairs, Seb? There is no way we can carry you all that way."

He nodded briefly and said, "Like this."

In the next moment, he and his wheelchair were rising in the air and floating among us. Our eyes went wide. Sebastian had apparently mastered the art of levitation.

Once we were on Level Thirteen, we'd proceed to the room and Sebastian would activate the Tesla Wand. He'd been playing around with it and found that it reacted with brain energy from the user's mind. What you thought is what it did.

"Right out of Harry Potter," piped up Molly Scott.

"Well, sort of," I responded, "except it's real."

After activating the Tesla Wand and neutralizing the reverse Tesla Field in the room, Dexter Chumley would walk inside and open the door so they could all enter the room. Then they would find out what was inside the lead container—his father or empty space. Sebastian assigned me to wait outside, to be a telepathic look-out and send him a mental thought if anyone came for us.

*Ready?* Sebastian had changed to speaking to us via his mind. Our eyes widened. It was still weird to have somebody's voice implanted in your brain.

*From here on in, we communicate by mind only. No talking. Got it.*
Each of us nodded.

*No, tell me.*

*Got it*, I thought. And I heard the others voice the same thing.

*Yeah, got it.* This was an added voice, not any of ours. And it was coming in the corridor directly outside the door to Sebastian's room. *Right, Greenburger.*

We had no choice but to let Grady O'Reilly come with us. Not surprisingly, he had slipped into Molly Scott's mind earlier that day and learned of Sebastian's plan. The plan was set and Sebastian didn't see how one more person could imperil it. And Grady's mind reading talent just might come in handy.

Sebastian floated as we walked down the narrow, dark, musty staircase to the lower depths of the Psi Cave. It was a somewhat icky experience. There were bats fluttering about and wet things slithering at our feet and on the staircase's damp walls. There was also a bad, sulfur smell. At one point, Grady said, "Okay, Greenblatt, enough with the broccoli farts."

Sebastian had told us to keep our minds shut during the descent and in addition to doing just that, for most of the walk down, I kept my eyes closed as well. Finally, after what seemed an incalculable time, we reached the bottom. Grady brazenly opened the door and peeked into the dark corridor of Level Thirteen.

*Grady, wait!*

But it was too late.

Grady held open the door. "Here they are. "He said.

There stood the X Squad, led by Captain Borden and Master Sergeant Reedy, backed by a platoon of psi-warriors and a small army of seven foot tall orc wraiths.

"Sorry, my fellow cadets," Grady said, still standing in the doorway smirking. "And even you, Greenblerg."

With one punch to Grady's nose, I wiped that aggravating

smirk off his face. "For the last time, Cadet O'Reilly," I said, "the name's Greenberg."

"You four again," Major Atkinson said in a huff as we stood before her desk at tense attention just fifteen minutes after Grady O'Reilly's treachery. And because Molly Scott was no longer with us, I supposed she had been part of Grady's betrayal.

After a time, Major Atkinson stood.

"Does someone want to tell me the meaning of your second breach of regulations?" she asked. "And, why you persist on trespassing in restricted areas?"

"First, tell us why Colonel Drake is locked up down in that room," I said, insolent now. My belief was stronger than ever that he was down there, held prisoner. And feeling that we'd definitely be expelled, I figured there was nothing to lose by being defiant.

"We've already told you, Cadet Greenberg," Major Atkinson said, her back stiffening and her frown now narrow and disagreeable, "that he is not down there. That he is dead. That what Sebastian senses is his residue."

"Residue, smesj-a-due," I said. "The whole thing's one big lie!"

"Henry!" It was Freda Morgenstern. She knew we were already in horrible trouble, and an insolent tone wouldn't help it.

Major Atkinson looked about ready to explode. She rocked back on her heels, but never got the chance to respond. Someone was knocking at her door. She frowned and called out, "Yes, come in."

It was Captain Borden the commander of the X Squad.

"We've been breached, Major," he said.

From outside along the length of the corridor, an alarm horn sounded, bleating in deep, low moans every five seconds.

"It's Colonel Zebb," the Captain said, "somehow, he's entered the Psi Cave."

I smiled. Now I knew that the Psi Academy was the place where dreams come true.

# Part 3
# Escape from the Psi Academy

# Chapter Forty-Three
## Rescue

The X Squad's Captain Borden gave Major Atkinson a quick update regarding Colonel Zebb's breach of the Psi Cave. Presumably, after wall walking into Level One, he had conjured a force of vicious, orc wraiths. They were last seen approaching the stairwell to Level Two and the psi-warriors defending the area were in serious retreat.

"He teleported inside," Major Atkinson said more to herself than anyone in the room.

"Ma'am?" Captain Borden asked.

She gave him a sharp look. "He didn't wall walk inside, Captain Borden," she said. "No man can wall walk through a mountain without becoming locked inside the rock. That's one reason Project Mind Bloom came down here. It's too thick, molecules too dense. No, it is far more likely he teleported in."

Major Atkinson closed her eyes, and a moment later, three large, hooded dark wraiths, scary triplet versions of the Grim Reaper, formed behind us.

"Take these cadets to the mess hall. And get the others there as well. But be forewarned," she added, "Colonel Zebb is out to capture this one," and she pointed at Sebastian "and this one," and then she pointed at me.

"Yes, Ma'am," Captain Borden said. He nodded for Master

Sergeant Reedy to get going but, after a step turned back to Major Atkinson.

"Captain?" Major Atkinson scowled with annoyance. "Is there something else? Time is of the essence."

"But, Ma'am," Captain Borden asked, "if Colonel Zebb can teleport himself, why didn't he teleport himself right down here. Where we're standing."

"Because he has no idea where they are," she said. "Or where Colonel Drake is for that matter. Remember, we have blocked his ability, and the ability of anyone else, to remote view inside the Psi Cave."

Captain Borden nodded, appearing embarrassed for asking such a stupid question.

"Now, get going."

Captain Borden, Master Sergeant Reedy and the three demon wraiths hurried us into the corridor.

"Did you hear that," I whispered to Sebastian. "It's true. Your father lives."

Sebastian looked up at me with a weak smile and tears welling in his eyes. After a moment, he nodded. The news, though not unexpected, was a shock to his system.

"This way." Captain Borden pointed to the left. I noticed that he and Master Sergeant Reedy had worried frowns as if at any moment, they'd be facing something bad.

At the other end of the corridor, popping literally out of thin air, stood Colonel Zebb. Somehow, despite Major Atkinson's assertion, he must have figured out a way to remote view our location and had come to get us. He stood for a moment with his arms folded across his chest and smirked and in the next instant, he was surrounded by crag-faced orc wraiths. They charged at once like rabid dogs and I hoped and prayed that they had been programmed by Zebb to take us, as well as Captain Borden and Master Sergeant Reedy, alive.

But they never got that far. They stopped and formed a barrier between us and Colonel Zebb as he marched forward to stand behind them. Captain Borden, Master Sergeant Reedy and the three demon wraiths formed defensive stances and an eerie silence gripped the corridor.

Colonel Zebb turned and his eyes found mine. Then, he winked at me.

"Been dreaming about this day a long time," he said. "Eh, Henry?"

My whole life, I thought, but I dared not say it. I gave a short nod and he smiled back at me and I knew that he had spoken the truth in all those dreams. He was a good guy, and he was holding something.

"He's got a Tesla Wand," Captain Borden whispered to Master Sergeant Reedy.

Colonel Zebb raised the wand over his head.

"He's reversed it." It was Captain Borden, his voice dull, beaten.

And that was it. First, Major Atkinson's demon wraiths became puffs of smoke and disappeared and then Captain Borden and Master Sergeant Reedy sat helplessly down on the floor, against the wall content to surrender without a fight.

"What happened?" I asked Sebastian.

"He neutralized their powers," Sebastian said, "and then tele-influenced them to stand down." He smiled. "Or, sit down."

Colonel Zebb turned to Sebastian. "Now, let's go rescue your father." he said with the same confident look straight from my dreams.

I knew I wasn't dreaming, but it sure felt like a dream.

Colonel Zebb looked at Freda Morgenstern. "Is it true you can summon the dead?" he asked her.

Freda looked at me for some reason, as if wanting to know if she should answer.

"Can you?"

"Yes," she told Colonel Zebb. "I, I think so."

"Then I need you to come with me, too," he told her.

"Why should we go anywhere with you?" I asked, as I had countless times before in my dreams.

"Because," Colonel Zebb said with a wink, "I'm one of the good guys." He nodded at Sebastian. "And his father's another."

Then, he looked at Sebastian.

"I need all of your help to do this. To rescue your father," he said. "And we need that wand you're sitting on too." Sebastian nodded and pulled out the Tesla Wand.

"Well, what are we waiting for?" Sebastian asked.

Colonel Zebb was tall and blond and didn't look his age. He was a strapping figure, strong and lean—a superhero kind of guy. I immediately liked him. And I liked him even more now that I knew he was a good guy.

We followed Colonel Zebb and his band of orc wraiths to the stairwell we had walked down an hour before. It was still dark and wet and slithery with unknown things crawling around in there, but it seemed safer now that we were with Zebb and his orc wraiths. Freda and I followed them down at a decent pace while Sebastian hovered close behind us, applying his levitation power to negotiate his wheelchair down the stairwell.

It would not be long before the effects of the Colonel Zebb's reverse Tesla Field would wear off enabling Captain Borden and Master Sergeant Reedy to regain their powers. They'd quickly report to Major Atkinson that Colonel Zebb had Sebastian and I and was on his way to rescue Colonel Drake.

Within a couple of minutes, we had ambled down all those stairs and opened the door to Level Thirteen. This time the corridor was lit and we saw that a platoon of psi-warriors and dark wraiths guarding the room where Colonel Drake was being held prisoner. Some of the psi-warriors held Tesla Wands.

We stopped some yards down the corridor as Colonel Zebb assessed the situation.

"Now what?" I asked.

"Now, Freda dead talks," Colonel Zebb said.

"Dead talks to who?" I asked.

"My mother," Sebastian answered for the colonel.

"Can you do that, Cadet Morgenstern?" Colonel Zebb asked her.

This was something I had never dreamed. The dream had always ended with us going off to rescue Colonel Drake, but what happened after that had always eluded me.

"I'll try," Freda said and swallowed.

"And then what?' I asked.

"And then we hope the magic works, Cadet Greenberg," was all Colonel Zebb said.

Freda sat on the floor and went into a trance, mumbling to herself as she supposedly called forth the spirit of Sarah Drake. I looked over at Sebastian. Freda had his full and undivided attention.

After a minute or so, a low moaning emanated from the space above Freda's head. A frosty, cold mass filled the room as if a section of the North Pole had settled down in the same space. The psi-warriors guarding the room started to shiver and look around clearly wondering what was causing this rush of frigid air.

Quite literally, death was in the air.

In the next moment, I saw something forming above us, at the ceiling; a wisp, a form of person, a ghostly cloud, a puff of blue ice-like crystals out of thin air. Then there was a voice, mumbling. A shudder coursed through me as I realized that the voice coming from the icy ghost cloud above us belonged to Sarah Drake. Had she truly entered our realm from the afterlife? I wondered. Was such a thing was possible?

This was not like what had happened in Sebastian's room—this time we could see as well as hear her. Then, a stillness settled over us as the import of this became clear: death did not exist.

I looked back at Colonel Zebb and saw that even his eyes were wide, full of expectation and curiosity. Sebastian, too, was wide-eyed at the wonder and beauty of what he was observing.

He had lifted up his Tesla Wand and I saw it float in the air for a time until his mother floated over and grabbed it. In the next instant, she floated to the door to the room holding her husband, Colonel Drake, and went straight through it.

For some reason, none of the psi-warriors or dark wraiths did anything to prevent her.

"What's happening?" I asked.

No one responded and I began to wonder if anyone had heard me. I also began to wonder if this, too, was just another dream.

"Sebastian," I whispered. "What's going on? Where's your mother?"

"In the room," he said. "Rescuing my father."

I wondered to myself why she had never done this before. Why had she waited so long?

"Because no one ever thought of summoning her before," Sebastian answered with some annoyance, having heard my thought. "Spirits of the dead cannot act on their own. They must be summoned. The entity helping my father right now is not truly my mother, but a portion of what she once was. All ghosts are shadows of space/time; threads from the universe of what was once real."

I wondered at the thought of that, and what little I understood of it.

The time ticked slowly by as we waited in silence and fear. The unease felt by all of us, friend and foe alike standing in the dark corridor, mounted. And then, the door to the room slowly opened and out came Colonel Peter Drake, in the flesh, wearing a drab gray prison uniform. Even after two long years of confinement, and whatever other torments he had endured, he still looked strong and handsome. He was tall and lean and though his hair was long and uncombed, he exuded spark and resolve in his clear, blue eyes. A true leader, is what I thought.

Colonel Drake wasted no time. Lifting the Tesla Wand Mrs. Drake had given him, he pointed it at the platoon of psi-warriors and dark wraiths in the corridor before him. From across the corridor, Colonel Zebb likewise held up his Tesla Wand and, in the next instant, a bluish, eye-enchanting electrified beam, an energy wave of some kind, emanating from the Tesla Wands of Colonels Zebb and Drake, joining together and directed as one thick beam into the midst of the psi-warriors. They bounced back then surged momentarily forward, as if drawn within the coursing beam, and then fell in unison unconscious to the floor. A moment later, the dark wraiths evaporated into nothingness.

A trumpet sounded from somewhere far away seemingly announcing that, at long last, Colonel Peter Drake was free. But there was no time to celebrate. He strode across the corridor right up to Colonel Zebb and gave him a long, hard embrace.

"Thank you, my friend," he whispered. Then, stepping back, he looked longingly at the ghost of his deceased wife hovering in the corridor only a few feet from him. Colonel Drake swallowed and took a step toward her but she raised a hand to stop him.

"You mustn't," she said, her voice a barely audible wisp.

But he took another step anyway and whispered, "Sarah."

"No!"

She thrust out her hand and again he stopped.

I looked over at Sebastian gazing up at his parents with a sad look in his eyes.

"We have to get out of here, Peter," Colonel Zebb said with some urgency. "Now. Before it's too late."

Zebb reached out and tugged at Colonel Drake's shirt-sleeve. But Colonel Drake seemed immobilized, unable to shake himself from staring at the ghostly image of his dear, dead wife.

The ghost spirit of Mrs. Drake turned to Sebastian. "My dear son," she said with a loving look. "I am so sorry to have left you."

"Mother!" Sebastian cried out. "Don't leave me again."

"I have to, my love," she said. "My time is no longer here.

It's in a different place where parts of our souls look after the living."

"Mother!" Sebastian cried.

In the next instant her ethereal form had darted toward him and then through him. And that was it. She was gone.

"Sebastian?" Colonel Drake asked as he knelt before his son. Sebastian seemed to be in some kind of trance. "Sebastian!"

But in the next instant, Sebastian let out a breath and blinked. He stared at his father with his mouth wide open. After a moment, he smiled. "Father," he whispered.

Colonel Drake also smiled. "Where's your mother?"

"Gone," Sebastian said. "Back to Heaven."

Sebastian's eyes were still wide with wonder as he looked around, reached down and touched his legs. I noticed that his arms and hands no longer trembled.

And then he slowly rose and stood up. And in the next moment, he stepped forward.

He did not fall down.

# Chapter Forty-Four
## Escape

It took us some moments to wake Freda from her trance. At one point, as the time was slipping away, Colonel Zebb suggested we may have to leave her behind. But Colonel Drake countered, "She is a talented dead talker, Zach, and we may need her."

I knelt down and gently slapped her wrists several times urging her to come out of it. And, if you must know, I was afraid for her and had admitted to myself that I liked her, that I was even fond of her freckles spread across her nose and forehead, and the lines of her pale face. They made her look, quite simply, vaguely attractive.

At last, she came to and looked at me as if I had awakened her from a bad dream in her bed back home.

"Henry?" she asked.

"You have to get up, Freda," I told her. "Rise and shine."

She blinked for a time, then frowned.

"What happened?" she asked. "Did Mrs. Drake—"

"No time for that, young lady," said Colonel Zebb as he reached down and pulled her to her feet. "Let's get moving."

And off we went, scrambling to the stairwell leading from Level Thirteen, a quarter mile below the surface, three hundred and ninety steps all the way up to Level One.

There was no resistance until we reached the entrance of

the Psi Cave on Level One where an army of psi-warriors and dark wraiths stood between us and the door.

"Now what?" Colonel Zebb asked.

He looked worn out like the last thing he needed was another fight. And behind him, Sebastian, Freda, Dexter and I, were out of breath with aching thighs after the long climb up all those stairs.

"The wands," Colonel Drake said. He held one and he nodded to the one still held by Colonel Zebb. He looked out toward the horde of psi-warriors guarding the entrance to the Psi Cave a hundred yards away.

"It won't work," Colonel Zebb asked. "They have wands, as well. And they have certainly taken their Wheaties, laced with Boost; maybe super Boost. This looks to be an impossible fight, Peter."

"We could become a z-Prime and teleport out of here," Sebastian suggested. He had literally run up all those stairs and seemed none the worse for it. "One for all and all for one, or whatever the saying is."

"It's all for one and one for all," said Colonel Drake, "but no matter, I think it's a great idea."

"A z-Prime?" Colonel Zebb said and mulled the idea over for a time. A hundred yards across the huge expanse of cavern, the psi-warriors and dark wraiths readied for attack. "That's only been done once before, far as I know. And without Boost, it can't be done. Not to mention trying to teleport a hive mind."

"No, it is possible, Zach," Colonel Drake insisted, "the cadets have been secretly pumped full of Boost over the last six weeks. It was a weaker dose, but an enhancing drug nonetheless. Isn't that right, Sebastian?"

Sebastian nodded.

"What?" I asked. "We've been given Boost?"

"To more quickly develop our powers," Sebastian said. "I've read it in the recesses of the minds of Major Atkinson and General Bosworth. Our food has been laced with Boost powder. That's why our psi powers have been advancing so quickly."

"We don't have time to discuss this now," Colonel Drake said. "The point is their powers are strong enough to help us form a hive mind, a z-Prime. With you guiding them through it, Zach, I think we just may be able to do it, join together and become one mind, and teleport the hell out of here."

"Me?" Colonel Zebb asked. "Why not you?"

"I may not be fully showing it yet," he said, "but two years in solitary lead confinement has taken its toll."

Colonel Zebb nodded. From near to the entrance to the Psi Cave, they heard the sharp bite of a command and the psi-warriors and their wraiths started marching forward.

"And looks like," Colonel Drake said, "there's truly no other option."

"Well, the other option just might get us stuck in hyperspace," Colonel Zebb said. "And by the way, for your information, I only teleported once in my entire life. And that was an hour ago."

Colonel Drake shrugged. "Well, it worked, didn't it?"

"Not for our three brethren who tried it with me," he said glumly.

The psi-warriors and their wraiths kept advancing toward us while Colonels Drake and Zebb debated our options. Finally, with a sigh, Colonel Zebb seemed to have reached a decision. He had us come in close as if we were in a football huddle.

"Just like in the Mind Games you've been playing," he told us, "you let yourself get sucked up into one mind. Form an Amalgam Man. And if that works, you leave the teleportation to me."

"Where are we teleporting to?" Sebastian asked.

"The cabin," said Colonel Zebb. "That's all you need to know. Y'all ready?"

We looked at each other and nodded.

The psi-warriors were maybe fifty yards away.

"Hold hands and let my mind become your mind," he whispered.

I closed my eyes and held hands with Sebastian and Freda. And it was just like in the *Psi Wars!* games we had been playing the last few weeks—becoming one mind, letting our thoughts and memories form into a single cloud of thought. A hive mind, orchestrated by Colonel Zebb. I gave into the control of that and waited for what came next.

"Alright," Colonel Zebb said. "Good. You are all with me."

"Now!" he said.

There was a whoosh and a movement forward. We were hurtling through space and time, in dark, cold lines, into a sea of swarming protons and electrons and quarks. Imagine yourself jumping into a hole in the ground and being swallowed up by something that feels like forever. Actually, as we had learned in Commander Marzo's class, teleportation involved punching a hole in space/time and jumping through it, like Alice through the looking glass.

And in a frozen instance, with the psi-warriors and wraiths almost upon us we were zipped up in that hole and gone. A micro-instant later, we re-constituted in a cabin deep in a dark woods.

All of us, except Freda Morgenstern and Dexter Chumley that is.

# Chapter Forty-Five
## The Cabin

"Where are we?" was the next logical question. It was completely dark.

Someone switched on a light.

"You are in the cabin," said Colonel Zebb, standing by the light switch by the front door.

"Where is it?" I asked.

"A stone's throw from the Psi Cave," Colonel Drake said.

I looked around at the group and noticed Freda and Dexter were not among us.

"They're fine," Colonel Zebb said. "I couldn't take them with us. It was hard enough teleporting a four person hive mind. Before we moved into hyperspace, I dropped Freda and Dexter off on a ledge up in the cavern overlooking the psi-warriors and wraiths charging us. Don't worry, they're safe."

We were standing in a lavish hunting cabin; more a lodge than a cabin really. In fact, it was fit for an aristocrat, a senator or CEO. It was constructed out of long, thick wooden logs with several rooms downstairs and up, and a wide veranda outside around all four walls. The spacious main living room, which we now occupied, was furnished with an assortment of antique chairs and ornately carved mahogany tables. There was a massive stone fireplace against the far wall and above the long mantel, a stuffed elk head.

Up a short flight of stone stairs was an open kitchen. A gray sparkling quartz countertop separated the two rooms. Just off to the side of the kitchen was an open dining area furnished by a large polished wooden table with ten elegant, antique high-backed chairs. A winding staircase on the other side of the great room from the kitchen led to the second floor with six decent sized bedrooms.

Upon our materialization in the great room, six psi-warriors stood and were aiming side arms at us. When they saw it was Colonel Zebb with Colonel Drake and two kids, they eased up a bit but continuing pointing the side arms at us.

"Whoa, fellas," said Colonel Zebb and he gestured for them to lower their weapons. "The cat in the hat has come back."

That must have been the password because they immediately stowed their pistols.

"And I do have company," Colonel Zebb added. "Our comrade, Colonel Drake, his son, Sebastian, and his friend, Henry."

The psi-warriors who greeted us included Major Tom Pedersen, Captains Ed Ford and Nick Messenger, Second Lieutenant Gail Hartley, the only woman, Master Sergeant Paul Moretti, and Staff Sergeant Larry Grooms. These were the supposed evil psi-warriors who had escaped with Zebb from the Psi Cave a little over two years ago. Missing, were the three psi-warriors mentioned by Zebb who had been unsuccessful in teleporting with him earlier. They had not succeeded in breaking through subconscious hyperspace and, although nobody was quite sure where they had ended up, it was presumed that they had become heroic casualties in the war they had been fighting. In the next moment, each of the remaining psi-warriors stepped forward and hugged and back-slapped both Colonels Drake and Zebb and patted Sebastian and me on top of our respective heads.

After a few moments, Colonel Zebb gestured for Sebastian

and me to follow him upstairs to the bedroom we had been assigned to share. They had stocked two dressers with skivvies and some shirts and pants apparently anticipating that Sebastian and I would make it to the cabin. The other five upstairs bedrooms were shared by the six psi-warriors and Colonels Drake and Zebb.

Colonel Zebb told us to freshen up and change into something comfortable then join the reunion downstairs. As he was leaving the room, I asked him, if we were that close to the Psi Cave, how was it that the real bad guys hadn't come after us.

"We're cloaked," Colonel Zebb said. "We've scattered the light photons around the cabin to become unseen. It's like you or me becoming invisible."

I nodded. Of course. Psi-warriors seemed capable of doing just about anything. Reading and controlling minds, bending spoons, becoming invisible, teleporting from point A to point B, levitating, and even talking to the dead.

And then, from downstairs, we heard a roar of laughter.

Colonel Zebb laughed.

"Listen to 'em," he said. "Best sound you ever heard, a psi-warrior laughing. No one parties better than a bunch of battle worn psi-warriors, not even Seal Team Six. And they don't drink no butter beer down here. It's been a long time since they've seen Peter Drake."

"It's been a long time since I've seen him, too," Sebastian added. "And it's been a long time since I've walked."

Colonel Zebb nodded and smiled at Sebastian.

"Both must feel real good," he said.

I had almost forgotten all about that little miracle. Sebastian's wheelchair, due to whatever the ghost of his mother had done, was history.

"Feels great," Sebastian told him. He squatted down to the floor, those rose up and jumped into the air and Colonel Zebb laughed.

After Colonel Zebb left us to join the celebration

downstairs, I stood and watched as Sebastian went through the dresser assigned to him and dug out a change of clothes. Finally, he turned to me.

"What?" he asked. He was holding a pair of jeans and a tee shirt.

"What?" I said and laughed. "The months I've known you, you've been a crippled kid stuck like forever in a wheelchair with drool coming out of your mouth. Now, you're standing before me like some kind of athlete."

He shrugged and turned away, and for an instant, truly did not seem himself. There was something distant about him, something troubling, aloof, as if he no longer wanted to be my friend. As if he really wasn't that same kid in the wheelchair.

And then I remembered what Colonel Zebb had told me in my dreams:

*And another thing, Henry, Sebastian, your friend, is not all that he seems.*

After we freshened up and changed clothes, Sebastian and I went downstairs to join the psi-warriors' party. I lingered behind him, still amazed that he was out of his wheelchair, that he could actually walk, that he didn't lisp when he talked and drool didn't leak out his mouth and flow down his chin and onto his lap.

As we entered the living room, Colonel Drake, who had been sitting on the arm of one of the chairs, walked over and gave Sebastian and long, warm hug. Afterwards, he stood back and held his son at arms-length and regarded Sebastian with a glad, loving look. Now, that was a dad, strong and stalwart, a dad any kid would want.

After a few moments looking at the son he had almost lost, he turned to me and stuck out his hand and I reached up and shook it.

"So this is the brave Henry Greenberg," Colonel Drake said. "All four foot nine of him."

"Four foot ten," I corrected him and he laughed and patted my head.

"Dad," Sebastian said, "he's a wee bit sensitive about that, his height."

I turned to Sebastian, annoyed that he had made a point of that.

"A wee bit is he?" laughed Captain Nick Messenger, and the whole platoon laughed, increasing my annoyance and causing me to glare down at the floor.

But then, Colonel Drake put his arm around my shoulder and said, "Henry's physical stature means nothing. Our comrade Henry has the heart of a lion."

I blushed and looked down at my sneakers, embarrassed but appreciative for the comment.

"Here, here, I'll drink to that," said Master Sergeant Moretti as he took a long sip from a can of beer. "Although the size of one's gut does matter in the ability to guzzle beer. Lots of it." The Master Sergeant sat forward and patted his stomach. He was a large man, with a squat frame, but I would hardly describe him as fat. He took another long swallow of beer and the other psi-warriors laughed as did Colonels Drake and Zebb.

And in that moment, I was amazed that this was truly happening. Could I possibly be in the same room with Colonels Drake and Zebb, a man I thought was dead and the other a villain in a video game and from my dreams? Each of them were the stuff of legends and now they were living, breathing men and I was in the room with them, watching them laughing and back-slapping their fellow psi-warriors.

Sebastian and I sat together on a couch and, being mere kids, kept to ourselves while listening to the friendly banter and talk among the adults. Colonels Zebb and Drake sipped soft-drinks while three or four of the psi-warriors drank from cans of beer.

"So what the hell did you do locked up in that room all that time, Colonel?" asked Captain Messenger.

"Waited patiently for you slugs to come get me," he laughed. "Naturally, I fell asleep in the process."

"Drifted off to Valhalla, did you?" said Master Sergeant Moretti as he popped open with a whoosh the tab on another can of beer.

"Something like that," said Colonel Drake.

What I later learned was that 'drifting off to Valhalla' was a term of art, a short-hand for describing someone escaping from the present, active realm of consciousness to a parallel universe of sorts. It was a kind of suspended animation requiring extreme concentration that had been perfected by mystics and shaman and prisoners of war throughout the ages.

"They kept at me, though," Colonel Drake said. "Kept playing with my head, trying to get me to give up you guys."

"But you didn't crack," another of them said, Major Ed Ford. He was so quiet it was difficult to hear him. He sat with a sullen expression, brooding deep within the corner of the couch at the opposite wall from where Sebastian and I sat. "You kept the faith."

Colonel Drake laughed, more to himself than anyone.

"Yeah, I kept the faith," he said, "but now comes the hard part."

# Chapter Forty-Six
# The Kinsman z-Prime

"So what's the plan, Colonels?"

The question was posed from out of nowhere by Second Lieutenant Gail Hartley during a lull in the banter and talk. From the inexpert appraisal of this thirteen year old boy who'd never had a girlfriend, Second Lieutenant Hartley was pretty enough, though certainly not gorgeous, with a masculine manner and tom-boyish charm. She had intense, deeply set brown eyes, a square jaw and a thin face with sharp lines framed by dark brown, pageboy hair. It was obvious that she had a chip on her shoulder, a brash, sassy in-your-face kind of attitude that came from a lifetime of being held up to the scrutiny and sometimes ridicule of her fellow, mostly male psi-warriors. Perhaps, she had been raised by a dad who had wanted a boy and treated her as the closest thing to that he could get. She was my kind of girl because I saw a lot of myself in her; and, like me, she was sometimes altogether too defensive and abrasive for her own good.

And as if to prove my point, she added, "Or are we just going to sit on our hands around here and wait for them to neutralize our cloak and come get us?"

Frowning, Colonel Zebb and Colonel Drake glanced at each other. It appeared that they were exchanging thoughts, how best to answer their brash, impatient subordinate.

"What's the plan?" Colonel Zebb said. "We attack. That's the plan."

"Attack? Good." It was Captain Ford. After a sip of beer, he asked, "Where? When?"

"The Psi Cave," said Colonel Drake. "First thing tomorrow morning. After a good night's sleep. Therefore, I would suggest that whatever beer you're drinking be your last."

"The Psi Cave?" Lieutenant Hartley asked, finally giving voice to her comrades' collective incredulity at the suggestion. "Why would we do that, Colonel, with all due respect? We just plucked you out from under it, did we not, at a not inconsiderable cost—the lives of Jarvis, Conley, and Bukowski?"

"We invade the Psi Cave, Lieutenant," Colonel Zebb snapped back, clearly growing annoyed with her obstinacy, "to capture General Bosworth."

"Capture General Bosworth?" she asked, not backing down one bit. "Excuse me, sir, but you really have lost me. What's to be gained by doing that?"

I cringed at her tone and attitude. To my innocent, Psi Academy cadet ears, it seemed she had gone too far, and perhaps was pretty close to crossing the line into downright insubordination.

"We have it on good information, Lieutenant Hartley," Colonel Drake chimed in from across the room, "that Bosworth is in league with the Kinsman z-Prime. That he's been supporting its efforts all along. We further suspect that his judgment has been compromised by Kinsman's tele-influencing abilities. But the fact is, all that has happened, our betrayal for instance, could not have happened without General Bosworth's support. So what we need to do, short of neutralizing the Kinsman z-Prime, of course…"

I leaned toward Sebastian and whispered, "Did you hear that, Sebastian? He said, Kinsman. Like in your dream."

Sebastian nodded and whispered back, "And like the kin in yours."

"…is to kidnap Bosworth," Colonel Drake went on, "so that we can convince the General once and for all that he is fighting for the wrong side. That we are the good guys and that Kinsman is not."

I had shuffled to the edge of the couch and leaned forward with my elbows on my knees to listen to all this. It astounded me to hear that General Bosworth, the Psi Academy's Headmaster, might be in league with a bad guy. I glanced over at Sebastian. His blank expression and shrug professed a lack of understanding equal to my own. But there was something else, some kind of inner knowledge or intuition as it is often called, informing me that deep down, Sebastian knew more about the subject than he was letting on, perhaps more about it than even Colonels Zebb and Drake knew.

Then the warning from Colonel Zebb's dream avatar came back to me:

*And another thing, Henry, Sebastian, your friend, is not all that he seems.*

"With all due respect, Colonel Drake," Lieutenant Hartley persisted, "what proof do you have that General Bosworth is in league with Kinsman?"

Colonel Drake sighed and his eyes focused narrowly upon her.

"What proof I have, Lieutenant," he said, "is that General Bosworth kept me a captive for two years. And during that captivity, I was tortured by psi-warriors supposedly under his command, seeking the whereabouts of Colonel Zebb and this platoon."

The other psi-warriors looked at each other without comment. It seemed the only one among them with any doubt was Lieutenant Hartley.

"Put a sock in it, Hartley," said Captain Ford.

"No, Captain," said Colonel Zebb. "It's a fair question. After all, we are claiming that either General Bosworth is a traitor or a fool who has allowed his mind to fall into enemy hands. Those are serious allegations that require proper vetting." Colonel Zebb looked at Lieutenant Hartley. "So, go ahead, Lieutenant, ask your questions."

Finally, she gave Colonel Zebb a deferential look, as if she suddenly realized that she had nearly crossed the line.

"No, sir," she said. "No more questions. I beg your indulgence. I am certainly with the program."

"That's wonderful to hear, Lieutenant Hartley," Colonel Zebb said. "Glad to have you aboard."

"So how do we go in and steal General Bosworth?" Captain Ford asked. "Teleportation? As we have learned today, not all of us are much good at it."

"No, not teleportation," Colonel Zebb said. "This time, we get inside the old fashioned way. We walk through the front door."

"How do we do that?" Captain Messenger asked.

"We have an inside guy," Colonel Zebb explained, "a friend of ours, who can open it."

And with that, the party ended. The mood had been broken anyway, and tomorrow promised to be a long, hard day.

The psi-warriors got up and tramped upstairs to their respective bunks and mattresses.

# Chapter Forty-Seven
# The Unvarnished Truth

Colonels Drake and Zebb stayed downstairs and told Sebastian and me to stay with them.

"It's time you boys learned the unvarnished truth," said Colonel Drake, looking back and forth at us as we sat wide-eyed on the couch before him. "Or as much as we know about it. Consider the next few minutes a little primer on how this Psi War came about, who's behind it, and where it might be heading."

It made sense for us to know. If we were to be on the front lines of a major league Psi War in which control of the world was at stake, it would certainly be nice to know what had started it and who the players were. Because up to now, with Colonels Zebb and Drake being considered the bad guys one day, and good guys the next, I was getting a tad confused.

Colonel Drake sighed as if weighing how and where in the time-line of it all to begin.

"I guess," he finally said, "I should start with Alexander Kinsman."

I looked at Sebastian and he looked at me. There it was again, from his dreams, kinsman.

"Alexander Kinsman," Colonel Drake continued, "is the bad guy. The villain of this little tale. Not that he started out bad." He sighed and thought a moment, then gave Sebastian and me a long, cold look. "You've heard of Voldemort, right, the evil wizard from Harry Potter?"

Sebastian and I nodded.

"Well," Colonel Drake said, "Kinsman is a million times worse than Voldemort. You know why?"

Sebastian and I shook our heads.

"Because he's real," Colonel Drake told us. "But just like the fictional villain, or any fictional villain in stories like that, for that matter, he wants to take over the world."

"See," Colonel Drake went on, "some years back, the United States government formed something called Project Mind Bloom."

"Yes, we know about that," I said, "Major Tom covered it in class. That and the Boost."

"What did he tell you?" Colonel Zebb asked.

"He said that you and Colonel Drake were put in charge of Project Mind Bloom," I said, trying to remember as best as I could the key points of the lecture, "after Colonel Drummond quit. And then, at some point, Boost was invented and the psi-warriors in the Psi Cave, including you and Colonel Drake, starting using it."

They were still looking at me, not caring to chime in right then, so I carried on.

"But Colonel Drake started realizing that maybe Boost wasn't such a good thing," I said. "Because of its bad side effects, like making people power mad. But you..." and I nodded at Colonel Zebb "...didn't agree with him, or didn't want to agree. And, sure enough, the bad side effects started affecting you. You went power mad, and you..." I looked away from him and added, "And you killed Colonel Drake."

"Well, we all know that that part of Major Tom's lecture isn't correct," said Colonel Zebb.

"No, I guess not," I said. "Is any of it true?"

"That Boost had bad side effects is certainly true," said Colonel Drake. "It was invented by scientists working to enhance one's psi powers," he went on, and now he looked at Sebastian, "including your mother. And it certainly did that—increased psi powers. And like Major Tom told you, after a little while, it drove the user power crazy.

"But it wasn't Colonel Zebb who refused to stop using it. It was Alexander Kinsman. And it was Kinsman who fought Colonel Zebb and me, and the other psi-warriors you've met today, and some you haven't. With Boost's help, Kinsman eventually became a z-Prime." Colonel Drake stopped and looked at us. "Just like we did when we teleported out of the Psi Cave. The psi powers of such a z-Prime are naturally stronger than any one individual. It's like the Amalgams who were formed in *Psi Wars!*. And a z-Prime is a difficult thing to fight."

"So why don't you just form a z-Prime and fight fire with fire?" I asked. "Just like we did in the Mind Games competitions?"

"Because forming a z-Prime is not something easy to do," said Colonel Drake. "In fact, it's next to impossible, without Boost, that is. But if you form it using Boost, the side effects of the z-Prime are magnified as well. Imagine a megalomaniac hive mind."

I was having a hard time processing all this. Hive minds, z-Primes and Boost. Was it really possible?

"So you can't form a z-Prime to fight the Kinsman z-Prime?" I asked. "Is that what you are telling us?"

"Unfortunately," said Colonel Drake, "that's exactly what we're telling you. Forming a hive mind to teleport out of the Psi Cave, as we did, is one thing. Forming a hive mind z-Prime, to limitlessly work to change the world, or fight another z-Prime, is quite another. We are therefore at a distinct disadvantage in this Psi War for the time being."

"One thing I don't understand Dad," Sebastian said, "is why Kinsman didn't kill you and instead kept you captive."

"Well, Colonel Zebb fortunately escaped with a few psi-warriors when the Kinsman z-Prime formed and took over the

Psi Cave," Colonel Drake said. "So, Kinsman, with General Bosworth's help, decided to use me as bait. They knew my friend, my very good friend…" and now, he looked over at Colonel Zebb…"would never leave me behind."

"No soldier worth his salt leaves a fellow soldier behind," Zebb said.

"So," Colonel Drake continued, "they kept me in that room in the Cave to lure Colonel Zebb back there, set a trap. That trap involved, we think, using Tesla Wands to create a reverse Tesla Field neutralizing our powers. And then, he'd have us, and either kill us or better yet, tele-influence us into his z-Prime."

"But the one thing they never figured on," chimed in Colonel Zebb, "was that a dead talker, your friend Cadet Morgenstern, could summon Mrs. Drake to thwart their plan."

I looked over at Colonel Drake. He had lowered his gaze and gone pale with the memory of his heroic rescue by the spirit of his deceased wife. After a swallow, he managed to say, "And that brought us here, and will bring us to tomorrow when we'll go back into the Psi Cave to capture General Bosworth, and see if we can knock some sense into that crazy, old goat."

"But where did this Alexander Kinsman come from?" I asked. "Is he a soldier like you and Colonel Zebb?"

"No," said Colonel Drake. "He's not a soldier. He's a secret agent of some kind, a spy, maybe CIA. All we know for sure is that he showed up one day in the Psi Cave to be part of Project Mind Bloom and became a psi-warrior like the rest of us. He was a strange egg from the get go. He kept to himself and didn't seem to have much regard for the rest of us. And pretty soon General Bosworth was favoring him. We suspected that Kinsman was tele-influencing the General, and some other psi-warriors down there, including Major Atkinson, and even Major Tom. In fact, the only psi-warrior he didn't seem to have any sway over, in addition to me and Colonel Zebb and the other psi-warriors you met here tonight, was Captain Lucius Fabian."

"That's my mentor!" I blurted out.

"A good man, that Captain Fabian," Colonel Drake said, and smiled. "If not a bit of a strange egg himself."

Colonel Drake gave Sebastian and me a long, cold look. "You guys getting all this?"

With a shrug, I looked over at Sebastian. Sort of, I thought to myself.

"The point is," said Colonel Drake, "Kinsman, whatever his background, wants to take over the world either for himself or somebody else. Or at least, it looks that way."

"Somebody else?" I asked. "Like whom?"

Colonel Drake shrugged. "The powers that be," he said. "That's all we know."

"And the other thing you need to know," said Colonel Zebb, "Kinsman isn't the only z-Prime who wants to control mankind. There are several other rogue z-Primes out there in the world and he's in a battle with them and everyone else in his path for world dominance. That what this Psi War is all about. World domin-ation."

So that's all this is? One guy, or a bunch of guys, who went power mad?

"That's exactly what it is," Colonel Zebb said, having read my thought. "A bunch of guys going power mad."

"Any questions?" Colonel Drake said.

"So that's where Kinsman's now?" I asked. "Why he isn't at the Psi Cave?"

"He left mysteriously one day a few months back," said Colonel Zebb. "We think to fight other z-Primes, the ones competing with him for world control. We aren't a hundred per cent sure. But lucky for us—it was a lot easier rescuing Colonel Drake with him gone, to say the least."

"But he's sure to return," added Colonel Drake. "He'll come back to the Psi Cave and finish what he started, consolidate his power and move against the rest of mankind. And that's what the Psi Academy is for, giving him a ready supply of recruits."

"Geez," I said, shaking my head. I thought suddenly of Molly Scott, Freda Morgenstern, Grady O'Reilly, Dexter Chumley, and all the other Psi Academy cadets, being groomed to be evil psi-warriors for the evil Kinsman z-Prime. Maybe Grady would fit into that nicely, but I'd hate to see Chumley, and especially freckle faced Freda Morgenstern fighting for the wrong team. Becoming one of the bad guys.

"And that is the sad, sorry state of affairs," Colonel Drake continued. "How Project Mind Bloom has ended up creating a monster. And how we have come to be holed up in a cloaked hunting cabin in the middle of a desolate forest a couple miles from the Psi Cave branded as the bad guys. It is also why we absolutely must get to General Bosworth and once and for all put a stop to the Kinsman z-Prime and all the other rogue z-Primes that have arisen out there in the real world."

My head was swimming as I tried to keep straight what was what and who was who; that is, who were the good guys and who were the bad guys. To some, Colonels Drake and Zebb were the bad guys, and Sebastian and I were equally bad by joining up with them. But to the ordinary guy on the street, who comprised 99.9999 percent of human beings, all this was just some fantasy that didn't matter one bit to their mundane lives.

Only problem was, all of this was real and did matter.

"So, make sense?" Colonel Drake asked with a kindly smile.

I sighed and Sebastian remained expressionless.

"And there's still more," chimed in Colonel Zebb, glancing at Colonel Drake. "You didn't tell them about Sybil."

"Oh, yes," Colonel Drake said. "How could I forget Sybil?"

"Sybil?" I asked.

"She used to be a psi-warrior with the rest of us down in the Psi Cave," said Colonel Drake. "Then one day a couple years back, she was simply gone. She was right up your alley, Henry, a precog extraordinaire. Supposedly, she could tell you the exact date and time of your death, though she wisely didn't use that power much. And every single one of her dreams came true. In one of them, she dreamt that Kinsman took over the world and every single human being, became automatons like robots or something. All dressing the same way, in drab gray outfits, talking the same way and thinking the same way."

"Like communists?" I asked.

"Yes, like communists," said Colonel Drake, "You ever have any dreams like that, Henry?"

I shook my head and told him, "I don't know, sir. I've had so many dreams and I can't always remember—"

And then it hit me. A dream some years ago in which me and my parents were walking toward some huge outdoor stage, dressed in drab gray uniforms. I told Colonels Drake and Zebb about this dream and they frowned.

"So do you think the Kinsman z-Prime has her, this Sybil?" I asked.

"We truly hope not," Colonel Drake said. "That would not be good for us, especially if Kinsman could tele-influence her to change a future for his benefit." He scowled at me. "You ever change the future, Henry? Change your dreams?"

I shook my head.

"Captain Fabian was showing me how," I said, "through lucid dreaming. But I hadn't gotten very far."

"Well, that's it, the unvarnished truth," Colonel Drake said. "That's all there is to tell. So tomorrow we go in and see if we can break the bond that General Bosworth has formed with the Kinsman z-Prime, before Kinsman accomplishes what he's determined to do."

"Because," added Colonel Zebb, "we have no desire to see you guys dressing in drab gray outfits and talking the same and thinking the same."

"Well," said Colonel Drake, "I think you've learned enough about the real world for tonight." He checked his watch. It was 10:00pm. "I think it's definitely time for bed."

He yawned and I did likewise. Next to me, Sebastian held his poker face.

"Well boys, up to bed with you," Colonel Zebb said. "You should be exhausted after all that you've been through today. And we need to get our sleep as well. Tomorrow promises to be one long, interesting day."

Sebastian and I stood up and went to the staircase leading to our room upstairs.

"Sebastian," Colonel Drake called after us.

Sebastian stopped and turned around to look at him.

"I love you, son," he said. "Sleep tight."

"I love you, too," Sebastian said. "Dad."

But all I could think of was what Colonel Zebb had told me in that damned dream. *And another thing, Henry, Sebastian, your friend, is not all that he seems.*

# Chapter Forty-Eight
## Friendly Frankie

Sebastian and I had washed up and brushed our teeth in the bathroom across the hall and were now preparing for bed. In our room there were two beds on each side of the room with a small writing desk in the middle, and a couple of squat dressers at the foot of each bed. Along the far wall opposite the beds were two narrow closets with two pairs of Psi Academy casual dress uniforms, the khaki shirts and pants, hanging in them.

After taking off our rumpled uniforms from a long day of adventure and depositing them in a laundry basket that had been placed into our respective closets, we crawled under the covers of our beds. I had been yawning and achy with fatigue even before climbing into bed.

Through a yawn across the blackness of the room, I said to Sebastian, "Must be nice to have your dad back. Kind of makes me miss my parents."

Sebastian didn't answer right away. "Sebastian? You up?"

After a few seconds, he answered from the darkness, "Yes, I'm up."

"Must be nice," I said. "With him back."

"Yes," Sebastian said. "Nice."

I frowned. Sebastian's voice seemed different. Heartless, like he was just telling me what I wanted to hear.

"I still can't believe you can walk, Seb," I said. "It still is making my head spin."

"Go to sleep, Henry."


*I am walking down the sidewalk straight up to the entrance of Colonel J. B. Weber High School when Frankie Nytz comes out of nowhere, out of thin air, and is standing in my path.*

*"Hey, Greenberg," he says, surprising me by calling me Greenberg and not some other mocking perversion of my name.*

*I stop and look up at him.*

*"Where ya been?" he asks, "you and that other kid, the one in the wheelchair. What was his name?"*

*"Sebastian," I say. "Sebastian Drake."*

*"Yeah, him," Frankie says. "Sebastian Drake. Where is he?"*

*I shrugged. Back in the room, asleep, I thought, in the cloaked hunting cabin. But of course, I couldn't tell Frankie Nytz that. But then I remember more, the odd distance of Sebastian's voice when talking about his father, and the sense that he wasn't really Sebastian anymore. And the words of Colonel Zebb again, from my other dream:* And another thing, Henry, Sebastian, your friend, is not all that he seems.

*And I immediately regret not asking Colonel Zebb, in real life, if he knew what his dream image could have meant about Sebastian.*

*"So, what's going on?" Frankie Nytz pressed, but not in a mean way. He was simply curious, acting like he cares. "You and Sebastian left school so suddenly, right after you guys saw me in the hospital. The two of you went poof."*

*I have no answer for that and just shrug. I really didn't know where I have been, and what he's talking about for that matter.*

*"It's been four months," he said. "You left in December and now it's April."*

*"Anyway…" He went on tell me that he had stayed true to his word. He wasn't the school bully any more. He even made the honor roll last semester. And he's on the junior varsity baseball team, a first baseman. He was going out for the football team next fall, tight end.*

*"That's great, Frankie," I say and cock my head to look up at him*

*waiting for him to drop this kinder, gentler persona and break into his old, nasty, bullying self. It was funny, too, in a way. I actually missed his old, cruel, nag self.*

*And then Frankie is gone and I am standing there alone, in a wide expanse of schoolyard. And there he comes striding right toward me. I know that walk anywhere.*

*It's Sebastian Drake.*

*But in the area behind him, not farther than the length of a football field, is a thick, ugly black cloud, like smoke from a factory, and a form is rising from it, a malevolent persona of something and someone I knew.*

*"It's your next of kin," I hear in my mind.*

*No, it's Kinsman, I think.*

*Kinsman coming after us.*

I came out of the dream, suddenly, unexpectedly, like breaking the surface of some murky, warm lake after being under way too long and desperate for a deep gulp of fresh air. And to highlight that sense of unease, a gurgling noise came out of my throat as if I had swallowed a mouthful of water and it was swishing around in my lungs.

"You alright, Henry?" I heard Sebastian ask. "You dreaming again?"

"Yeah," I said after a moment.

"What about?"

"Frankie Nytz again," I told him. Then, I thought a moment. "And again, he wasn't a bully anymore. He was well, friendly." I sighed. "And you were in it, too, Seb. In my dream."

"I was? Doing what?"

"Not much," I told him. "Walking towards me in the schoolyard. From a long way away." I hesitated a moment, and for some reason, I decided not to tell him about the smoke creature lurking behind him in my dream. "Then, then I woke up."

"That was it?" he asked. "Frankie, and me walking toward you?"

"Yep," I told him. "That was it."

"So what does that foretell?" he asked. "That after all this, we end up back at Colonel J.B. Weber High?"

"Well, I was back there," I said. "I don't know where you were coming from."

After a few moments, Sebastian let out a laugh.

"And Frankie really was a nice guy?"

"That he was," I said.

"That I got to see."

"Maybe you will," I said. "I'm a precog, remember. My dreams come true."

"Yeah, I know," Sebastian said, then he yawned, too. "Night Henry."

"Night, Seb."

It was odd, because for the moment, anyway, the old Sebastian was back when he wished me goodnight, the real one, my best friend, not the one that Colonel Zebb had warned me about, not the one I feared Sebastian might become.

# Chapter Forty-Nine
## Captain Fabian to the Rescue

I slept soundly after that and when I next woke it was morning. Still, it was dark in the room, and it seemed as if no time had elapsed at all. But when I looked over at the small alarm clock on the night table, its red digits told me that it was already 8:14am.

I looked over at Sebastian's bed and saw that it was empty and made. He must have gotten up and gone downstairs—probably to see his father and the psi-warriors off on their mission to the Psi Cave.

I went over to the small window overlooking the thick forest surrounding the cabin and pulled up the shade. A thick, foul, gray-black fog filled the landscape, like the exhaust of a thousand old cars stuck in some enormous traffic jam on some busy freeway. The suffocating fog nearly blocked out even the nearest stand of trees across from the cabin. After a quick shower, I dressed into a clean, crisp Psi Academy uniform and ventured downstairs.

About halfway down the staircase to the lower floor, I stopped when I saw Lieutenant Hartley sitting at the kitchen table, sipping a cup of coffee. I had to take a deep gulp of air to regain my composure before I spoke. "Good morning, Ma'am," I said as I walked toward her trying not to feel so self-conscious. I even looked down at some point to make sure that the zipper on my trousers was up.

"Where's your cohort in crime?" she asked.

I stopped and looked around. Did she mean Sebastian?

"I thought he was already down here," I said.

Lieutenant Hartley frowned, shook her head.

"Haven't seen him all morning, and I was up at 0500 hours seeing off the detail," she said. "You check the bathroom?"

"Yes, Ma'am," I said. "I—he's not there."

Lieutenant Hartley took a sip of coffee. Frowning, she stood.

"Wait here," she said.

She trotted upstairs, presumably to look around for him. A couple minutes later, she was coming down the steps.

"You're right," she said, "he's not up there. Where the heck?"

She looked around the great room and kitchen and even opened the small closet near the front door.

"Well, where is he?" she asked and looked at me as if I was hiding something from her.

"I have no idea, Ma'am," I said with a shrug. "Why are you still here, Ma'am?"

She sighed with some annoyance.

"Orders on high," she said. "Colonels Drake and Zebb told me they needed someone to stay behind and keep an eye on the cabin, and babysit you two. And it looks like with that kid's disappearance, I'm not doing such a good job at either."

She sighed and paced the great room for a time.

"Maybe he went outside."

She stepped to the front door and tried opening it. But when she pulled back on the doorknob, nothing happened. The door did not budge.

"What the?"

She reached out and pulled again, this time crouching to give herself some traction, and still nothing happened. For a few seconds, she fumbled with the lock mechanism, mumbling to herself, cursing, then gave it another pull.

"I can't open the darn thing," Lieutenant Hartley said as she looked back at me. "We're locked in."

Lieutenant Hartley closed her eyes and, I surmised, tried using her telekinetic powers to open the door.

"Geez," she said, suddenly out of breath, as if she had just carried a great weight. "It just won't budge."

She ran to the back of the cabin where a small foyer led to the back porch. I followed after her and watched as she pulled at the knob of that door without any luck. She trotted from there, with me right behind her, back into the great room and tried opening the window overlooking the front porch. But that too was stuck. Then, she took off her boot and smashed it against the window pane but it only bounced off. She banged it several more times with the same result. Finally, out of breath, she turned to me.

"We're definitely locked in," she said.

"Why?" I asked. And where the hell was Sebastian?

"I have no idea," she said. "But it's damn disconcerting. And there's that damn fog outside."

"Did Colonels Drake and Zebb get inside the Psi Cave?" I asked.

"I haven't heard from them either," she said and checked her watch. "And they should have reported in by now."

And then, we both noticed that the knob of the front door was slowly turning. Someone or something outside was trying to get in.

Lieutenant Hartley's expression hardened. She gestured me over and I scrambled to her side. *Keep absolutely silent and still.* She said into my mind.

She took out her silver pistol and tightly closed her eyes, trying to use some power to determine the identity of the intruder. We both were wondering, was it man or beast.

And, just as the door to cabin had cracked open ever so

slightly, a sliver of energized light and air began to swirl in the middle of the living room not ten feet away from us. By the time the front door had fully opened, revealing a seven foot, silver mechanical man, whose face was a formless mask with only a red slit for eyes, a body had materialized from the energy field and stood looking at us.

Lieutenant Hartley's training was on overdrive. Her mind was spewing out garble as she pointed her pistol at the person who had materialized into the cabin.

"No, don't shoot!" I shouted. "It's Captain Fabian! He's one of the good guys!"

# Chapter Fifty
## Traitor

Captain Fabian strode over and stood with us as we faced the faceless, remorseless looking metallic creature standing in the doorway.

"It's an automaton," he said, "controlled by a psi-warrior back at the Psi Cave. It will do whatever the psi-warrior wants it to do."

I sensed that there were other creatures like it on the porch also waiting to come in.

"We've got to get out of here," Captain Fabian said. "Now."

"How?" Lieutenant Hartley asked.

"Like this," he said and held out a hand to her. "Grab onto her waist, Cadet Greenberg."

The automaton was lurching toward us as other creatures like it had ambled into the cabin.

"Then what?" Lieutenant Hartley asked.

But Captain Fabian didn't answer. Instead, he turned to me and when he saw I had reached around Lieutenant Hartley's slim waist, he winked.

"Ready, set, go," Captain Fabian said.

"You're teleporting us?" Lieutenant Hartley said.

But before she could add, "That's not possible," it was happening.

Like yesterday, my body and my mind and my soul

were being transformed, pursuant to Commander Marzo's impossible equations, into infinite wavelengths of pure energy. I found myself sucked into a vortex of sorts, swirling down a long, narrow tube into an eternal abyss.

A millisecond later, we were standing out in the middle of the forest somewhere a pretty good distance from the cabin, hidden behind some thick brush. All around us was the soupy, smelly fog that hung down from the sky like a bad case of rust belt pollution.

Lieutenant Hartley squinted at Captain Fabian, still doubting whose side he was on.

"You can put the gun down, Lieutenant," he said. "As Cadet Greenberg told you—"

"Yeah, yeah," she said, "You're one of the good guys."

"Yes," he said.

"Well, what are you doing here then?" she said

"We've been betrayed," he told her and he lifted his chin back at me. "By Sebastian Drake."

"Sebastian?" Lieutenant Hartley said that with wonder in her voice.

But I wasn't the least bit surprised. Another of my dreams had come true.

"What happened?" I asked him. "How did Sebastian turn traitor?"

As quickly as he could, Captain Fabian described what happened. He had been the inside guy Colonels Drake and Zebb had mentioned yesterday. His job was to set the front door of the Psi Cave to open at 0600 hours to coincide with the arrival of their psi platoon. And that part went off as planned. They had crept through the open door with a small army of orc wraiths behind them and appeared ready to go down to Level Nine where General Bosworth was nestled in his bunk snoring away oblivious to his pending capture. That, it was hoped, would change the course of the Psi War and lead to the demise of the Kinsman z-Prime.

But they were stopped in their tracks. An even larger army of orc wraiths commanded by General Bosworth and Major Atkinson stalked out of the shadows and confronted them as they approached the main elevator.

"Surrender!" General Bosworth had boomed. "Or die."

And at the moment, Sebastian stepped forward from the shadows behind his father and Colonel Zebb, the other psi-warriors and their platoon of orc wraiths. He held a thin black tube over his head, a Tesla Wand, and all at once, the orc army melted into a useless gray cloud that soon dissipated. And Colonels Drake and Zebb and the platoon of psi-warriors suddenly had no psi powers with which to defend themselves. But they did not surrender. Instead, they fought, charging forward into the General Bosworth's orc wraith army.

"What happened to them?" I asked, fearing the answer.

"I was up on the maintenance ledge overlooking the lobby of the main entrance," Captain Fabian said, "trying to stay hidden. So, I couldn't see all that well. But I did see some of them fall. Not all of them. I'm not sure who and what happened next, because I teleported out of there and headed toward the cabin. That's when I noticed this horrible fog and stumbled around trying to find you. And when I finally did, I knew that you were no longer cloaked. And worse than that, there was a regiment of automatons surrounding the cabin."

"What about Colonel Zebb?" I asked, fretful now that all was lost. "Colonel Drake?"

"I told you, Henry," he said. "I don't know."

"You ran away?" Lieutenant Hartley asked.

He glanced sharply at her.

"There was nothing I could do for them," he said.

From the direction of the cabin no more than fifty yards away from us, there was a flash of light followed by a terrifying explosion. Kaboom! We looked away then crouched down close to the ground and winced when another explosion rocked the air and shuddered the ground beneath us. The automaton platoon sent to capture or kill us had blown up the cabin.

Captain Fabian gestured that we needed to get away from there. The fog had decidedly lifted but had not completely dissipated. There were still pockets of its nastiness in the deep crevices of the dark forest and hills around us.

"Let's get moving," he said.

And Lieutenant Hartley and I followed.

# Chapter Fifty-One
## Last of the Good Guys

Keeping low and trying to stay quiet, we hustled through the low brush away from the smoldering cabin. Around us we heard the scattering of creatures, automatons and orc wraiths, no doubt searching for us.

"Where we going?" I asked as we started up a short hill.

*Silence!* Captain Fabian shot into my mind. *You must turn off your mind to everything.*

Soon enough, we were far enough away from the cabin so that we could stand completely upright and trot. At some point, Captain Fabian stopped us and gestured for us to get down again.

"What is it?" I whispered.

*Drones.* He said into my mind. Then, he turned to me and pointed to his right temple. *You have to learn to talk with this—your mind.*

Lieutenant Hartley heard that as well, nodded her agreement and I nodded in return.

Soon enough, I heard the drones, buzzing like frustrated insects above the tall pine trees or zooming between them to get a better look at the landscape, and whomever or whatever lurked down there. And I remembered back to my dream of the furious insects searching after me in the forest. Another dream was coming true.

These drones were pretty much based on the same idea as the remote-controlled aircraft used by the U.S. military to fly spy and attack missions into hostile places such as the deserts of Iraq or mountains of Afghanistan. Except these drones were a lot smaller, no more than a couple of inches or so in length and, like the automatons sent to find us and destroy the cabin, they were not controlled by radio transmission from some military base or Navy ship but were operated by the minds of psi-warriors from somewhere deep inside the Psi Cave.

I thought back to my dream about the drones and remembered that we had found a dark, narrow cave in which to hide from them. And I suddenly knew exactly where it was.

*This way!*

I broke into a trot and after gawking at each other for a moment, Captain Fabian and Lieutenant Hartley followed. Finally, we came to an outcropping of rock on a high ridge (exactly as I had dreamed it), composed of grayish rock, granite or something. It seemed to be exactly the cover we needed, a narrow, deep cave carved into the ridge.

"In there," I said, pointing to it, and Captain Fabian smiled, nodded.

"Well done, Henry," he said.

He got down and edged his way into the slit in the rock that led into the cave. I hesitated a moment, despite what I had dreamt, but Captain Fabian called for me to follow him and I lowered to my hands and knees and crawled into the cramped blackness. Once inside, I panicked and rolled onto my back and pressed my hands up against the rock ceiling of the place only three feet or so above where I lay. I called out to Captain Fabian and he harshly shushed me. Lieutenant Hartley had entered directly after me and we lay side by side in the uncomfortable, unpleasant cold, damp, claustrophobic space.

"This is perfect," Captain Fabian whispered.

"Perfect?"

"You would like the Holiday Inn, Cadet Greenberg?"

That quote was directly from my dream.

"How did you know about this place?" Lieutenant Hartley asked.

"I dreamt it," I said. "A few weeks ago."

"Appears you just made our future," Captain Fabian said.

I sighed. My eyes were finally adjusting to the dark cave and I saw that Captain Fabian was no more than three feet across from me on his side with his back up against the far rock wall. Lieutenant Hartley was about a foot below where Captain Fabian laid propped up on an elbow stretched out from the opening of the cave. I was the third line of the triangle, a small figure, crunched up in the oppressive darkness. No more than three feet above us lurked a ceiling of thick, damp rock.

*Now what?* I thought the question, hoping Captain Fabian would receive it.

*What did you dream?* He asked.

*Nothing I can remember after finding this cave.*

He emitted an unintentional wave of foreboding.

*All we can do is wait, I suppose,* he thought. *And keep quiet. Rest.*

He closed his eyes.

*We get some needed shut-eye, then wake up around two o'clock in the morning and head out. Try to make it back to civilization and make a report to someone, okay?*

*Like who?* I asked.

*The good guys.* He reached out and after I turned to him, he grinned at me.

*If there are any,* I thought back.

*Sounds like a plan.* That was Lieutenant Hartley. *Now let's go to sleep.*

She yawned and tried to stretch out her arms.

I wiggled around to get comfortable and closed my eyes but I kept thinking back to the day's events and how miserably wrong it had gone. Colonels Zebb and Drake and the psi-warriors they commanded, the guys I had met just last night, were dead or captured. And even worse than that, Sebastian had fulfilled a dream intuition by becoming one the worst traitors known in the history of mankind, worse than Brutus, worse than Benedict Arnold, as bad perhaps as Judas even. He had not only betrayed his father, his country, his friends and comrades in arms, but his entire species.

*Why'd he do it?* I wondered as I stared out in the blackness of the cave.

*Because it wasn't Sebastian who did it.* Captain Fabian answered me.

*What do you mean?*

*Sebastian was infected by a mind parasite.*

*What's a mind parasite?*

*A mind parasite is a thought or series of thoughts, a thought process, if you will, that is embedded in the mind of another. It lurks there, sometimes for months, years, until one day, it's activated and little by little, it takes over the thoughts, emotions and actions of the host. That's different from mind control, you see, because where a psi-warrior controls another's mind and actions temporarily he needs to be nearby. However, once a mind parasite is implanted, the psi-warrior can disappear, confident that at some future date, the mind parasite will activate. Implanting a mind parasite is an old art that has been practiced for centuries. And there have been some pretty famous cases of suspected mind parasites. Lee Harvey Oswald immediately comes to mind.*

*In Sebastian's case*, Captain Fabian added, *a mind parasite was probably embedded at the same time he was crippled. Probably by the Kinsman z-Prime.*

*So Sebastian was some kind of puppet or something all along, a puppet of the Kinsman z-Prime? He was allowed to come to the Psi Academy and all that so that he could set up his father and Colonel Zebb and the other psi-warriors they commanded?*

*Something like that*, Captain Fabian said. *Let's just say he became an ace in the hole, a trump card for the Kinsman z-Prime. But the bottom line, it was not the real Sebastian who became a traitor. It was a mind parasite who made him do it.*

Captain Fabian finally let go of a deep, tired yawn.

*And that's why we must remain free*, he said. *I truly fear that we three may be the last of them.*

*The last of what?* Lieutenant Hartley asked.

*The last of the good guys*, Captain Fabian said and then he yawned again.


Several hours later, someone was pushing at my shoulder. I had been laying on my belly in a dreamless sleep. It struck me as I rolled onto my side that I was stuck in a narrow, damp cave surrounded by orc wraiths, automatons, drones and whatever other evils the Kinsman z-Prime could muster.

It was Captain Fabian who had been poking at me. Now, he lay on his side, propped up by an elbow, glaring at me.

"She's gone," he hissed.

I looked around. He was right. The space where Lieutenant Hartley had sprawled out as we went to sleep last night was empty. At some point during night, she had left the cave.

Captain Fabian closed his eyes and moments later, a dark figure was sitting near the cave entrance, a wraith he had just conjured up, or concocted, as he liked to say. It had a scary, mean face, like an over-stressed gargoyle.

An instant later, it got up and hovered out of the cave.

"Where'd it go?" I asked.

"Outside," he said, "to see what's what." Captain Fabian closed his eyes.

"What's he see?" I asked.

Captain Fabian shook his head. "He's gone," he told me.

"What do you mean, gone?" I asked.

"You know," he said, "dissipated. Poof!" He sighed. "Some-one or something neutralized him."

In the next moment, I heard Sebastian's voice.

"Henry, it's me, Sebastian," he said. "Why don't you and Captain Fabian come out? It's over."

"Yes, Henry," said another voice, Lieutenant Hartley. "Come out. Time to give up. You're surrounded."

"Damn it," spat Captain Fabian. "I'll ring her neck. She let down her guard."

So she had become a traitor, too, I thought. Another unrequited love of my life, ruined. Well, perhaps I still had Freda Morgenstern. And then I wondered, how could I be thinking of that at a time like this?

"What should we do?" I asked.

Captain Fabian did not offer me an option.

"Captain?" I whispered.

But he had gone stone silent. Frozen where he lay beside me like a statue.

"Captain!"

Then smoke had oozed into the cave and surrounded us. I coughed a moment, tried to think what to do. But in the next moment, the smoke thing grew tentacles that encircled and settled into my body. And then, I was being dragged out of the cave. The next thing I knew, I was on my back in the dirt outside the cave staring up at Sebastian's evil grin. Next to him leering down at me was Lieutenant Hartley and encircling them both was a platoon of orc wraiths and automatons.

For a moment, I glanced past Sebastian and Lieutenant Hartley up into the field of stars against a velvet black, moonless sky that chilly night in early April. Then, I turned and saw the stiff figure of Captain Fabian lying a few feet from me. He was still, and I feared he was dead.

Lieutenant Hartley crouched down and her face came within inches of mine. I could smell her sweetness. I yearned for her to kiss me despite what an evil witch she had turned out to be. She was so pretty, her face with his sharp, lovely lines was difficult to despise.

And then she smiled down at me.

Sebastian stepped into my field of view above her, still smiling.

*It is finished, Henry.* Sebastian told me. *You are defeated.*

"And you are a traitors," I whispered out whatever strength I could muster. "Worse than dirt."

*No, Henry,* Sebastian said, *we are the good guys.*

And then someone made my brain go numb and everything went dark like sleep.

# Chapter Fifty-Two
## Mind Wash

I woke up in the mess hall of the Psi Academy sitting in a chair in a row of chairs facing the stage. My fellow Psi Academy classmates were seated with me.

"Pst! Greenacres." I looked to my left. It was Grady O'Reilly, several chairs down. "You alright?"

I gave a brief shrug. Right after that, another of my classmates down the row of chairs from him turned to me and asked the same thing. Sitting next to me was Cadet Gallardo, and on the other side of Grady O'Reilly, Molly Scott. Next to her was Freda Morgenstern, and down the row was Dexter Chumley and Cynthia Raymond. Turning around in the row forward was Francis Palmer.

"You alright?" they all wanted to know.

"Yes," I said. "Fine."

I blinked several times to get my bearings and looked about the room. Most of my Psi Academy classmates were looking back at me. I seemed to have become quite the celebrity. My exploits on the run with Colonels Drake and Zebb and their band of evil psi-warriors, and my dramatic capture, had become the stuff of legends in the coming annals of the Psi Academy.

As for Sebastian, I did not see him amongst the cadets around me.

"Where's Sebastian?" I asked.

Grady shrugged and so did some other of my classmates. No one knew.

"He's a damned traitor," I said and that drew even more stares, all of them disagreeable. "You're full of it, Greenbug," O'Reilly said.

"I'm telling you—"

But I never got the chance to finish the statement. At precisely that moment, Headmaster Bosworth, Major Atkinson, Major Tom, Commander Marzo, Captain Stanwyck, and a host of other psi-warriors strode onto the stage. General Bosworth stood at the podium and glared out at us as if he knew this had been a bad day. Next to him, Major Atkinson stood at grim attention. "I regret to inform you," General Bosworth said, his voice booming, angry, "that our mission has been compromised. This morning, as you know, we were invaded by a rogue element that has been working against the mission of this Academy, indeed against the United States of America."

I could not stand it anymore and stood up.

"Where is Captain Fabian?" I shouted up at him.

"Captain Fabian?" the Headmaster General shouted back at me. "He is part of the rogue element about which I am speaking. He is, as you would put it, Cadet Greenberg, one of the bad guys."

"No," I shouted back. "He's not. You are!"

"Henry!" Molly Scott scolded and she was joined by some other of my classmates.

"Where are Colonels Drake and Zebb?" I shouted up at General Bosworth. "And where is that traitor, Sebastian Drake?"

And as if on cue, Sebastian entered from stage right and strode to the podium. He glanced out at us with a smile and a short wave.

"He's walking," I heard some of my classmates whisper in amazement to each other or no one in particular.

"Where's your father, Sebastian," I shouted as he stood at the podium. "Where's Colonel Drake?"

At the podium now, General Bosworth stepped aside and patted Sebastian on the back. Sebastian looked out as us and found me.

"Cadet Greenberg," he said. "You are mistaken. You have been duped. The forces with whom you mistakenly sided were the bad guys. They have been defeated and my father has been rescued."

Sebastian glanced to his left at someone off stage.

"Dad," he said. And in the next moment, Colonel Drake entered the stage and strode up the podium. Upon reaching it, he and Sebastian embraced.

After a moment, General Bosworth started clapping, and this gesture was followed by Major Atkinson, Major Tom and all the other psi-warriors on the stage. And then, the cadets around me stood and applauded. Only I remained on my seat, glaring up at what seemed to me a phony show of reconciliation on the part of Colonel Drake and Sebastian.

"Bravo!" General Bosworth said, still clapping.

Sebastian and Colonel Drake joined General Bosworth at the podium and patted each other on their respective backs. Major Atkinson hugged Colonel Drake and kissed him on the cheek. I soon noticed that Lieutenant Hartley was among the contingent of psi-warriors on stage who had joined in the reunion like one big happy family.

After a time, I stood up and pointed at them.

"They are not Colonel Drake or Sebastian Drake!" I shouted. "This is a complete fraud! A grand lie!"

"Sit down and be quiet," Grady O'Reilly told me from across the row.

A few others joined in telling me to keep quiet.

"No, let him speak," said General Bosworth.

He had stepped forward and was now speaking into the

microphone while Sebastian and his father, their arms over each other's shoulders, looked out at me with marvelous grins.

"Let him speak," General Bosworth repeated.

I may have said something, though now I do not remember what.

The next thing I recall is waking up in my bed back home.

# Chapter Fifty-Three
# Home Sweet Home

"Henry! Henry!"

I opened my eyes and there she was. My mother. She was still shaking me by my shoulders and seeing my eyes blinking in the morning light, she straightened and looked down at me with a grave frown. It had been a full week since my last bad dream, shouting in my sleep, shaking, then waking up drenched in sweat.

As she stood over me, I remembered what was going on, what the story was. I had suffered some funny kind of pre-teen nervous breakdown just before last Christmas and had to be hospitalized, sent away. After three months of therapy, my scrambled mind had been put back together, or something like that, and I had been released, sent home to the care of my parents.

"Henry," she said softly. My mother was smiling, but it was not a happy smile. "You were having another bad dream." She hesitated a moment before asking, "Was it the same one? About the..."

"Academy?" I asked.

Yes, I thought to myself. That one. About psi-warriors and mind wraiths, a game called *Psi Wars!*. Colonels Drake and Zebb and the Headmaster and a strange, magical kid by the name of Sebastian Drake. And something about a kin of mine, a z-Prime, whatever that was.

I sat up and stretched out my arms, yawned, then told her, "No, Mother. Not that one. I—I can't even remember what this one was about. But it wasn't that one. Don't worry."

My mother shook her head with that old, worn out look of hopeless concern. I had been released from the clinic only two weeks or so ago and the last three months truly seemed like an irrational, lost dream to me. I was still mostly unconvinced that I had gone off the deep end and needed treatment for the sudden and unexpected onset of a childhood mental sickness that hopefully would be cured with the help of an assortment of colorful pills. Either that, or, as my father said, it was just growing pains.

But that had not quite happened yet, a cure, at least according to the much respected and highly recommended child and teen psychiatrist, Dr. Jacques Rideau. I still saw him once a week to talk out those 'Daddy and Mommy issues' that had, supposedly, resulted in my bizarre dreams and other fantastic claims over the last three months. Those claims, or 'delusions' as Dr. Rideau assured me they were, concerned my being a central character in some kind of important military escapade the success of which might entail the salvation of the human race. And it was this escapade that had resulted in my current state of mental confusion. It was all part of my disorder. Dr. Rideau had assured me and my parents it was a symptom of a larger, authentic psychological problem that plagued my mind. And it was his job to get to the bottom of it. It was the job of the drugs he gave me to stop me from having these bizarre 'delusions' and the bad dreams.

At first, I argued with Dr. Rideau that I did not suffer from mental illness, I suffered from amnesia. But over the long weeks of therapy, I had long since learned that playing along with Dr. Rideau, even flattering him, and pretending that I was indeed a warped, demented teenage kid who needed psychoanalytic treatment, was the best approach. Or then again, as Dr. Rideau claimed, even this delusion was just another symptom of my mental disease. Fighting him might earn me another trip to the clinic or nuthouse as my father called it, for a few more weeks, or even months, of more hands-on treatment. Not only were most of the doctors working at the clinic self-important quacks, but it housed and entertained many truly mentally and emotionally deranged teenage kids, some I was sure were destined to become serial killers, child molesters, spouse abusers or suicides. And having survived three long months there, I certainly wanted no further part of that.

What troubled me most was that I had no recollection whatsoever as to what had led to my commitment. I could remember only vague snippets of the last days leading up to my alleged breakdown. These memories were like the stuff of the bad dreams I had been having ever since.

Still, I continued to secretly resist the proposition advanced by Dr. Rideau and others that I was suffering from delusions resulting from a disease of the mind. Instead, I held firm in my private, secret belief that there was something beyond my life, an extraordinary experience and world from which I had been intentionally removed.

And that world was the world of the bad dreams I was having.

My mother tucked me in (well, I was only thirteen), and I quickly fell back to sleep. I had no more bad dreams that night, at least none that woke me up screaming, or that I could remember, about the strange Academy and psi-warriors and mind wraiths, or any dreams for that matter. My alarm went off at 7:00am and I got out of bed and went downstairs to the kitchen. My mother was at the stove already flipping pancakes. When I padded over to the kitchen table and sat down, she looked back at me with a kindly smile.

"Do you still feel like going to school today, Henry?" she asked.

It was to be my first day back at old Colonel J. B. Weber High School after the months away recovering from my alleged mental breakdown. I knew not going that morning, as planned, would be considered a major setback by Dr. Rideau.

"Sure Mom," I said. "I want to go. I'll be fine."

I ate and went upstairs and got dressed for school. When I came back down, my father was in the kitchen eating a bowl of cereal while squinting at the sports section of the morning newspaper spread out on the table before him. He had been decent to me during the treatment of my sickness. When I entered the kitchen, he looked up from the paper and gave me a nod and a smile.

"Don't take any guff from anyone," he told me. "Not even that idiot, Frankie Nytz."

"I heard Frankie's reformed," my mother said.

My father grunted then dug a spoon into his cereal and resumed reading the sports pages.

My mother drove me to school and let me off in front of the same exact place where now nine months ago, I had first seen Sebastian Drake being dropped off in his wheelchair. Had that really happened? Sebastian had been real. Only he wasn't at the school anymore. He had dropped out around the same time I went crazy and was sent to the clinic. Nobody was quite sure where he went. His kindly Aunt Dottie and Uncle Brad had left town with him.

As I got out of the car and started up the sidewalk to the entrance to the school, my mother shouted after me, "Try and have a good day, Henry."

I looked back at her and waved and smiled, but my smile was entirely fake.

# Chapter Fifty-Four
## Skipping School

I was about half-way up the sidewalk when Frankie Nytz popped out of nowhere.

"Well, if it ain't Henry Greenberg," he said wearing his usual cocksure grin.

"Isn't," I told him and kept walking.

He sidled up and started walking with me.

"Isn't what?" he asked.

I took a couple more steps then turned to him. If we were going to have it out, we were going to have it out right now, first thing.

"You said, 'ain't'," I told him in a snotty, almost arrogant tone. "You should say, isn't. That's proper English."

"Ain't, isn't," he said. "What's the difference? My point is, it's you. Back at good ol' Colonel J. B. Weber." He slapped me on the shoulders like an old friend. Then, he leaned forward an inch from my nose and whispered, "We all heard you went bonkers. Is it true?"

"So they say." I frowned at him. "And what did you call me? Greenberg?"

"That's your name, ain't, I mean, isn't it?"

I sighed, nodded as if I didn't care, and resumed my slow walk toward the school.

Then I had that funny feeling that threw me off kilter for

a moment, what folks called a *déjà vu*. I had lived this scene before, or maybe it had been one of my crazy dreams; or, perhaps it had only been a dream within a dream; or, better yet, a dream from another life in a galaxy far, far away. Or maybe I had dreamed up the whole thing. Another of my silly delusions. I laughed to myself over that last one.

"So where you been, Greenberg?" Frankie called as he trotted to catch up to me.

I shrugged and kept walking.

"And that other kid," Frankie said, "the weird one in the wheelchair. What was his name?"

I stopped and looked at him.

"Sebastian," I said. "Sebastian Drake."

He nodded dumbly as I checked my watch. It was still five minutes to the warning bell.

"Yeah, him," Frankie said. "Old Sebastian Drake. Where the hell is he?"

I shrugged. Back in my dreams, I supposed, at the Academy that didn't exist. And then this came to me, something somebody said to me once, perhaps in a dream as well. *And another thing, Henry, Sebastian, your friend, is not all that he seems.*

"So, what's going on?" Frankie Nytz pressed me, but not in a mean way. He was simply curious, acting as if he cared. "You and that Sebastian left school so suddenly, right after you guys talked to me in the hospital, made me see the light, changed my ways. The two of you went poof."

I had no answer for him and just shrugged.

"Where'd we go?" I told him. "I can't remember. It was like I blacked out."

"For four months?" he said. "You left in December, it's April."

He went on to tell me that he had stayed true to his word. He wasn't the school bully any longer. He even made the honor roll last quarter. And he was on the junior varsity baseball team, a first baseman. He was going out for the football team next fall, tight end. Who knows, he said, smiling, he might get scholarship.

"That's great, Frankie," I said, remembering that I had heard all this before.

I cocked my head and looked up at him waiting for him to break out of this kinder, gentler persona and break into the old, nasty, bullying Frankie Nytz. It was funny, too, that in a way, I missed his old, cruel, nagging Frankie Nytz self.

The warning bell rang and Frankie looked anxiously at the school.

"See you later, Henry," he said and trotted off toward the entrance.

I stood there for a moment, feeling weird inside, as if I didn't belong here at all. Maybe, Dr. Rideau was right. I was nuts. Schizo.

And then I heard the voice.

*Henry.*

"What the?"

*Skip school.* The voice whispered. *You have more important things to do today.*

Suddenly, I realized whose voice it was.

*Walk over to Griffith Park.*

It was Sebastian Drake.

*Go to the picnic area and look for a black van. We're there.*

"Who?"

From the front entrance, I saw Frankie Nytz waving at me.

"Hey, Henry!" he shouted. "Hurry up! You'll be late."

But I turned around and ran. I was skipping school.

# Chapter Fifty-Five
# The Return of Sebastian Drake

Griffith Park was an expanse of mowed grass and thick woods at the edge of Griffith Lake only three blocks from the School. My understanding was that the park and the lake had been named after some World War II hero. I had played plenty of little league ball games in that park and my parents had taken me there for picnics a couple times every summer during which my father spent those warm afternoons guzzling beers, eating chips and grilling hot dogs and hamburgers while listening to oldies but goodies on a cheap CD player.

I hurried past the entrance pillars and the wood sign blaring the name 'Griffith Park.' It was deserted at that time of day, about 8:00am. I walked through the park, past various playing fields and down a worn asphalt road until I came to a spacious picnic area divided by countless small shelters. This was where Sebastian's telepathic voice, if it was real, had told me to look for a black van. But the shelters were deserted like the rest of the park and a black van was nowhere in sight. Perhaps I had imagined the whole thing. Perhaps I was hearing voices, another symptom of my mental illness. I imagined Dr. Rideau wringing his hands joyfully when he heard that I had skipped school and went to Griffith Park because I heard the voice of Sebastian Drake in my head.

But, finally, there it was, a black van heading straight for me. Because of its tinted windows, I couldn't see the van's occupants as it slowed and rolled to a stop crunching the gravel along the shoulder of the road where I stood waiting. A moment later, the passenger door opened and out jumped Sebastian Drake.

"Sebastian?"

I recalled that before my hospitalization, Sebastian and I had become friends during the weeks following his arrival at Colonel J. B. Weber High School. And I also vaguely remembered the Sebastian I had known had been a crippled kid in a wheelchair.

Upon exiting the van, Sebastian walked up to me wearing a silly grin. "Hi, Henry," he said. "How ya doing?"

I shrugged and gave him a sideways look. "You can walk?"

It was certainly odd seeing Sebastian on his feet, standing before me, with his motorized wheelchair nowhere in sight. Furthermore, he didn't speak with a lisp and saliva wasn't dribbling out of his mouth and down his chin as he spoke.

"Yes, Henry," he said and grinned. "I can walk." His look turned serious. "Heard you had it pretty rough the last three months."

"Rough?" I said. "Only if you think spending all your time with teenage lunatics and popping pills that turn you into a zombie rough."

"Well," he said, "sorry about that," as if it was his fault.

"So how is it that you can walk, Seb?" I asked.

"Why don't you come with me in the van, Henry," he said. "I'll explain everything."

I frowned and stretched forward trying to look into the van. I could see the dark silhouette of a driver waiting for us.

"Who's that?" I asked him.

"An old friend." he said. "C'mon in and find out. And we really should be going. It's not wise standing out here in the open."

As if on cue, whomever was driving the van honked the horn.

"What's going on, Sebastian?" I asked.

"Just trust me and get into the van," Sebastian said.

I shrugged. What the heck, maybe this was all part of some hallucination, another symptom, as Dr. Rideau might suggest, of my schizophrenia.

Sebastian held out a hand offering me entrance the van. As I took it and stepped inside, the driver turned and looked at me. He was a guy in his late twenties with grinning eyes.

"Hello, Henry," the driver said. "I'm Lucius Fabian."

I nodded. "Glad to meet ya," I said sheepishly. "Henry Greenberg."

"I know," Fabian said as Sebastian entered the passenger side and closed the door. "Named after the ballplayer."

Fabian turned around and put the van in drive and off we went. He made a U-turn and headed for the entrance to Griffith Park.

"So what's this all about, Sebastian?" I asked. "And how the hell were you able to get your voice into my head."

And then it hit me, a dream. With Sebastian walking toward me with a black cloud following after him, like smoke leaping from a fire.

"This look familiar, Henry?" Sebastian asked.

"Why don't you just tell me what the heck is going on."

"That's exactly what we plan to do, Henry," he said. "Replenish your mind."

"Replenish my mind?"

"Yes," he said. "Fill in the blanks. Clean up what was washed out and filled in."

By now we had reached the entrance to Griffith Park. Captain Fabian took a right turn and off we drove.

"Just in the nick of time," Captain Fabian said to Sebastian as he nodded forward. "That is certainly one of their cars. They are most certainly onto our scent."

There was a dark sedan driving in the other direction back toward Griffith Park. I looked back and saw it turn left into it.

Sebastian sighed. "That was close. All the more reason to get this done quickly."

"Get what done quickly?" I asked.

Sebastian turned around. "Replenish your mind," he said.

"Replenish?" I asked. "What the heck are you talking about?"

"First thing I need you to do, Henry," Sebastian said, "is close your eyes."

"Why, I—?"

"Just do it, Henry. Trust me."

I sighed, felt something inside my mind that told me I should listen to him. I nodded, then did as Sebastian said and closed my eyes. The next thing I knew there was a flash of light and I made a sort of 'Wow!' sound.

Then everything came back to me in an instant right from the beginning to end.

*The new kid in the motorized wheelchair was dropped off in front of Colonel J. B. Weber High School by a special van... Then everything came back to me in an instant right from the beginning to end.*

And all the rest in between.

Being bullied by Frankie Nytz; the government test; my acceptance into the Psi Academy; traveling there with Sebastian and Molly Scott and Grady O'Reilly; meeting Major Atkinson and the Headmaster, General Bosworth, and the other Psi Academy cadets and instructors; the classes on psi powers taught by Major Tom and Commander Marzo's wacky equations; mind wraiths; my mentor, the very same Captain Fabian driving the van; the appearance of Colonel Zebb in real life out of my dreams and rescuing Sebastian's father, Colonel Peter Drake, with the help of the spirit of Sebastian's dead mother, Sarah Drake, and her curing of the disease that had crippled him; a Tesla wand and reversal of a reversed Tesla Field; the escape from the Psi Cave to the cloaked hunting cabin and meeting the psi-warriors, the supposed good ones; Second Lieutenant Gina Hartley, over whom I still had a crush; my escape with that very Lieutenant Hartley and Captain Fabian to the low, damp cave; Sebastian's treachery; my capture and return to the Psi Academy.

And, lastly, the washing of my mind.

So that's what happened. And why I couldn't remember. But now I could.

And then I learned that the last three months had been a sham, that my mind had been programmed to remember a mental clinic that really wasn't, and that my parents had somehow been tele-influenced to remember the same thing. I had not been there at all, but at the Psi Academy all that time.

Finally, I learned that even Dr. Rideau was one of them, one of the bad guys.

I looked at Sebastian and he smiled, knowing I was back.

I nodded and almost returned the smile. But I was a little scared, too. "But you, you became a traitor. The, the mind parasite. Then, how...?"

"How am I here?" Sebastian sighed. He reached over and gently patted Captain Fabian on his right arm. "In escaping from the Psi Academy, the Captain neutralized it. Set me free."

There was much, much more to learn about what was going on—how he and Captain Fabian had escaped from the Psi Academy, for instance.

And there were more adventures, I knew, certain to follow. Many more.

The Psi Wars had just begun.

"So where're we going now?" I asked.

"You'll see when we get there," Sebastian said.

# Join Us

Thank you for reading our novel, *Escape from the Psi Academy*, and for supporting speculative fiction in the written form. Please consider leaving a reader review so that other people can make an informed reading decision.

Find more great stories, novels, collections,
and anthologies on our website.
Visit us at DigitalFictionPub.com

Join the Digital Fiction Pub newsletter for **infrequent** updates, new release discounts, and more:
Subscribe at Digital Fiction Pub

See just some of our exciting fantasy, horror,
crime, and science fiction books on the next page.

# Also from Digital Fiction

Digital Fantasy Fiction Anthologies
Short Stories Series One
Uncommon Senses – Book 1
Ignis Fatuus – Book 2
Casual Conjurings – Book 3

Digital Fantasy Fiction Novels
The Black River Chronicles: Level One –
David Tallerman and Michael Wills
The Messiah – Vincent L. Scarsella
Three Wells of the Sea – Terry Madden

Digital Fantasy Fiction Short Reads
Fantasy Short Stories – Various Authors

# About the Author

Vincent L. Scarsella is the author of speculative, fantasy, and crime fiction. His published books include the crime novels *The Anonymous Man* (2013) and *Lawyers Gone Bad* (2014), as well as the young adult fantasy, *Escape from the Psi Academy*, Book 1 of the *Psi Wars!* Series originally released in May, 2015. Book 2 of the series, *Return to the Psi Academy*, followed in 2016.

Scarsella has also published numerous speculative fiction short stories in print magazines, such as *The Leading Edge*, *Aethlon*, and *Fictitious Force*, various anthologies, and in several online zines. His short story, "The Cards of Unknown Players," was nominated for the Pushcart Prize and has been republished by *Digital Science Fiction* (an imprint of Digital Fiction Pub).

Scarsella's full-length play, *Hate Crime*, about race relations in the context of a legal thriller, was performed in Buffalo on September 13, 2016 and is scheduled for a reprise in late May of 2016. *The Penitent*, about the Catholic Church child molestation scandal, was a finalist in the June 2015 Watermelon One-Act Play Festival.

Scarsella has also published non-fiction works, most notably, *The Human Manifesto: A General Plan for Human Survival*, which was favorably reviewed in September 2011 by the Ernest Becker Foundation.

# Copyright

**Escape from the Psi Academy**
Written by Vincent L. Scarsella
Executive Editor: Michael A. Wills
ISBN: 978-1-988863-02-3 (ebook)

This story is a work of fiction. All of the characters, organizations, and events portrayed in the story are either the product of the author's imagination, fictitious, or used fictitiously. Any resemblance to actual persons or dragons, living or dead, would be coincidental and quite remarkable.

DIGITAL FICTION
PUBLISHING CORP
DigitalFictionPub.com

Made in the USA
Lexington, KY
26 December 2017